BELLE'S RUIN

Joseph McRae Palmer

Copyright © 2023 Joseph McRae Palmer

www.josephmcraepalmer.com

This book is a work of fiction. The characters, incidents, and dialog are drawn from the author's imagination and are not to be construed as real. Any resemblance to actual events or persons, living or dead, is fictionalized or coincidental.

No part of this book may be reproduced in any form or by any electronic or mechanical means, including storage and retrieval systems, without written permission from the author, except for the use of brief quotations in a book review.

ISBN (paperback) 978-1-961782-00-6

Editing: Claire Ashgrove, Sean Leonard
Cover art: Planet by 1971yes as provided by iStockPhoto.

For Betty, who strengthens me

Acknowledgments

When I completed the second draft of *Belle's Ruin*, I was pretty happy with it. Nobody had yet seen it.

Months and multiple revisions later, I have something I like even more. It wouldn't have gotten there without the following people:

First, thank you to my editors, Claire Ashgrove and Sean Leonard, for not only editing my drafts but also teaching me how to write a decent novel.

Next, thank you to my family members who read early versions of this work and gave me feedback: Beatriz Palmer, Alexander Palmer, Cecily Palmer, and Nathan Palmer.

Lastly, and most important, thank you to my wife, Beatriz, for her endless patience with my projects. For letting me dream of better roads, supporting my attempts to walk them, and holding my hand along the way.

Part One

Outward Bound

1

"Charlie One Niner Five, Clinton Departure," Belle Machado heard in her headphones. "Cleared to depart on heading one-fifty, elevation seventy, contact Clinton Control on one-four-eight-point-four-five."

"Clinton Departure, Charlie One Niner Five," Borya Utkin, her co-pilot, replied, "cleared to depart on one-fifty and seventy, switching to one-four-eight-point-four-five. Have a nice day."

Belle had just lifted the barge, *C195*, off its pad at Clinton Base, and they zoomed along at a low level over the jungle on their take-off vector. Every bump of turbulence caused something in the thirty-year-old heap of junk to complain, and the expansion bottle's temperature fluctuated just like the crew chief had forewarned her.

"Keep an eye on that bottle, Borya," she said while holding their attitude and speed.

Belle sat in the pilot's seat of the cramped cockpit of the rattling, old, ground-to-orbit barge—now converted to tending survey sensors at remote locations on Clinton. As a pilot-candidate, she, for the first time, acted as pilot-in-command.

Borya sat in the co-pilot's right-hand seat, wearing an orange, single-piece, fire-resistant flight suit identical to hers. In the center jump seat behind them, situated aft of the center console, sat Phil Curtis. Formerly her pilot-mentor when she'd been a pilot-apprentice.

The barge typically carried a two-person crew on the three-day sensor tending runs, but this run was atypical. As a pilot-candidate, Belle's employer, Kepler Research Corporation, was considering her for promotion to pilot-commander. Phil, a qualified check-pilot instructor, would evaluate her performance during the next three days while Borya acted as her co-pilot.

Belle punched their departure parameters into the autopilot. But rather than enabling it, she put it into an armed state—she might need them on a moment's notice in case of an emergency abort. *But darn it, it's not every flight that's one's first as pilot-in-command.* She forbade the crusty flight computer to steal her moment.

Gripping her control stick with a steady hand, Belle banked *C195* toward her assigned heading, pulled back on the stick toward the departure vector, and shoved the throttle to maximum. The bottle's temperature jumped but then stabilized, rock-steady and well within its safety margins—again, just as the crew chief had told her it would do—and the occasional creaks became a short scream as the old ship's structure adjusted under the new forces.

The thrust pushed Belle into her acceleration couch. Tears welled from her eyes, and she let out the triumphant exclamation of her Peruvian Morochuco ancestors: "Yee-haw, *montala, vaquera!*" Phil wouldn't mind her outburst and probably was smiling right now. Though Borya gave her an odd look.

She'd done it. She'd just logged her first successful departure as pilot-in-command. This tub might be old and less capable compared to a full-fledged starship, however, the company measured its worth in the tens of millions of credits. Yet they'd judged her sufficiently trustworthy and competent to take charge of C195 and its crew for the three-day run.

Since she'd been a middle schooler, she'd dreamed of one day becoming a starship captain. Her father's last words to her before he died were, "Belle, find those stars."

Ninety seconds later, they entered Clinton's stratosphere, and she enabled the autopilot. No pilot was precise enough to perform the necessary orbital maneuvers ahead, other than in extreme emergencies, and she'd had her fun. She settled back in her couch, contentedly smiling, and watched the countdown to thrust cutoff.

The thrust cut at twelve minutes, and they were in freefall. Two more burns were scheduled: one five-minute orbital plane change in twenty minutes, then a deorbit burn thirty minutes later. In less than ninety minutes, they would arrive at their first destination and her first logged *landing* as a pilot-in-command.

"Clinton Control," Borya said into the radio, "Charlie One Niner Five requesting deorbit burn in sixty seconds."

Belle heard in her headphones: "Charlie One Niner Five, Clinton Control, you are cleared for deorbit burn at your discretion."

Belle watched the burn countdown tick its final seconds, and then felt the kick of thrust, which lasted only thirty seconds. During the thirty-minute coast to the atmosphere's edge, she looked out the small cockpit viewports at the planet rolling slowly below her and imagined what awaited them at the landing site.

Clinton was the most Earth-like planet humanity had found thus far—if that comparison was made versus an Earth of three hundred million years ago. Clinton existed in its version of the Carboniferous geological period. A single endless ocean covered three-quarters of the planet and the other one-quarter was covered by a supercontinent named Wordonia lying on its equator. Clinton's total surface area was about ten percent greater than Earth's, so the total land area was roughly the same as Earth's.

Like Earth's Carboniferous Period, Clinton was marked with soaring oxygen levels, over fifty percent higher than Earth's. Vast rainforests covered Wordonia, inhabited by invertebrate animals. Towering trees and giant oxygen-fueled bugs dominated the land.

Belle's heartbeat raced at the thought of the pictures she'd seen of two-meter-long megapedes, a poisonous centipede-analog. She imagined stepping on one and watching as it wrapped its long, yellow and black chitinous body around her legs, immobilizing her. Then being repeatedly stabbed in the stomach with its long fangs and injected with acidic venom. Afterward, hoping to die quickly from anaphylactic shock because the alternative was a slow, painful, smelly, and messy death caused by gangrene from the resulting tissue necrosis.

She was so glad nobody was required to exit the tender.

A chime and notification light brought her out of her ruminations: The navigation computer had confirmed her landing site but needed clarification. *What in the world?* She had already programmed it with everything necessary to complete the landing sequence.

Studying the notification details, Belle realized what was wrong. "Borya, did you fill the reaction mass tanks?"

"Yes... Was I not supposed to?" Borya said.

"No, we're overweight for the landing. I need to burn off some mass." She looked at Borya. "Check our flight plan next time before you order the tank filling. It will avoid this kind of error."

As the pilot-monitoring, Borya's job was to ensure fuel and consumables were at proper levels before departure. However, as pilot-in-command, ultimate responsibility fell on Belle.

She quickly went to work calculating how much mass needed to be dumped and how she would do it. Just barely over. A two-minute burn at fifty percent thrust would get their weight down enough for the gravinegator to handle, but she would have to perform the burn immediately before landing. There was no time to do it now without throwing the craft too far off course.

No actual harm was done. The reaction mass tanks contained filtered water. Nothing more than untainted tap water. And the required dumping wasn't a reportable incident; pilots had to correct minor errors like this all the time. But she was still disappointed in herself for letting Borya's oversight slip by her. Phil was probably making a note about it.

A little while later, *C195*'s slow deceleration through the atmosphere brought its airspeed below supersonic. Looking at her terrain map, she plotted a circular orbit around the landing site, took manual control, and pushed the throttle to fifty percent. "Beginning reaction mass dump," she said to the cockpit.

Landing under the gravinegator lift was necessary because the fission torch would incinerate the towering rainforest canopy, resulting in a forest fire.

As she reached the end of her plotted course, Belle confirmed the tender was below the max gravinegator landing mass. She executed a turning descent toward the landing site. Just another featureless stretch of trees like the other ten thousand square kilometers currently in view.

Now began the most distasteful part of piloting—the gravinegator descent. Belle's stomach turned as she anticipated the waves of nausea and disorientation she would experience when the lift system became energized. For a small craft like *C195*, no gravinegator in existence could produce the smooth lift gradients of larger vessels. Though advantageous for landing in dense jungles, it was hell for the human nervous system.

Belle enabled the autolanding sequence. They would soon be almost wholly incapacitated, only able to hold enough attention (hopefully) to make an abort decision if something were to go wrong. She tightened her restraints and steeled herself for the coming discomfort.

As the airspeed approached the tender's stall speed, the flight computer energized the gravinegator, and Belle's world turned upside down. She closed her eyes and focused on what she could hear. The flight computer verbally reported its progress, knowing the humans were suppressing as many of their senses as possible while fighting waves of nausea.

"Five-hundred, one-fifty."

"Two-fifty, fifty."

"Two hundred, holding."

"Deploying jungle penetrator."

"Deploying drone."

"Landing site is hazard free; please confirm site clearing procedure."

Belle pressed the confirmation toggle on the flight stick, her thumb momentarily hovering over the abort toggle as another wave of nausea nearly overwhelmed her.

What seemed like an eternity later (but probably only

sixty seconds), the flight computer said, "Landing site is clear; please confirm landing procedure."

Belle pressed the confirmation toggle again, then felt the world go topsy turvy as *C195* adjusted its gravinegator fields to begin the descent.

"One-fifty, two hundred."

"One hundred, one hundred."

"Fifty, one hundred."

"Forty, fifty."

"Thirty, sixty."

"Twenty, sixty."

"Ten, thirty."

"Five, thirty."

"Touchdown."

Briefly closing her eyes, Belle felt her sanity return as the flight computer de-energized the quadruple-damned gravinegator from hell.

She had brought them to a safe landing.

Phil would hold Belle under a microscope in the coming days. Every command she issued checked for its suitability to the event it responded to. Her efficiency in piloting the ship compared to established minimum performance thresholds. Her skill in communication with the crew and Clinton Base measured for clarity and content. Her technical knowledge of the tender's many systems graded, be it the flight computer, the power plant, the mechanical systems, or even the living quarters plumbing. Her knowledge of astrogation and navigation. Her personality and professionalism.

Yes, Belle felt like a lab rat. She disliked the constant measurements demanded from her profession, always needing to prove to the organization that she was a qualified pilot. But conversely, she loved the freedom of being in command, of being out on the range—be it on a horse at her family's ranch or a survey tender on an uncolonized planet. Of being responsible for an expensive, complex vehicle and knowing how to guide it to complete a job.

She was probably the first of her graduating class up for promotion. She'd taken this job with Kepler mainly because it would present more command opportunities, even though it was less glamorous than a position on a spaceliner. Belle just needed to see that they completed their assigned tasks on this run, then returned the vehicle and crew home safely, on time, and with minimal wear and tear. If she could do that, she was almost guaranteed to meet Kepler's piloting standards and qualify for promotion.

2

Dr. Benton Valero entered Kepler Research Corporation's Clinton Operations Center. It was a large room filled with a dozen control consoles organized in three rows of desks and tables. The front wall was covered by a large computer display. At present, it showed a 2D map of the entire planet with markers indicating Kepler's vessels, installations, and personnel. Four staff members sat at consoles.

As the Clinton Base chief scientist, Benton normally worked in the Science Building. But he frequently visited the Ops Center to provide consultation when requested, or, like now, to provide operations directives when needed.

He approached Silvestre Jenkins, who sat at the on-duty operations officer's console in the back row. "Silvestre," Benton said, "I have a geological anomaly that needs to be sampled. It's in Grid 18M071399."

As the on-duty Ops officer, Silvestre was responsible for coordinating resources and schedules of Kepler flight crews and their vehicles.

The Union of Anglo and American Nations' (UAAN) Department of Planetary Exploration (DPE) funded Kepler's survey on Clinton. An updated DPE Phase Two Survey contract required Kepler to investigate an unusual rock monolith recently found in the remote sensor data from the Phase One Survey that was completed one year ago. According to the DPE, the monolith emitted radiation anomalously higher than background levels.

Silvestre cross-referenced his ops schedule with the grid. "Pilot Belle Machado is out with a crew and is scheduled to perform sensor installation there in two days. This morning, she left with a crew in a tender on a three-day sensor tending run. Grid 18M071399 is scheduled as her last location before returning. Would you like me to modify her work order?"

Benton had to think for a moment. "I don't recognize the name."

Silvestre looked at his computer display. "She is a pilot-candidate. This run is her final pilot-check ride. Phil Curtis is with her as the pilot-check instructor. My records say she's qualified to perform surface geological sample collection. Their tender is equipped with a sensor boom and robotic arm. They should be able to collect samples without extravehicular activity."

Benton paused in thought. The monolith radiation levels were high enough to be a contamination risk to anybody who approached. Not particularly dangerous in the short term, but potentially messy. If the crew or the vehicle became contaminated, it would cost Kepler substantial time and money to cleanup. Better if a more experienced crew took this task.

"There is a radiological contamination risk at this monolith," Benton said. "The sampling also has to be done at the end of their run, when they're tired. Could we, instead, schedule a visit by our Special Missions Survey Team?"

Silvestre didn't even look at his schedule. "No way, Dr.

Valero. Special Missions is booked solid for at least the next six weeks. They're busy surveying several active volcanoes in southern Wordonia. Unless you would like to wait until then?"

Benton clenched his teeth. Kepler possessed a Special Missions Survey Team for undertaking unusual scenarios, particularly where there was elevated risk to crew or vehicles. For situations like this.

"What is the point of having a Special Missions Survey Team if they're never available to perform...*special* missions," Benton said. "Come on, Silvestre! When will you guys in Ops realize that keeping assets at 100% utilization means they aren't available for other uses? That makes using them for discretionary needs and unexpected scenarios impossible—*just like this one.*"

Silvestre was silent, sitting in his chair with his arms crossed.

Benton sighed. "And we can't wait on this. Our updated contract with DPE explicitly requires us to study this at the next opportunity. When is that grid scheduled to be visited again? I'm guessing not for a while."

"Correct," Silvestre said, "it will be six months until the next tender visit. I'm sorry, Dr. Valero, but Special Missions has been given assignments per company policy. There isn't much I can do, though if you were to escalate your concerns to the executive committee, I might get permission to reassign them."

Because of his position, Benton would probably get his way if he went to the executive committee. But then, Special Missions would be forced to adjust their schedule. It was an expensive outfit to operate, and a last-minute rescheduling would hit the company's bottom line. Operations would likely have to play scheduling gymnastics with the calendar to meet their other obligations.

"Can you swap grid assignments and give this one to a more experienced crew?" Benton said.

Silvestre made some adjustments to his computer. He said, "We have eighteen other teams out on various missions, of which, about half are adequately equipped to sample the anomaly. However, none are in a fuel and supplies situation where they could handle the grid without first returning to Clinton Base for resupply.

"Frankly, it would be cheaper and faster just to pull a crew that's currently off assignment."

"What would that do to your schedule?" Benton said.

"Nothing, but it would mean cutting a crew's rest period short, and the expense of flying a tender all the way out to the grid point."

Benton quickly shook his head. "As much as I would like that option, I don't want to disrupt crew who are resting if it's unnecessary."

Silvestre didn't say anything, but he looked relieved.

Benton decided he would chance assigning the task to Ms. Machado and her crew. Technically, they were qualified. He didn't want to look overly cautious in front of the executive committee and cost the company money because he felt uneasy.

"Let's let the girl do this," Benton said. "You said Phil Curtis was riding along as an instructor?"

"Yes, sir."

"Okay, that makes me feel better. It means a long workday for the crew—and on the last day of their run. But they'll be fine." He lifted a finger in emphasis. "Just make sure you remind Ms. Machado of potential contamination risks when you send her the assignment changes."

"Yes, sir, I will definitely do that. And thank you for your understanding and willingness to work with the operations team to find a solution."

Benton Valero gave him a quick grin and a wave and walked out of the Ops Center.

3

Belle's body hovered above the jungle floor. Over the low background hum of the motors, the sounds of the jungle arose. Snapping, whistles, clicks, and other noises she could not identify. She was surrounded by massive trees with trunks two meters in diameter.

She turned her head and saw *C195* in the distance, partially obscured by vegetation.

Below her, Belle watched a spiderbot install a seismic sensor on the jungle floor. The eight-legged ground drone was drilling a deep hole down into the bedrock. A second spiderbot approached and dropped a new seismic sensor next to the first bot, ready to be hammered into the drilled hole.

After dropping its load, the second bot walked back to *C195*. A *chittering*. A crash of branches near the bot. A flash of bright yellow.

A megapede leaped out of the soil and wrapped itself around the bot. Squeezing its body around the bot, it snapped two legs and caused the sensor assembly to implode. The megapede disappeared into its hidden burrow with the bot.

Damn. Belle snapped out of her quadcopter perspective and back into C195's cockpit. "Borya, I just lost another spiderbot!" she yelled to her co-pilot, who was working in the drone workshop. The wildlife at this location was some of the worst she'd ever seen. At this loss rate, they would be out of spiderbots before they completed the run.

After landing at their first grid assignment, Borya and she immediately set to work deploying a new batch of unattended sensors. They didn't do the physical work and were not supposed ever to leave the safety of the tender unless the most dire situation occurred. Like a reactor accident or failure of the life support system. Instead, most of the work was done by an army of spiderbot drones.

Belle monitored and controlled the work from her pilot's couch while Borya worked in the tender's workshop, fixing the results of Clinton's abuses on the robots.

Phil sat quietly, watching Belle work. Always evaluating.

Belle's neural implant interfaced directly with cameras and microphones on the tender's two quadcopter drones. This allowed her to roam around the jungle, monitoring work, without leaving the safety of the tender.

They were currently at the third of their four assigned sites for the day.

Borya appeared at the cockpit hatch. "Okay, I'm uncrating a new spiderbot. Had to pull it from our reserves. We've got nine left."

Belle stretched out on her cot, nursing a mug of hot tea while waiting for her dinner to finish heating in the kitchenette's tiny oven. They'd just finished the fourth and last assignment of what had become a sixteen-hour workday.

The three-person crew shared a tiny living space with

three bunks, a kitchenette, food storage, and a lavatory that lacked a shower. Just six square meters of ship floor area, located directly astern of the cockpit. They were only one day into the run, but the living quarters already stank of unwashed bodies and lavatory chemicals.

By now, Belle was accustomed. She'd spent the previous year on tender runs with Phil as pilot-in-command. She enjoyed the crew-rest time. That's when Phil told her stories of his career. The man had been piloting for planetary survey firms for almost thirty years.

Phil lay in the bunk across from her, making a face. "I still don't understand how you can drink that stuff."

"I don't have a titanium gut like you," she said. "Ginger tea helps calm the cramping from the gravinegator."

Borya was in the tender's tiny lavatory, bathing himself.

They had a six-hour block of rest until they needed to depart for the next grid assignment tomorrow morning. With her feet finally out of her flight boots and propped up in front of her, she yawned and stretched her arms.

At the previous site, several spiderbots had disappeared. Eaten by some overly aggressive Clinton fauna. It had been necessary to dip into their bot reserve in order to stay on schedule.

At this current site, she'd almost lost one of the quadcopters after a motor overheated and began smoking. In Clinton's high-oxygen atmosphere, it had been seconds away from bursting into flames by the time Borya recovered it.

The entire day, Phil sat quietly in the background, judging Belle's every action. Now with Borya in the head, he opened up a bit to her. "Technically, I'm not supposed to comment to you on my report, but you did well today. You handled the error with the landing mass well, though I'm going to ding you for not catching it."

Belle growled softly, looking into the distance.

"It's a small error. I'd be concerned if you kept making similar mistakes, but you haven't."

"Thanks, Phil, you're too good to me. It was a stupid mistake."

Phil gently kicked her bunk. "Don't think that just because I like you I'm going to go easy on you. I've got a reputation to maintain." He winked at her.

Though a friendly guy, Phil was widely known as a brutally strict flight instructor. Especially to his former apprentices.

The timer on the oven dinged, and almost simultaneously, the cockpit comms behind her head also began to chime. "I wonder who that could be." She had submitted their daily report not twenty minutes ago, so it must be somebody at Ops with follow-up questions or instructions.

With her mug of tea in hand, Belle walked the three steps to the cockpit and put on her headphones. "Charlie One Niner Five, standing by."

"Charlie One Niner Five, Clinton Ops, we have an assignment modification for you; say when ready to copy."

"Clinton Ops, Charlie One Niner Five, understood. Hold for thirty." Belle took a gulp from her mug, carefully set it down in a cup holder, and got her electronic planner ready.

"Clinton Ops," she said, "Charlie One Niner Five, confirming ready to copy instructions."

"Charlie One Niner Five, Clinton Ops, this is Silvestre Jenkins speaking. Hello, Belle. How are you doing this fine evening?"

Belle sat a little straighter in her chair. "Hello, sir, we are doing fine. Preparing to eat some dinner before bedding down for the night. How can I help you?"

"I have a change of orders for one of your grid assignments on Thursday, in two days' time, as follows: Pilot Belle Machado, you are hereby ordered to conduct sample collection at Grid 18M071399. The collection shall be done using the sampling arm and sampling saw; spectrometer measurements shall also be recorded of exposed surfaces. The target is an unusual and prominent rock monolith located in the northern half of the grid, the only one visible by lidar. How do you copy?"

She repeated back the instructions.

"Affirmative, and, Belle, Dr. Valero asked me to warn you of a potential radiological contamination hazard at the monolith. Please be careful and advise us immediately of anything unusual you observe."

Like all Kepler flight crews, Belle had received training on handling radiation and radiological contamination. But she'd never had to put it into practice.

"Do you have any additional details on the nature of this hazard?"

Was it radioactive dust? The monolith itself? Contaminated groundwater?

"No, that's all I have."

"Understood. Good night, sir, Charlie One Niner Five."

"Charlie One Niner Five, Clinton Ops, good night to you also."

She hung her headphones on their designated stowage hook and sat back in her seat for a minute. That seemed like an unusual call. Dr. Valero rarely got directly involved with the day-to-day tender operations, and she had never been introduced to him personally. What did he know that would make him forward a caution message via Ops?

It would all be okay. This was standard operating

procedure.

As she sat in solitude listening to the night, through the thin bulkhead, the racket sounded of Clinton's giant arthropod fauna murdering each other. Belle considered the spiderbot that was ambushed by the megapede earlier. What it would be like if that was herself. Dragged underground by an alien jungle monster.

She clutched her arms to her chest.

4

Belle looked out the cockpit window at the jungle below as she circled Grid 18M071399. It was the third and final day of the mission, and this was the last survey site of the day. She was tired and ready to go home. The tasks ahead of them, plus the two-hour return flight, were all that stood between her and a promotion and satisfied sleep in a warm bed back at base.

Their orders stated that the monolith sat in the northern half of the grid and was the only prominent object in the area. She programmed a loose circular flight pattern over the grid into the navigation computer and enabled the autopilot.

Confirming that *C195* flew stable and tracked the pattern, she next reached for her central flight display and changed its mode to lidar ground scan. Adjusting its settings for canopy penetration, mapping of terrain elevation, and scanning the entire grid.

Belle initiated the scan. While waiting, she kept her attention on the flight path ahead, looking for flight hazards.

There it is! That had to be the rocky monolith up ahead. She didn't have the lidar scan results yet, but that must be it.

The jungle—a featureless canopy for thousands of square kilometers around her—suddenly thinned out. A dip in the ground. No. The trees dipped, becoming shorter and less dense. The stunted trees had a sickly yellow hue. The canopy they formed was so thin, the jungle floor was visible below.

"Look't that, guys!" she called out to the others. "You ever see something like that on Clinton?"

"No," Borya said.

"Sort of," Phil said, "but never anything that regular in shape. And what's wrong with the trees?"

In the middle of the canopy depression lay a small rocky plateau, perhaps ten to twenty meters above ground level. There were no trees growing out of the prominence. Though the canopy of nearby trees partly shrouded the plateau from directly overhead, those were stunted, reaching a height of perhaps only forty meters above the ground.

The monolith was strange. *What an odd object.* "Object" was the correct word. "Monolith" wasn't. That described a giant natural boulder, but this one was symmetrical in shape. More like a thing than a terrain feature. She'd seen nothing like it in this region over the last three days. The ground was unbroken. Not so much as a boulder stuck above ground. What's more, the trees of Clinton's rainforests tended to grow not just between inanimate objects, but also on top of them, like the giant banyan trees of Earth. Yet there wasn't even a stick growing on top of the monolith. The object could be mistaken for a building.

As the tender neared its closest approach to the monolith, the master warning light illuminated along with its chime.

Belle checked the status board. An elevated background radiation level had been detected. At the closest approach of five hundred meters, it peaked at 0.01 millisieverts-per-hour (mSv/hr). Not spectacularly high, but she understood what interested the science team.

About ten minutes later, after running two-and-a-half loops, *C195* completed the lidar scan. Belle confirmed that the rocky feature she observed was the target of interest. What at first appeared to be a plateau was, in fact, more of a low dome shape with an irregular bumpy surface.

Its height peaked at about twenty meters above ground in the center and sloped gradually to the soil. The area above ground—the sloping sides suggested the monolith extended below the visible terrain—was oval. About one hundred meters long west to east, and fifty meters wide north to south, though part of the western end fell off sharply. It presented a cliff face of about five meters in height.

Belle considered their plan of action.

They still needed to perform the originally scheduled sensor deployments. That should take about three hours and would be conducted from a landing site near the center of this 1km square grid.

After that, she would reposition *C195* just to the west of the anomaly, near the exposed cliff face, within reach of *C195*'s sampling arm and sensor boom. That should permit them to collect all the requested samples before daylight ran out.

Three hours later, they landed at the monolith's cliff face. The jungle penetrator had cleared the site in record time because of the sparse undergrowth and thin canopy. The sky was visible in all her cockpit windows. *That's a first.* Usually, the canopy completely covered the landing site, despite the best efforts of the penetrator. Although the hour was late, the increased sunlight significantly improved the illumination she was accustomed to working in.

At this location, radiation levels were 2 mSv/hr. Quite high. A human lacking augmentations would suffer serious health problems if they remained there long term. But all three of them had blood nanite augments. Microscopic robots swam around their bodies, repairing cell and tissue damage. They could tolerate radiation levels a thousand times higher. Necessary because these small tenders had lightweight reactor shielding that routinely exposed the crew to levels exceeding one millisievert-per-hour.

She prepped the sampling arm and sensor boom. Running through its self-tests, she noted everything was in order and began planning the sampling.

"I'm going to step into the workshop," Borya said. "I still have a little drone maintenance to finish up. Let me know if anything exciting happens."

Belle nodded as he walked to the stern. With Borya gone, the rock face of the monolith appeared through the starboard cockpit window, about ten meters away. Despite the distance—about six-and-a-half times her body length— the rock dome loomed above the tender.

"Belle," Phil said, "I don't need to evaluate your sampling. It's outside the scope of a check-flight. So while you're doing that, I'm going to use the radio to upload my next report. No reason for me to sit here idle." Phil reached forward and configured the tender's radio for data transmission.

Belle smiled stiffly. Was he uploading her completed evaluation? Was she done? Surely not until after she returned the crew and ship safely back to base. Better to assume that.

She forced her attention back to the task at hand. Phil wouldn't usually interrupt her, but he tried to be efficient.

She unstowed the arm from its internal cradle, extending it out about two meters away from *C195* toward the cliff face. The arm had binocular optics, a microphone array mounted directly behind the hand, and a short forearm.

She enabled the feeds into her optical and audio nerve neural interface. Belle became the arm as new visuals and audio signals flooded her mind.

She could still feel the arm control sticks under her hands, and it only took a split second to switch between the perspective of the arm feeds and her own senses, if necessary, but still, the view exhilarated her.

A massive dragonfly-analog zoomed by her vision. It seemed almost within touching distance. The *thump-thump-thump* of its wings beating Clinton's thick atmosphere sounded, and reflections of *C195* repeated thousands of times in its large compound eye array, the size of a dinner plate. The splash of sunlight through the giant insect's thin wing membrane refracted into beautiful rainbow patterns.

Wake up, Machado, get with it. She must really be tired if her mind was wandering that much. There would be plenty of time for sightseeing on another occasion, but now, she had work to do.

The sensor boom contained a suite of additional sensors and tools, including a rock grinder, rock saw, chemical spectrometer, magnetometer, and radiation detectors. Working the external arm, she grasped the sensor boom and withdrew it from its own cradle, inserting it into its dedicated socket underneath the arm's hand so it could be easily extended and retracted as needed.

She extended the fifteen-meter arm toward the rock face ten meters away. As she approached, Belle kept an eye on the radiation detector and saw a slight increase in the level, rising to 4 mSv/hr. That meant that, whatever the radiation source, it was farther away, or the level would have increased a hundredfold as she came nearer instead of twofold.

The entire cliff face was coated with a moss-analog, more like a thick coating of blue lichen. She looked for a spot with less moss, but it all looked like the same featureless furry rock. Belle picked a position a meter above the ground, extended the boom, and took multiple still photographs using the hyperspectral imager.

Next, she extended a scraper and cleaned the moss off her target, storing samples in a sample basket. The rocky surface under the moss looked just like black granite. She extended the boom's chemical spectrometer, moved it up next to the rock, and recorded some measurements.

So far, so good. Time to do some digging.

She needed to remove the rock's weathered surface to get a suitable spectrometer reading. If they were going to become contaminated, this would be where it happened. The grinding wheel produced copious amounts of dust. If the rock were radioactive, that dust would be radioactive, and if it sprayed all over the tender—or worse, got into the life support system—they would have a mess for the hazmat teams to clean up when they got home. However, radiation levels were steady, so she retracted the spectrometer, extended the rock grinder, and spun it up.

The radiation level jumped as the grinder's diamond-tipped head dug into the rocky surface.

It kept increasing.

She stopped grinding. But the level continued increasing past 50 mSv/hr, then 250 mSv/hr.

"What is going on here...? Background radiation is rising," she said to Phil.

He had finished his report and was sitting back, watching Belle work. "Stop grinding."

"I already did." It should have stopped rising as soon as she halted grinding, then slowly dropped as the dust settled. That wasn't happening.

"What's it at?" Phil asked.

"Now it's at 500 mSv/hr."

Then there was a huge spike. In only two seconds, detected radiation climbed to 10,000 mSv/hr.

Belle gasped. That could be lethal if they stuck around. Their blood nanites couldn't fix damaged cell walls and DNA fast enough.

There was a *crash* in the drone workshop, like something heavy fell from a workbench onto the deck.

"We need to leave here now." She turned in her seat. "Borya, return to the cockpit immediately," she yelled. *Oh, for an intercom on this boat.*

Belle pushed the transmit button on her radio and said, "Clinton Ops, Charlie One Niner Five, um… I'm getting some strange re—"

The whooping of *C195*'s master alarm sounded. Then its computer screamed, "CORE OVERHEAT! SCRAM! SCRAM! SCRAM!"

Belle switched out of the sensor feed and saw the cockpit panels lit up like a Nuevo Peruvian cantina.

The master alarm klaxon whooped in her ears. *C195*'s reactor core was overheating. Melting down!

A tremendous loud boom reverberated from the stern of the tender. Her ears popped, and her head slammed into the cushion of her acceleration couch.

The cabin air smelled of ozone, hot metal, and burning plastic.

Smoke.

Phil coughed. "What in the blazes just happened? Did we just lose the reactor?"

The whooping alarm started again. "FIRE! FIRE! FIRE!" screamed *C195*.

Belle raced to detach herself from the straps of her seat. Finally, she got loose. She jumped up on her seat and turned around.

5

A wall of flames spanned the rear of the cabin. Thick black smoke accumulated on the ceiling. The path to the drone workshop passed through the fire.

Belle yelled, "Borya! Get out of there!"

Her training kicked in, and she glanced at *C195*'s status panel. A cabin fire, a fuselage breech, and *C195* had dumped its reactor core. *That's what that great bang was.* Radiation levels were dropping below 1,000 mSv/Hr.

Which environment was safer? Stay inside this burning vessel, try to fight the fire, and make contact with Clinton Base? Or evacuate into the hostile jungle and the monolith? Belle had to make a decision.

Nothing she could do would stop that fire. Because of the cabin breach, Clinton's oxygen-rich atmosphere had penetrated and fed the flames. Even metal would burn.

C195 was doomed. They would soon be also if they remained here. But first, they had to survive the fire long enough to get out.

Each wore fire-proof flight suits, boots, and gloves, with integrated fire hoods folded into the collar. Portable full-face oxygen masks were located on their couches. These could supply oxygen indefinitely as long as they had a supply that could be filtered. They also included a thermal imager in the eye shield to see through smoke.

"Hoods and masks!" she said.

She deployed the hood from her collar and wrapped it around her head, leaving only her eyes, nose, and mouth exposed. Then she put on her mask—covering those body parts—turned on the oxygen supply, and enabled the thermal imager.

She checked on Phil. He had finished donning his equipment.

No sign of Borya.

Phil rose from his seat and tried to get to the stern. "Borya!" he yelled, but there was no reply. "Borya!"

Phil stumbled back to the cockpit. "The flames are too hot. I can't get back there!" Their suits were fireproof but had little thermal insulation. They couldn't stand in fires.

"Evacuate!" Belle said. "We'll try and extract Borya from the outside at the rear escape hatch."

Phil gave her a thumbs-up in agreement.

Belle quickly went through her emergency evacuation mental checklist. Comms were down, so there was no calling base. And there was no reactor left to shut down.

She stood on Phil's seat, directly below the cockpit emergency egress hatch. Lashed to the inside was a crew survival pack.

The cabin temperature rapidly rose. They were seconds away from a flashover. Everything inside the cabin would spontaneously combust, and they would cook inside their fireproof suits.

She smashed the IN CASE OF EMERGENCY BREAK GLASS cover over the hatch's latching mechanism with her elbow. Gave it a tremendous haul and pushed.

Belle scrambled up and out onto the upper surface of the tender.

The hatch opened outward so she could detach the survival pack and put it on like a backpack.

Phil exited behind her a few seconds later. They paused to assess the situation.

The rear half of the tender blazed like an inferno. Tongues of flame moved across the metal surface like it was a lit match. The stern egress hatch burned. It had never been opened.

"I think Borya's trapped!" Belle said. "We need to rescue him!"

Flames rushed toward them.

"No!" Phil said. "It's too late. If he hasn't already escaped, then he's lost. Nothing we can do. We need to get to the ground!"

The ground. Full of megapedes and other hidden monsters. But surely they would stay away from the fire. Would they? Wouldn't they be safer on the ground?

"We're trapped!" Phil said.

The flames had already reached the main service ladder leading to the ground. Their escape route.

Belle suppressed a whimper. Shocked indecisiveness crept into her mind, corrupting her decision-making. *Stop it! Think!*

She would rather take her chances with the megapedes and the monolith than die by fire.

The drop to the ground was a long four meters from where they stood. And onto an uncertain surface covered with timber and foliage cut down by the jungle penetrator, then crushed by the weight of *C195*'s undercarriage. All of it steamed and smoldered. They were likely to break a leg jumping down. Then be forced to watch the little ship burn down on top of them.

Looking to starboard, she spied the extended sampling arm still reaching out to the cliff on the western end of the monolith. She'd left it extended in her rush to deal with the emergency. They might manage to walk hand-over-hand down the arm to safety if they could reach it—however, the arm's shoulder connected at midships, where it burned with bright yellow flames.

She walked to the very bow of the upper fuselage and gestured for Phil to follow.

"We need to leap across the gap between the fuselage and the external arm and grab it." Belle looked at the overweight fifty-year-old man. "Can you do it?"

With a brave face, he said, "I'll try. You go first!"

Belle turned around and gauged the distance to the arm. She took off in a sprint toward the stern and the flames. She pivoted her trajectory to the left at the last second and jumped, arms stretched out to catch the thick steel tube. *Dios, ayudame!* Airborne.

She felt cold steel slam into her upper chest. She wrapped her body around it like a snake, holding to it desperately with her gloved hands. *Don't look down.* She needed to clear the way for Phil's jump. She started walking herself down the arm, hand-over-hand.

The sound of running and Phil's grunt as he leaped met her ears. The metal bar she gripped jumped to the side. Then Phil yelped. A crash echoed below.

Belle looked down between her feet, which dangled three meters above the ground.

Phil had fallen. His body was motionless on top of a large log, his head twisted unnaturally.

"No! Phil!" she cried. "No, no, no!"

Violent heat was at her back. Flames undoubtedly licking

her neck. At that moment, she wanted to curl up and cover her ears. She nearly lost her grip. Memories of her father's death flooded her mind. "No!" she screamed.

Belle forced away thoughts of Phil for the moment. She brought to her mind the jungle gym she used to play on in her elementary school. She walked one hand over the other. Then that one over the other. And again. Again. Again.

The muscles in her arms screamed.

Again. Again. Again.

The heat on her back lessened. The ground rose toward her. The sample she'd targeted rested almost at the base of the cliff. When she was halfway to the external arm's hand, she jumped safely to the ground.

She turned back to the ship to look for Phil, but it was too late. The place where he'd fallen burned. His broken body was motionless in the arms of the flames. Eyes open, he stared sightlessly into the distance as if lost in deep thought.

Belle sobbed. Then she whispered, "I'm sorry. I'm so sorry."

She bid her dead crew-mates farewell and ran the rest of the way to the cliff, tears wetting her cheeks. Unable to wipe them away because of the oxygen mask. Not caring if a megapede took her.

C195 was no more. Roaring flames consumed the entire tender. Thick black smoke rolled toward the north on a southerly breeze. Belle flinched as a sharp *bang* reverberated off the monolith and forest. Definitely an overpressurized compressed gas cylinder. She cowered. There were still all kinds of nasty materials on the burning tender.

An even more enormous smoke plume lay to the south, five hundred meters distant. What could it be?

In a last desperate act to save itself and the crew, *C195* had dumped its reactor core. The molten slag of the metal casing, moderator, and radioactive fuel pellets ejected with enough force to carry it half a kilometer downrange.

The core underwent a catastrophic meltdown. It was likely to remain a glowing radioactive hazard for the next few years. An everlasting ember now resting in the middle of one of the densest forests known to humanity. Surrounded by millions of tons of living and rotting biomass. Shrouded in an oxygen-rich atmosphere.

The wind blew the flames northward, and nothing would stop it from burning everything in its path. Including Belle.

She needed to distance herself from both the wreck and the reactor fire. There was only one place she could go and be confident she wouldn't become trapped in the flames: Up.

The rocky, domed monolith was just that: a dome. A sloping surface ran along most of its perimeter. Only on the side where she stood was it a cliff.

She ran toward the north along the western edge of the cliff, away from the flames. The cliff's lip sloped down about twenty meters away until it met the ground.

On hands and knees, she scrambled up the steep rocky face. After a meter, her feet slipped as the moist moss detached from the rock. It was impossibly slippery once it came loose. Like climbing an ice wall.

She tried again, this time with a running start. She made it a few more meters but slipped and fell onto her stomach. She slid back to the ground.

Next, she tried going up backward, digging her heels into the stone. Using her hands to support her weight up off the moss. Also a failure. And this time, she tore a hole in the back of the right calf of her ship suit.

Belle hadn't thought it would be this difficult to scale the monolith. She needed traction.

She dropped the survival pack where she stood and

sprinted back to the cliff face. *Good!* The end of *C195*'s arm—and the sensor boom—were still intact, though flames were minutes away from reaching them. Her hands danced over the boom, looking for the cutting tools. She found the scraper. She detached it using the multitool strapped to her belt.

Then she switched to the external arm's hand. It had a crowbar-like spike used for gripping surfaces. Made of hardened tool steel. She removed that also.

Wisps of smoke floated by her head. Glowing flames were closing in. She ran back to where she'd dropped the survival pack—more of a fast walk, because the thickening smoke made it difficult to see. If it weren't for the oxygen mask she still wore, she would have likely already passed out from smoke inhalation.

Belle put the bag on her back again. She ran another fifty meters along the rock edge toward the northern edge of the dome. There, she found a spot on the ground slightly higher than where she'd tried to climb previously, where the rock was consequently less steep.

Using the pry bar like a spike and the scraper like a steel fingernail, she stopped herself from sliding down the slippery slope while she climbed. She got about fifteen meters from the edge. The hill flattened enough that it was no longer a slip risk. She stowed the scraper in the pack but kept the spike ready in her right hand.

She scaled the slope the rest of the way to the dome's center. Belle stood twenty meters above ground level. High enough to see all around the dome, but still half the height of the surrounding jungle canopy.

It couldn't have been more than ten minutes since the accident, but the forest to the south of the dome blazed. Flames reached hundreds of meters into the sky.

Belle had been so desperate to reach safety that she'd ignored the potential radiation hazard on the dome. The survival pack had a medical computer that included a radiation detector. She pulled it out and checked.

4 mSv/hr. The same level as before she began grinding the wall. Even with the reactor fire nearby. How could this be? If it had been contaminated, the wind would have spread radioactive dust over the entire monolith. Maybe not a lot, but it would have been measurable.

She put the medical computer back in the pack.

The sun set as she rested there, watching. Believing she was safe. Transfixed by the spectacle. *Why are humans drawn to fire?* With the growing darkness, hot embers became visible, floating a thousand meters up into the sky to be carried for kilometers into the distance.

Not wanting to grieve for her friends yet. Not wanting to think about the consequences to her career of losing her command during a check-flight. Not worrying about whether she would live to see her family again. Just watching Clinton's jungle burn to the ground.

But the giant forest fire didn't take long to spread toward the north, south, east, and west. Clinton's dense, oxygen-rich atmosphere fueled it, and the impenetrable waterlogged rainforest might as well have been tissue paper withstanding a blowtorch.

It quickly grew into a firestorm.

Trapped—not safe—on top of the exposed monolith, Belle again found her life in jeopardy.

6

Hurricane-force winds howled over the rock's surface as they rushed forward to feed the raging firestorm.

Belle placed the survival pack flat on the stone. Then she grasped the spike in one gloved hand and the scraper in the other. Spreading her limbs as far apart as possible, she lay face down on top of the pack.

Fortunately, her oxygen mask recharged itself from the atmosphere. Otherwise, she might have died right then and there from the ghastly gas mixtures released by the superheated biological matter being cooked by the fire.

The blue-green moss covering the monolith shriveled in the dry heat, then seemed to turn to dust. Its ashes blew away in the powerful winds. Belle now lay on bare, hard, and gratefully cool granite.

Despite the flight suit being rated for shipboard fires, these conditions definitely invalidated the manufacturer's warranty. And through the small hole in her suit's right leg, the exposed flesh screamed as it burned. She shifted the fabric around until the stone hid the hole.

Some strands of her hair fell loose from underneath the firehood. It curled from the heat, then turned to ash and blew away. Just like the moss.

The firestorm raged on for hours. Belle lost track of time.

During the worst part of the storm, she feared her suit would fail. Oh, for a proper fireshelter, like those carried by the wilderness firefighters back in Nuevo Peru. However, the granite surface of the dome remained cool. Belle clung to it, letting it sap excess heat from her body.

But the flesh on her back screamed, and the roaring storm deafened her hearing. She became delusional from dehydration and possibly heat stroke. Belle taunted its fury, daring it to bring worse.

Now she grieved for her lost crewmates, especially Phil. Over the last year, he had treated her like a daughter. Acted like a father preparing his child for the dangerous world. Now, he was gone.

Memories of Dad flooded back, and she let them.

Her first memory of him taking her for a ride on his horse around the family ranch. Teaching Belle how to ride a pony when she was five. Defending her honor when she was sixteen, killing a man because of it.

Father going to jail, only to be released nine months later on compassionate grounds after being diagnosed with terminal, inoperable cancer.

Dying in his bed at their family home. Surrounded by Mom, herself, her brother, and four sisters.

There were evil men. There were good men. Her father had been good. She would honor his name.

She would also honor Phil Curtis, a good man.

Two men who'd sacrificed so that she might live a decent life. Belle would not disrespect them by giving up now.

A cathartic lament released from her chest, expanding out to the universe. It carried away an awful weight.

Eons passed. The howl of the storm attenuated to a roar.

Then a moan.

Belle came to herself suddenly from whatever fugue held her captive. She lived and breathed, sucking air through the oxygen mask.

She rolled over onto her back and sat up, bending arms and legs. All her limbs were still attached. A sharp pain pulsed in her right calf where it had burned. Probably a good sign. Worse if it had been numb.

Belle took water out of the survival pack and drank deeply. Then she lay back down on her back, looking at the black sky. She might still survive this ordeal.

Her ship, *C195*. Her first and only command. Lost. What would happen to her? The careers of captains who lost their ships tended not to go well, no matter the circumstances behind the loss.

What had happened to cause the meltdown? The reactor hadn't even been running at that moment. It was on standby, secured for ground operations. Was the radiation spike caused by the failure, or was it symptomatic of whatever triggered the meltdown?

These questions weren't worth answering if she didn't survive. And for that, she needed to be rescued.

Because of the firestorm, she hadn't deployed the survival pack's automated rescue beacon. But conditions had calmed sufficiently.

Using the spike as a grip, she levered herself to a standing position on stiff legs. Belle looked dizzily around her.

It was a wasteland. Smoke-covered piles of ash for as far as the eye could see, which wasn't much. The heavens were as black as the night. What time was it?

She queried the time from her neural implant. Twelve hours had passed since she'd evacuated the tender! It was midmorning, but the skies were black.

Obviously, the monolith had saved her life. Its isolation kept her from the flames, and its cool mass protected her from overheating.

Belle rummaged around in the survival pack, taking stock of her supplies. Besides the tools she had scavenged from the external arm, she had a three-person shelter, rope, a blanket, a lantern, and a water filter. A fully equipped first-aid kit. Twelve days of emergency rations and water. A combination of O_2 supply and CO_2 scrubber. A flare gun with four flares and a one-way emergency radio beacon. A power cell to run everything.

She needed to remove the mask to use the emergency beacon, but couldn't do that in the open because of the thick smoke. Belle deployed the shelter—which was little more than an incredibly rugged and roomy sleeping bag—stuffed everything inside, and then herself.

She hooked the O_2-CO_2 combo into the shelter's integrated life support system and powered it up.

Once it was operating correctly—she owed the maintenance people back at the base a drink—she removed her mask and took a deep breath. The place smelled like canned air and campfire. *Wonder why.*

The one-way beacon was just a handheld radio. It operated at shortwave frequencies and had a large antenna that needed to be unfurled.

She put her mask back on and scrambled out of the shelter to deploy it. Connected it to the handy impermeable cable interface provided outside the shelter. Then she got back in her shelter and unmasked.

While inspecting the radio, she ate an energy bar and forced down more water. Though not hungry or thirsty—she suspected she was in shock—she knew she was dangerously dehydrated and hypoglycemic after twelve hours in the firestorm.

Belle turned on the radio in standby mode. She held the record button and said into its small microphone, "MAYDAY, MAYDAY, MAYDAY, to any station, this is Charlie One Niner Five actual on automated beacon. My vehicle is abandoned, one soul stranded, requesting rescue at northern edge of Grid 18M071399."

She flipped the status lever to transmit, and that was it. Her message was now transmitting once a minute in the open on the planet-wide search-and-rescue frequency.

Stretching out on the floor of the tiny shelter, Belle intended to think about recent events. Instead, her exhausted body dozed off and slept for several hours.

She awakened around noon. Ate another protein bar and drank more water. Belle felt much better.

The shelter had a small window. Through it, the sky was still filled with black smoke. There would be no rescue until this cleared up.

What caused *C195*'s reactor to have a meltdown? What was the sequence of events leading up to the meltdown? Radiation levels had held steady until the grinding wheel dug into the dome's stone. Then there was a rapid rise over perhaps fifteen seconds until the alarms started going off in the cockpit.

The first alarm was *CORE OVERHEAT! SCRAM!* An alert about the core overheating, followed by an order to scram the tender's power plant fission reactor. That didn't make sense.

C195 was too small to use a fusion plant. Only medium and large ships employed those. And the largest ships actually used black-hole, matter-annihilation power plants. But the advantages of fission plants over fusion or black-hole plants were their compact size and high power-density.

Scramming a fission reactor was an emergency shutdown during a malfunction. But at the time of the incident, *C195*'s reactor had been in standby mode, secured for ground operations. Ship systems were running off their stored-power cells. The core wasn't in a critical state, so there was nothing to scram. Yet mere seconds after the scram alarm sounded, the automated systems had dumped the core in an attempt to save the ship.

Belle had an idea. She opened the first-aid kit. The medical diagnostics computer included a blood nanites interface module.

She powered it up, then interfaced it with her neural implant. Commanded it to analyze the state of her blood nanites. Her implant could do its own analysis, but the kit's medical computer was more capable.

Graphs and spreadsheets scrolled down the screen on the computer's display. She dug through the data and looked at time stamps. There was a notable dip in her nanite blood count right about the time of the radiation incident.

That would only be possible from powerful gamma or neutron radiation. Furthermore, her nanites were currently tracking elevated levels of activated radionuclides in her blood. Timestamps indicated those rose simultaneously with the dip in her nanite count. Radionuclides were created in materials when bombarded by neutron radiation.

Belle had been hit with a powerful pulse of neutron radiation. That was the only explanation for the drop in nanite count and rise in blood radionuclides.

Her physical health was no longer in danger from the pulse because her nanites had already returned to their nominal levels. They would quickly repair the cell damage caused by the rabid radionuclides rampaging through her body. But the pulse would have been fatal to an unaugmented human within days. If not, hours.

Had the pulse originated from the reactor? Or from somewhere else?

It was physically impossible for it to have originated from the reactor. It had been on standby. Its fuel pellets isolated from one another and surrounded by neutron absorbers. Held in a non-critical state.

The academy's mandatory nuclear power engineering classes had taught her how to create a critical mass of fissionable material. One method for doing it with a nominally subcritical mass was to shoot a neutron beam at it. If powerful enough, it would go critical.

Could the neutron radiation pulse have been strong enough to make *C195*'s reactor go critical? That seemed unlikely if its energy was emitted in all directions equally. Sufficiently high levels would have instantly killed her and her crew. But what if it was a directional neutron beam? Perhaps Belle's body only caught the outer edge of the beam's neutron flux.

Maybe this explained why Borya hadn't escaped from the fire in the drone workshop. It was adjacent to the reactor compartment. Caught by the beam, he would have died before the fire began.

Belle had questions, and it would be hours until the smoke cleared enough for rescuers to find her. Where had the hypothetical beam originated from? What hints might she find back at the wreckage?

7

Benton Valero's office phone rang. He answered.

"Dr. Valero, your presence is requested in the Operations Center."

"I'm in the middle of something," Benton said. He was typing a memo and, if interrupted, wouldn't remember where he was. "I can stop by in about thirty minutes."

He heard shuffling on the phone, then a different voice. "Dr. Valero, it's Silvestre in Ops." Jenkins sounded excited. "We just picked up a mayday beacon from Belle Machado's tender. It's urgent that we consult with you immediately."

This changed things. Ops had lost contact with *C195*'s crew twelve hours ago and reported their return to base overdue early this morning. These things happened, sometimes due to equipment malfunctions halting flights. Or sometimes delays because of operational complexities. But a mayday beacon meant there was more to this than just a broken radio or temperamental drive system.

"I'm on my way." Benton hung up. He saved his memo, then left his office on a brisk walk. The Ops Center was two buildings away on the base.

He entered the Center and found Silvestre sitting beside

an Ops Center staffer at a control console. Benton approached them from behind. On the console's large display, there was a satellite image and graphs of telemetry.

"You heard a mayday?" Benton said.

"Yes, sir," Silvestre said. "C373 picked up the beacon as it flew over C195's last known position." He pointed to a location on the satellite image.

"Is that smoke? Is this image recent?"

"Yes, and yes. There is a forest fire burning."

"Where exactly are they? Can you zoom in?"

The staffer zoomed in on the image until clouds of smoke rising into the atmosphere covered most of it.

"C373 geolocated the beacon to right in the middle of the fire," Silvestre said. He pointed to a dot on the image.

"Did the beacon provide any useful information besides the mayday?"

"Yes. Play the recording for Dr. Valero," he said to the staffer.

Over speakers, Benton heard a woman's hoarse voice. "*MAYDAY, MAYDAY, MAYDAY, to any station, this is Charlie One Niner Five actual on automated beacon. My vehicle is abandoned, one soul stranded, requesting rescue at northern edge of Grid 18M071399.*"

"What does she mean when she says *actual*?" Radio jargon and etiquette were a foreign language to Benton.

"It means it is the actual vehicle commander speaking. We're listening to Belle Machado."

But there were three crew members assigned to C195. Phil Curtis crewed the flight. "She says, '*one soul stranded.*' Where are the other two?"

"Presumed missing. She's only supposed to report on the number of living persons under her charge."

The grid coordinates Machado had named sounded

familiar. "Do you have the digital elevation map handy from the Phase One survey? Can you pull it up and superimpose it over your satellite image?"

"Sure, give me a moment," the staffer said. After a few minutes, a black-and-white elevation map appeared overlaying the satellite image. The geolocated beacon was located precisely in the center of the rock monolith.

Benton felt a sudden coldness at his core. "Do we know what happened? Any ideas?"

"We're still piecing together clues," Silvestre said. "But it happened sometime after they relocated to collect the sample from that rock monolith we spoke about." He pointed at it on the display. "Is that it?"

"Yes. Anything else?"

"Their last transmission is garbled but has some clues. We think it may be from the moment they ran into problems. Play that recording for Dr. Valero," Silvestre said to the staffer. "The one we were analyzing."

Benton heard Belle's voice again. "*Clinton Ops, Charlie One Niner Five, um... I'm getting some strange re—*" A cockpit alarm interrupted her voice, and the recording terminated.

"That's it," Silvestre said. "We've heard nothing else since."

"How long after they relocated was that transmission sent?"

Silvestre paused for a moment and said, "About fifteen minutes."

"They would have been in the middle of the sampling operation."

Silvestre nodded.

To Benton, it sounded like Belle was reporting *strange readings* or *strange results* when the alarm interrupted her. At the same time, they were in the middle of sampling the monolith.

What could have gone wrong? Nothing in the Phase One data indicated a severe threat. Crew and vehicle contamination should be the most serious risk they would encounter. Not something to dismiss, but at worst, it would have meant isolating the crew for a week and ordering a hazmat team to decontaminate the tender.

"Is Ms. Machado still alive?" Benton said.

"We have no way of knowing unless she updates her beacon," Silvestre said.

"Are you planning a rescue attempt?"

"Just beginning, sir. If you have a few minutes, I'm expecting Grant Stewart here any moment. To discuss the rescue operation."

"Yes, thank you, I'd like to listen in." Benton considered the risk of sending another crew near the monolith. However, he wanted to rescue Belle. Not only because it was the humane thing to do, but he wanted to know what she had learned. But how could she possibly survive alone out in that jungle? And in the middle of that forest fire?

A fit young man entered the Ops Center. He wore drab olive combat fatigues. He was tall and of Filipino descent through his mother's side. Benton was friends with Grant Stewart's father. They had been roommates in college many decades ago. However, he didn't know Grant all that well. He was the team leader for one of Kepler's search and rescue teams.

"Hello, Grant. Nice to see you again. How is your father?"

"Dr. Valero, good to see you also. Dad is great. Staying busy at the State Department."

Silvestre gave an overview of the situation to Grant. Then asked, "If we insert your team at this location"—he pointed to the monolith—"can you safely extract the pilot?"

"Hold on," Benton interrupted. "I'm not comfortable putting them down right onto the monolith. We don't know what happened to the vessel, but it seems related to the monolith."

Maybe the transmission coincidently cut out while they sampled. But Benton didn't believe in coincidences.

"We could be putting Grant's team in danger."

Silvestre listened to Benton, then gestured to Grant for his opinion.

Grant paused for a moment. "Well, I think your point is valid, sir. I have two additional concerns. First, there's too much smoke in the area for a dropship to insert us. It needs to clear some before we go in."

"Your second concern?" said Benton.

"I know these jungles well. I've a hard time believing this pilot will survive out there alone, without shelter, for more than a few hours. It'll be an allergic reaction if the wildlife doesn't get her first. Or a respiratory fungal infection. Or the fire, for that matter."

"Are you recommending we postpone rescue?" Silvestre said.

"Yes, indefinitely. Until the situation improves."

"Then what are your insertion criteria?"

Grant held out a hand and extended a finger. "One-kilometer visibility at ground level." He extended a second finger. "The pilot updates their beacon message. Then we'd know they're still alive."

"Dr. Valero?" Silvestre said.

"If we satisfy those restrictions, then I ask we not insert directly on top of the monolith. And the SAR team approaches with extreme caution. Send in your best people, Grant." They were all good people in the SAR teams. Almost exclusively former special forces combat medics. But not all of them were as experienced with the Clinton ecosystem as they should be.

Grant nodded.

"Okay," Silvestre said, "then the rescue op is canceled until further notice."

Benton felt terrible for the poor pilot—assuming Belle was still alive. And he grieved the loss of the other two missing crew members, particularly Phil Curtis, whom he had known for many years. But throwing more people into the dangerous situation likely would only increase the body count.

8

It is actually a dome. Belle stood outside her shelter, looking at her surroundings. The smoky sky had changed from pitch black to dark gray, but there was enough light and atmospheric clarity to give about a hundred meters of visibility.

During the firestorm, all the moss covering the rocky monolith had been burned and swept away. What was left was a bare granite surface, a smooth and featureless low dome.

At least there was nowhere for jungle creatures to hide in the stone. Assuming any were left alive after their home burned.

She stood at the dome's exact center and doubted that once she descended she could get back up again. So she chose to pack up her shelter and all her supplies.

The radio beacon she left transmitting, hanging from her shoulder, but disconnected and stowed its large antenna. That would decrease its transmission range by about tenfold until she could redeploy it.

Before descending, she walked a wide circle around the top of the dome. It was not wholly featureless. She found seams in the stone that formed hexagonal shapes about three meters across at two locations. The seams were close-fitting. The blade of her multitool was too wide to insert into the gap.

There is no way this structure is natural. But Clinton was an uninhabited planet. Furthermore, in the universe, humankind had not yet met another intelligent alien species, extinct or alive. The implications of her conclusion were too much to think about right now.

With all her possessions on her back in the survival pack backpack, the spike in one hand and scraper in the other, she carefully walked down to the dome edge from where she initially climbed.

Five meters before the edge of the rock, it became too slick to walk on. It was covered with ash sprinkling from the sky, making it slippery. She would have to descend the rest of the way on her backside.

Before doing that, she assessed the state of the ground. Looking for potential megapede hiding places.

The ground was littered with hundreds of burned-out exoskeletons. Indeed, nothing could have survived above or below ground. She was safe to walk.

After sitting, she scooted herself down the slope until she touched the ground.

It looked like a moonscape. Light puffy ash covered everything and continued to fall and accumulate. The silence was profound.

In the distance were giant tree stumps that still burned. In countless places, the ground smoked from fires that continued to smolder underground.

The land looked nothing like the jungle of yesterday. If it weren't for the landmark of the stone dome, she would be hopelessly lost right now. Belle kept close to the northern edge and slowly walked to the western cliff face, retracing the steps she'd taken yesterday.

The cliff face emerged from the murky gloom. Like the dome's upper surface, the cliff's face was now also moss-free. She needed to pause and take it in.

Bare smooth stone was not what remained. Quite the contrary; it was tiled in large hexagonal stones about one meter in diameter. From the ground to one meter short of the dome's roof, suggesting the dome had a solid stone roof one meter thick. The gaps between stones were nearly seamless, so closely fitted, just like the two larger examples found on the roof.

Many of the ground-level hexagonal stone faces were carved with mysterious symbols. Belle approached one. The cuts were of uniform depth and width. Definitely made with tools of some sort. So clean and precise were the cuts, it was like the creator worked clay with scrapers and knives, then in one step transformed it to solid granite.

In addition to being carved with symbols, the faces of two hexagons were also inlaid by smaller hexagons about twenty centimeters across. Could those be protective panels to some kind of door-opening mechanism?

Belle eventually made it back to the remains of the external arm and sensor boom. Despite being constructed chiefly of metal, little remained.

Temperatures down here had been sufficiently high to melt the aluminum and even burn some of the materials that must have contained high quantities of magnesium. Some of the remaining tools on the boom, and the fingertips of the hand, were made of hardened tool steel and survived, though their tempering was lost.

Here were the remains of the binocular camera—from which she had supervised the cutting that triggered all of this. It was a charred wreck of wires and melted optical assemblies.

On the cliff face was the cut she'd made yesterday. The grinding wheel barely scratched the surface of the hard granite, only removing the outer weathered surface. The newly ground surface was rougher than the original, lightly polished granite.

Belle checked radiation levels. 4 mSv/hr. The same as when they had begun the cut.

C195 was almost completely gone. It had burned hot, and ash, puddles of aluminum, and bent and twisted sheet steel were all that remained. It was colored a purplish hue from high temperatures. Nothing was salvageable.

She searched for the remains of Phil and Borya but without success. The fire had been so hot that even their bones and flight suits had burned. Temperatures amid the flames exceeded even the fireproof flight suit's max rating. There was nothing left to return to their families.

Shame on Belle for failing to bring them home. As pilot-in-command, she was responsible for crew safety. How could she face Kepler management without even the bodies of her dead crew? This run would become a safety case study. Belle's name would be forever immortalized in the textbooks of student pilots.

She sat on the ground and wept, reliving the grief she'd experienced during the firestorm.

Get a hold of yourself, Belle! She was blowing things out of proportion. She composed herself and stood back up.

Belle slowly walked around the wreck in a widening spiral, wondering at the devastation. Suddenly something snagged her left foot. A root maybe?

Stabbing pain shot through her heel.

A giant centipede-analog, a megapede, had latched onto

her foot and sunk its mandibles into her heel. The monster had been hiding underground, the soil protecting it from the fire.

The three-meter ambushing megapede tried to drag her underground into its burrow.

Adrenalin surged in Belle's blood. She dug her right foot into a dead stump to halt the creature's progress, and took the spike in her right hand. Furiously, she plunged it in and out of one of the megapede's compound eyes.

It instantly released her foot, made a horrible chattering sound, curled up on itself, and disappeared underground.

Recoiling in horror, Belle stumbled to her feet. She half ran, half limped in a beeline to the cliff face.

Her breathing was rapid. She could feel her chest tightening up. Sitting against the wall, holding the ichor-covered spike out in front of her to ward off imaginary pursuit by the monster, breathing became more difficult.

Anaphylactic shock!

Clinton's biology was incompatible with Earth's. That megapede had no hope of gaining nutritional value from Belle's body—though its tiny brain didn't know that. Whatever venom it had injected into her body was also unlikely to act in the intended manner, but it didn't matter. Her immune system had detected the alien biological agents injected into her body and responded with a massive allergic reaction.

Her first-aid training kicked in. Belle had only a few minutes of consciousness remaining. She took the survival pack off and dug out the first-aid kit.

She connected her neural implant wirelessly to the medical computer. Waited a moment for it to do its thing.

It instructed her to inject herself with a dose of epinephrine, conveniently giving her colored numbers matching the correct pouch in the kit where it was located.

From it, she grabbed a syringe and uncapped it. There was the bright gleam of a long needle. Belle stuck it into her thigh muscle, pushing through her suit. Squeezed on the plunger.

Within seconds, she felt her throat loosen and her heartbeat slow down. She withdrew the syringe and tossed it away.

Overcome by a sudden rush of nausea, she pushed the oxygen mask away from her face and vomited her meager lunch onto the ground.

The medical computer beeped and ordered her to take an antihistamine pill. Her blood nanites were dutifully disposing of the acid-based allergen the megapede had injected into her bloodstream.

There was tissue damage to her left heel. Now that the adrenalin and endorphins were wearing off, the pain was excruciating. She commanded her neural implant to deaden the nerves in her left foot. Belle felt immediate relief.

She stripped off her boot. Her ankle was swelling rapidly. There were two large puncture wounds surrounded by angry red, inflamed skin. They were leaking a nasty green fluid. Using the first-aid supplies, she cleaned the wound and bandaged it.

Belle ingested an anti-inflammatory medication, wrapped her foot with a medical boot, and put her damaged boot in the survival pack. She wouldn't use that for a few days until the swelling went down.

Belle was dizzy and tired. She felt a shiver of cold. Despite the effects of the epinephrine, she must be suffering from residual shock.

She cleared a spot of ash and debris near the cliff and redeployed the shelter. Then she stumbled inside and sealed away the outside world.

Belle commanded her implant to awaken the nerves in her foot. Otherwise, the deadened nerves would impair her nervous system's attempts to repair it.

Oh, the pain! Like the worst case of a sleep-numbed limb. She squirmed in discomfort on the floor of the shelter.

There was a quick way out of this. She commanded her implant to induce a four-hour medical sleep. Belle fell into a deep state of unconsciousness.

9

Belle awoke eight hours later. She had come out of the medically induced sleep after four. But her implant ordered her to eat and drink, then immediately go back to sleep. Now it was the middle of the night.

Her head hurt. Her burned calf and swollen heel ached. She wanted to lay here and go back to sleep. Her hopes of becoming a starship pilot were shattered.

Tomorrow will be a better day.

Belle forced herself out from under the blanket. At the least, she needed to eat, drink, and clean her wounds.

A chattering sound and motion nearby. Was she being attacked? Belle flashed the lantern out the tiny shelter window.

Where she had vomited earlier, about eight meters south of her shelter, there was a roiling mass of creatures. More of Clinton's fauna had survived than she thought possible. These were the scavengers who tunneled underground and evolved precisely for these sorts of ecological disasters.

They were feasting on the corpses of the dead. Some had found their way to Belle's vomited lunch. However, being biologically incompatible, they died as soon as they ate. And those dead bodies attracted even more carrion eaters.

It was just a question of time until they tasted her shelter, with or without her inside it. Belle needed to relocate.

She quickly cleaned and re-bandaged her painful wounds, put the medical boot back in place, and prepared to evacuate.

Her options were limited. She might try climbing the dome again, but injured as she was, she was unlikely to make it up the slippery slope. And even if she did, what would ensure safety from Clinton's dangerous fauna?

Rescue was likely still hours away. Only after the first daylight.

The domed monolith was a ruin of some kind but seemed impervious to the Clinton environment. Despite the thick layer of moss that had built up over the years, there was no evidence any other vegetation or wildlife had penetrated. If she could enter the structure and reseal it, then she might be safe until rescued.

Belle also wanted to know if the monolith had been the source of the neutron beam that had destroyed her ship. Any evidence she found supporting that hypothesis would help her justify the loss and recover her career.

There were potential problems though. The ruin needed to be investigated by proper scientists. She might get into trouble for disturbing it. However, she preferred that and survival over the...alternative of becoming lunch for some crazed megapede.

With the lantern attached to her head as a headlamp and oxygen mask on her face, Belle stumbled out of the shelter and packed everything up except for the emergency beacon and its antenna.

She relocated the beacon a little farther away from the mass of dead and dying creatures but left it open. The radio's transmissions would not reach the outside world from inside all that granite.

Pressing the record button on the radio, she spoke into it, "MAYDAY, MAYDAY, MAYDAY, to any station, this is Charlie One Niner Five actual on automated beacon. My vehicle is abandoned, one soul stranded, requesting rescue at northern edge of Grid 18M071399. Attempting entry through the western wall of monolith in search of improved shelter." Her updated message would tell anybody searching for her that she might be inside the ruin.

Next, she walked to the cliff and turned her attention to its granite hexagonal-tiled face, puzzling how to pass. Approaching one of the tiles that was embedded with a smaller hexagonal tile, she probed it. She tried to pry it out using her multitool, but the seam between it and the surrounding tile was too narrow for her to gain any leverage.

Then she took out a mallet she had recovered from the sensor boom wreckage and lightly tapped the stone around the panel, listening for any change in the pitch of its pinging. There was no noticeable difference. All sounded like the same solid stone.

Next, she tried pushing on the panel, hoping it might be some spring-loaded hatch. First nudging it with a finger, then pressing with her hand, then finally pressing her shoulder against it with all the force she could muster. The panel did not budge a micrometer.

Belle then repeated the same probing tests with the second tile with the same panel style but experienced a similar result: the tile face was unchanged by her exertions.

While she worked on her door experiments, twice she paused to strike out at megapedes with her spike when they approached too close. Her headlamp attracted attention, and what's more, the smell of wounded megapedes drew treacherous brethren who saw a chance for an easy meal.

Belle was quickly running out of time. Should she give up on entering the dome and instead reclimb it?

Branches snapped, and the earth turned. She looked behind her. A gargantuan four-meter megapede approached her cautiously. Weaving across the ground, looking for a weakness.

Belle turned to face it. She held her spike with a two-handed grip diagonally across her chest. This was by far the largest megapede she'd ever seen.

It halted about a meter from her, raised its head and the first few body segments off the ground, preparing to strike. Deadly dripping fangs appeared in its mouth.

It struck. She dodged to the side, and the megapede hit the stone wall with a resounding *thunk*.

Not pausing for a second, she turned, raised the spike over her head, and rammed it down into the armored head of the megapede, burying half its length into its body.

The megapede's body spasmed and curled up. Then it lay still.

Belle recovered her spike and cleaned it in the ash and dirt. She tried to shove the megapede corpse to one side, but it was too heavy.

She turned to face the unmoving panel in the cliff wall. Belle fell to her knees, breathing deeply, heart beating out of her chest. Her forehead rested against the panel. In growing desperation, she cried out in her mind, *Please, let me be well, let me be safe, help me!*

A mighty *clunk* arose deep inside the domed structure, like a giant clockwork mechanism turning over. Then the stone she was leaning against produced a humming vibration. The hexagonal tile to her right moved!

She stumbled onto her feet, stepped back, and watched

the tile slide backward into the structure.

This door had been unopened for many years. Heaps of soil were built-up in layers. The floor upon which the door slid was about one meter below ground level. Two tiles slid back on rails embedded in the stone floor, one tile on top of the other, moving as a single piece of stone. The soil had entirely hidden the bottom tile.

When the tiles had retreated about one meter into the face, they stopped and slid to the side, revealing a dark void beyond. Shining her headlamp into the doorway illuminated reflections off a granite wall some five to ten meters deeper into the structure.

With more creatures at her heels, Belle wasted no time leaping the meter down to the floor and stepping into the unknown interior.

10

"You earned a Purple Heart on the moon," an incredulous Tom, the new kid, said.

Grant Stewart smiled. *Storytime.* "Yup, back in 2170 during the Nigeria-Brazil war. A Nigerian sniper put a bullet through my right clavicle."

"Oh, man! Let me see it!" The kid was leaning over the card table.

Grant pulled the neck of his shirt down until the old wound in his brown skin was exposed. It still bothered him to this day, especially when carrying loads above his head.

"Look at that!" Tom said. "You can see both the entry and exit scars. I bet that hurt like the devil!"

"Afterward, yeah. But I don't remember much from when it happened. Just an impact on my chest, like somebody kicked me. My suit lost air pressure, and I passed out." Grant covered himself and stretched his right shoulder. "The suit sealed itself and put me under until I was rescued."

"Yeah, the rescuer had to be rescued," Tom said.

"The doctors put six pins into my clavicle, and I spent four months in physical therapy. Missed the rest of the war."

Grant was on call in the search and rescue ready room at Clinton Base with fellow rescue parajumper medic Tom and two dropship pilots. They were playing a casual game of poker.

He was the leader of his team of rescue parajumpers. Assigned to Kepler's Special Missions group, they spent half their days on duty, waiting in the ready room for calls.

"Hey, what happened to that crew that crashed in the jungle yesterday?" Tom said.

"Ops says they didn't crash. There was a problem of some sort while they were collecting samples from a rock," Grant said. "We were supposed to go in this morning and rescue them, but I recommended it be called off. The accident site is in a forest fire. Too much smoke for us to approach."

"Poor suckers. Can you imagine being stranded out in these jungles overnight?"

An alert sounded on the dispatch channel. Tom got to the radio first and answered.

While surveying volcanoes in Southern Wordonia, a volcano next to the one a group of geologists were on had unexpectedly erupted. A landslide blocked the return to their base camp, with reports of injuries.

They dropped their cards on the table and suited up in their gear. Grant heard the ground crew prepping their Sentry dropship for takeoff outside the ready room.

Grant and Tom were donning the mark of their trade—man-packable gravinegator lifts. The military-grade harnesses could lift one combat-loaded parajumper and one casualty out of harm's way.

One minute after receiving the call, they and the pilots were loaded into the Sentry. The pilots powered on the systems, and Tom and Grant verified all their medical and rescue equipment was ready and secured.

The Sentry was a medium-lift utility dropship capable of delivering twelve passengers or two thousand kilograms of cargo between ground and orbit or anywhere on Clinton within sixty minutes.

"Flight time will be twenty minutes," the co-pilot said over the intercom. "Prepare for takeoff."

Grant sat next to Tom on a forward-facing acceleration couch in the passenger compartment. He felt momentary nausea as the dropship's gravinegator was energized, but his military-grade neural implant quickly compensated.

The Sentry lifted off the pad, and Grant remembered the night fifteen years ago when he had almost died. He and some older friends were cruising around town when the driver wrapped the car around a tree.

Grant had suffered a skull fracture and a broken left femur. His leg had bled profusely, and he'd nearly died from blood loss. The timely care of two life-flight paramedics who'd rescued him and stabilized his vitals saved his life.

Ever since that night, his greatest desire had been a job that helped people through life-and-death situations. As the Sentry accelerated into the sky, he recognized that he was preparing to do that again. Running *toward* an exploding volcano, living the pararescueman motto: *These things we do, that others may live.*

When they arrived at the disaster scene, they found a much worse situation than was reported. Not a landslide, but a lahar had cut the six scientists off.

They had been in a valley between two volcanoes when one erupted unexpectedly. Its snow-capped peak instantly melted, and the muddy mix of ash and meltwater raced down the mountainside through their valley.

The group escaped to higher ground but was trapped on a cliff. The lahar's raging waters were eroding the cliff.

"We'll hold a hover over the group," the Sentry's pilot said, "but that mountain is still erupting. We may have to pull out without warning."

Grant acknowledged, then prepared to jump. Tom would stay in the dropship to attend to the wounded as Grant brought them onboard.

He opened the rear hatch and lowered its ramp until he could stand up and look out the back. They were directly over the victims, who panicked and waved at the Sentry.

"Jumping," he said over the radio, then energized his gravinegator lift and pushed himself out into the void.

Controlling the lift using his neural implant, he lowered himself until he was just out of reach of the victims. "How many injured?" he yelled to them.

Some pointed to a woman crouched behind them on the small ledge, cradling an arm.

Grant signaled for them to give him space. "I can only lift one person at a time!"

The group tried to give him more space, but the ledge had little room. Clods of dirt fell off into the roiling flood below.

Grant was worried about a panicked victim jumping on him when he went for the woman, but there wasn't time to establish more space. He zoomed forward and looped his rescue harness around the woman. The other victims exercised good discipline and stayed out of his way.

He commanded his lift to return to the dropship, and they quickly rose from the ground.

The woman began vomiting. That was common for people under the influence of the gravinegator who lacked the proper implants.

He deposited her into the back of the Sentry, and Tom immediately began treating her wounds.

Grant dropped three more times to rescue individual victims. There were now only two left on the ledge.

He had retrieved the second-to-last and was lifting him into the Sentry when he heard over the radio, "It's blowing! Do you have them all?"

"One more!" Grant responded.

He looked out the back. Then he heard a tremendous blast, and the ground shook. The ledge under the last victim —a man—crumbled, and he slid into the raging waters.

"We need to get out of here!" the pilot said.

"Twenty seconds," Grant said. He pushed himself out and freefell until almost to the water before engaging the lift. Then he flew after the man floundering in the turbulent, muddy water.

Grant glanced behind him and saw the top of the mountain had exploded. A pyroclastic flow of superheated volcanic gas and ash was racing toward them at aircraft speeds.

He caught up to the man, then, like a dragonfly, he dropped on top of him and embraced him with arms and legs. Icy water soaked through his clothes. He hoped his lift would be able to raise them both out.

He commanded his lift to go up. They slowly rose out of the water. Grant could hear a great roar behind him, like a ship lifting off into orbit. Water was draining out of their clothes. The lift rate increased.

The man was struggling. Panicking as he spit up water and coughed.

"Hold still!" Grant said. "I've got you, be calm. You'll be okay." They continued to rise, and he looked for the dropship.

The Sentry's pilot had maintained a hover over Grant, skillfully following him as he flew downstream after the victim.

"We need to go now!" the pilot screamed at him over the radio.

"Five seconds!" Grant said. He throttled the lift into emergency mode, and the victim began violently vomiting all over Grant's chest. However, their rate of climb increased significantly, and soon, they entered the Sentry.

Grant dropped the two of them into the back of the dropship, pounded the close button for the rear hatch, and yelled to the pilot, "We're in, go!"

Out the rear of the closing ramp, a hellacious boiling black cloud raced at them, just seconds away. The Sentry's rockets engaged, and everybody in the passenger cabin slid toward the rear as they accelerated. With the passengers not fully secured, it was a dangerous maneuver.

Then the ship bounced in turbulence, and Grant heard pings and bangs against the hull. Foul-smelling black vapors leaked through the partly closed hatch, making them cough until it finally sealed itself. The acceleration shifted backward to downward as the ship pulled into the sky.

The ride smoothed out, and the acceleration decreased. He heard the pilot say over the public address system, "We're clear. Passengers and medics will please strap into their seats."

Everybody was safe. It was a twenty-minute flight back to base.

Grant was sitting back in the ready room, relaxing. Medical personnel picked up the victims when they landed, and the rescue team waited around until their shift ended.

Tom walked in and gave him a high five. "Woo! That was some awesome flying you did back there! I thought that guy was a goner for sure."

"He's fortunate I got to him in time. Another thirty seconds, and he'd have drowned. We cut that so close." He was looking for the pilots but didn't find them. They must still be closing up the Sentry. "I thought our pilots were about to leave us behind."

"You should've heard them when you jumped out again. The co-pilot was cursing up a storm! But you made the right call." He slapped Grant on the back. "You are the man!"

Grant's mobile rang. "This is Stewart," he answered.

"Hello, Mr. Stewart. This is Silvestre Jenkins in Ops. The rescue beacon from tender C195 was just updated. At least one person is alive. Smoke has also cleared significantly at the accident site. Your rescue criteria are met, and you are cleared to execute the rescue at the next available opportunity."

"Yes, sir," Grant said.

"Remember that you are not to insert on top of the monolith. Keep your distance as much as possible."

"Yes, sir. Any other information?"

"The crew's updated beacon message indicates they sought shelter inside the rock monolith. You must land and approach it on foot. Only pilot-candidate Belle Machado is known to be alive. The other two are missing."

"Very well. I will assemble my team and make the rescue attempt at first light local time."

They ended the call. Interesting. Somebody had survived the night out in the jungle and was still awaiting rescue. He looked forward to hearing their story, but wanted to avoid the monolith. This crazy person had entered it.

He decided he would take Tom on this rescue. Grant was

impressed by how well he handled himself during the return of the geologists.

11

As soon as Belle cleared the doorway, the door—which had come to rest behind the wall adjacent to the entrance—slid back into place and sealed her inside the ruin. The *clunk* of some powerful locking mechanism sounded again and then complete silence.

There were no interior lights visible. The air was clear of smoke. She carefully removed her oxygen mask.

She expected the air to smell like the mildewy odor of old structures or soil, but it was surprisingly fresh and dry, with just a faint whiff of ozone and whatever debris she had tracked in.

At first, she could hear her heaving breath, thumping heart, and rushing blood. But after a few minutes of standing there calmly, she detected a faint but steady low-frequency hum in the background.

The air was warm, twenty-seven degrees centigrade, dry, and with a faint breeze blowing toward interior spaces.

The room she stood in was rectangular, made of the same granite as the exterior, but tiled with much smaller ten-centimeter hexagonal tiles. It was about four meters wide—equivalent to four of the exterior tiles in width—eight meters deep and six meters tall.

Though the roof sloped upward toward the twenty-meter summit, this chamber had a flat ceiling. In the rear was a one-meter hexagonal passageway leading deeper into the dome. Near the top were several small openings, hexagonal in cross-section, possibly part of whatever ventilation system flowed through the structure.

Belle pulled out the first-aid kit's radiation detector and noted the elevated background radiation levels of 5 mSv/hr. This would be a harmful place for an unaugmented human to live long-term.

Indeed, the high radiation was probably part of the reason Clintonian fauna had made no headway invading the ruin. But her blood nanites would protect her. There was no serious risk to her health.

This chamber seemed to be some supply room and was clear of dust. Several empty containers made out of some woven composite material were in a corner.

On their sides were raised symbols in a style similar to those cut into the stone faces of the cliff. What they usually held was a mystery.

Nearby were three two-meter stacks of hexagonal granite tiles of various sizes that looked like they were spares for doing structure repairs. Each stack probably weighed ten tonnes. They could be one month old or one millennium old. She had no way of knowing.

She turned toward a faint clicking sound in the distance. It sounded like tiny legs walking on stone and was growing louder. Gripping the spike in her right hand, she prepared to defend herself. *Sounds like a megapede.*

She finally noticed the sound was approaching from one of the small hexagonal openings near the ceiling. Out of it, a curious creature appeared. Definitely not of Clintonian biology. It looked more like a machine than an animal.

Its body comprised a stack of three hexagonal plates about one centimeter thick. Out of the bottom plate were attached six legs, and out of the upper plate were attached six wispy antennas or arms. From the center of the top plate sprung an array of six stalks. Eyes?

Belle froze in fear that it might be an armed sentry. Had it noticed her? It was too difficult to know where it was looking. The first few times it paused, she cringed. Had it noticed her and was preparing to attack?

The small creature's body measured ten centimeters in diameter and three high. It looked like a six-legged starfish carrying hexagonal plates, with spindly legs of three segments bent at ninety degrees for use as locomotion. The body plan was hexaradial. That is, it had a radial symmetry of six slices around the axis of symmetry.

The walking starfish creature ignored Belle, moving out of the opening and smoothly transitioning to walking suspended from the wall like a spider.

Occasionally, it would stop and pick at unseen objects, though only for a moment, then continue. Belle hunkered down in a distant corner, observing it cautiously as it made a circuit of the room along the wall about three meters up, out of her reach.

When it passed over her location, she held the radiation detector toward it and saw a sharp rise in levels. It then disappeared down a different opening from whence it had come five minutes earlier.

She decided the starfish creature was harmless and wondered if it was a caretaker of some kind. All the surfaces seemed so clean and free from dust.

This dome didn't feel like a ruin. It felt inhabited, despite the lack of lighting.

Her bladder felt suddenly loose, and she decided she couldn't rest unless she explored more. Perhaps she could find the source of the neutron beam.

The one doorway out of the chamber, which held no obvious door, was a one-meter hexagon in cross-section. She had to crouch down almost to a crawl to get through it.

On the other side was a low-ceilinged passage running from left to right, the other end of the doorway facing the passage wall. The ceiling was about 1.2 meters high. She had to walk in an uncomfortable stoop. Its width was just over two meters. The walls comprised the same ten-centimeter granite tiles as the storage room/foyer.

Going to the right down the passage took her to a series of two doors that entered a larger room just south of the foyer. They shared a common wall. By her calculations, this larger room should be where the other doorway in the cliff led, and she found evidence of door tracks on its floor.

The room was rectangular. Like the foyer, six meters high and eight meters deep, but a much wider ten meters.

There were more of those empty containers in a corner. However, the most interesting object was a large box in the center of the room, about three by four by three meters, made of the same woven composite material as the containers, though thicker. There were no clues to what it held, but it was heavy. She couldn't budge it.

At the end of the passage, there was another one-meter granite tile with a smaller hexagonal plate, which she now recognized as a locked door. She didn't know how she had managed to gain entry into the dome and failed to open this new door.

She found two more locked doors at the other end of the passage, to the left of the first foyer.

Halfway down the passage segment was a narrower

passage leading to the west and down, where she found three doors on the left and one on the right.

The three on the left probably led to small rooms that shared a wall with the foyer, but the doors were locked. However, the one door on the right was open. It was slid back into the room behind and stowed behind the wall, clearing the doorway.

The room was packed floor to ceiling with containers neatly stacked in racks and shelves. Most were unrecognizable. A few looked like portable pressure vessels for holding air or combustible gasses.

Just inside the door was a large, open container holding water, into which dripped a slow but steady stream from a source in the ceiling. *Could this be a cistern? Or was somebody cleaning up after an annoying roof leak?* Regardless, she had a water source, though she'd need to test it for contaminants.

On a whim, she put on her oxygen mask, turned off her headlamp, and enabled the thermal imager.

The room appeared in blazing detail. The ceiling had multiple heat sources. Belle touched them, but they weren't warm.

She found a stack of intricately worked tablets on one shelf, made of the same dark-gray woven composite as the containers. However, these flat tablets were printed with thousands of tiny symbols similar to those engraved into the granite.

There must be hundreds of tablets. Most of them were held together in groups by metal rings. If the material and symbols hadn't been so exotic, she would conclude they were binders of documents.

Belle rubbed her fingers across the symbols, expecting to feel the texture of the engraving. But they were smooth. She turned off the thermal viewer and turned on her headlamp.

Now the tablets were blank, and the ceiling heat sources were black.

The thermal imager was sensitive to infrared wavelengths of light. Could the rooms and tablets be meant to be viewed in infrared?

She turned the headlamp off and the thermal imager back on. The symbols on the tablets appeared again. She left the imager on.

Most containers in this storage room were sealed, and she wasn't ready to force them open. Doing so would surely anger somebody—the scientists back home, or worse, somebody here.

As she explored these three rooms, on two occasions more of the starfish creatures appeared, doing whatever mysterious task they did. With the thermal imager on, symbols became visible on their bodies.

The walls of the building also had prominent geometric figures and lines that were viewable in infrared. There were also infrared light sources—for, indeed, that's what they were—at regular intervals on the ceilings in all hallways and rooms.

The inhabitants of this structure viewed the world in infrared wavelengths. Human-visible wavelengths were probably invisible to them.

It all felt so *alien*.

Another shiver went down her spine. Her heart palpitated. Had she stepped from the dangerous jungle into an even more dangerous world? High background radiation levels. Infrared light sources. Infrared paint and print. Oddly shaped and sized doors. Ceilings not quite the correct height. Exotic autonomous robots.

Despite her misgivings, Belle was exhausted. Even after the solid eight hours she'd slept earlier in the night.

Fortunately, Belle had her mobile home on her back. After exploring for a few hours, she returned to the foyer where she had entered.

Surprisingly, it was not the same as she had left it. In the middle of the room, there was a piece of furniture. Somebody, or *something*, had constructed or assembled a low table made of the dark gray composite. It was just half a meter across and thirty centimeters off the ground—more of a platform than a table—but its purpose was clear. The table top was a hexagon with six stubby legs, one at each corner.

Somebody was aware of her presence. They must have been, because somebody had allowed her to enter. But she didn't feel secure.

After unpacking her gear and deploying her small shelter next to the new table, she ate a little food and drank water.

After her meal, she needed to use the restroom but had seen no facilities of that sort—yet another difference from human buildings. Everything was so clean. She felt guilty even thinking about doing her business in a random corner somewhere. She got one of the empty containers and adopted it as a chamber pot.

Finally, she carefully cleaned her wounded foot, gave herself a napkin bath, and sealed herself into her shelter. She felt safer, even though the thin walls afforded little additional protection. At least she was invisible to whoever was watching.

Belle reflected on her status. Her crew and ship were lost. Without question, she had failed the check-pilot evaluation. But perhaps she could salvage something from the situation if she could prove that an external source—namely, this structure—had been the source of a disabling neutron beam.

Furthermore, if this structure were of alien origin, it

would be the first of its kind. Might she convert the fame of being the person who discovered it into something that would save her career?

Belle had not completely lost control of the situation. After she rested a bit more, she would make additional efforts to explore the ruin. If it injured or even killed her, it couldn't be a worse fate than she'd already suffered.

12

In the back of a Sentinel dropship, Grant sat strapped into an acceleration couch next to his fellow pararescueman, Tom. The g-forces pressed him into his couch as they descended through the upper limits of Clinton's stratosphere at hypersonic velocity, leaving a kilometers-long trail of ionized gas behind. He remembered some combat drops he'd made as a special ops soldier.

After two years of college, bored and with poor grades, he'd decided it wasn't for him and enlisted in the UAAN Space Force. Mom had been furious. Being a professor of English Literature, she had always assumed Grant was following in her footsteps. Boy, had she been surprised.

Out of basic training, he qualified for and attended pararescueman school. The hardest thing he had ever done, but he excelled, especially at the medic training. It fed his desire to put his body to work to save others. He subsequently graduated, and then spent eight years as a spaceborne pararescueman for UAAN Special Operations Command. He remembered his jumps into Nigeria, the moon, Primavera III, and others.

Sitting in the back of this Sentinel was a life of luxury

compared to other places he had worked. That didn't mean that every day was a vacation. On the contrary, he and the rescue team would usually be out babysitting scientists and engineers while conducting various field operations around Clinton. Protecting them from megapedes, pulling them free from stumpholes, rescuing the wayward from mountain tops, or treating bumps and scratches. Saving them from exploding volcanoes—like yesterday.

Today was different. Today, he and Tom got to do an *actual,* for-real, downed-pilot rescue. His first in years, but what he and Tom had initially trained for. That's why he was reminiscing about the old days.

Belle Machado's crew had gotten themselves into a heap of trouble. They were stranded in the middle of the jungle fifteen thousand kilometers from Clinton Base. Details were sparse; the crew could already be dead, but their situation was unquestionably dire.

"How're you doing, Tom? You ready for this?" he called out to his companion over the building roar of the atmosphere outside the dropship's hull.

"Hell yes, I am! About time we had some excitement," Tom said with a huge smile.

"You mean yesterday wasn't enough?"

Tom leaned closer to Grant. "This morning, I woke, and my first thought was, 'If I get asked to pull Johnson out of another stumphole, I may just leave him there until dinner.' You know what I mean?"

"I hear you, brother. For being a xenobiologist, you would think he'd know to look before he steps!"

"I need a day off from babysitting scientists. I really appreciate you taking me out on this mission. I know the other guys on the team all wanted to go, but I'm glad you picked me."

"Was an easy decision. Don't tell any of the others, but you're my best medic," Grant said, "even being the new guy on the team. We have reason to believe some of the crew may be injured. No, I don't expect this will be a milk run!"

"Well, regardless, sir, drinks are on me when we return tonight."

Grant smiled at Tom, shook his hand, and said, "I won't say no! But I have a feeling somebody else will soon want to buy us those drinks. In, oh, about five minutes, I'd estimate."

They sat quietly for several minutes, mentally preparing themselves for the unknown. Then, over the intercom, they heard, "We are subsonic, two minutes to the landing zone. Light smoke is in the air, and visibility is about eight-hundred meters. Less than we were told, but we can manage.

"From here, it looks like the entire forest around the site has burned to the ground. Lots of stuff still smoldering."

Grant said, "Roger, fire hazards are visible on the ground."

Switching to the intercom channel he shared with his partner, he said, "Tom, this is how I want to proceed. The pilots aren't going to want to land. Too much debris." Illustrating with his hands, he said, "I'm going to have them approach in a hover, and I'll go first under lift. You get on the chain gun and cover me from wildlife until I secure the site, then you follow me down. Okay?"

"Yes, sir, I'll cover you while you jump. I'll jump in behind you when you give the all clear."

"Very well. Hooyah!"

"Hooyah!"

Grant switched back to the general intercom. "Pararescuemen are ready. Team lead will jump first under manpack lift and clear the zone while first assistant covers on the gun, then assistant'll drop once he gets the all-clear. You fellas, please hang around for us."

"Acknowledged, we'll maintain a hover over the landing zone. Stand by, beginning approach."

At about one hundred knots, the dropship did a low-powered pass several times around the monolith to get a good view but keeping its distance before going under the gravinegator.

Both pilots and jumpers were equipped with military-grade neural implants that mitigated the worst side effects of the gravinegator. However, it was still best to engage it only at the last possible moment, just in case of an implant malfunction.

The pilot called out, "Engaging lift now!"

Grant waited for momentary nausea to pass, then unstrapped from his couch and checked his lift harness for the third time.

He cycled the dropship's rear loading ramp, lowering it until he could comfortably stand at its end.

Tom unstowed the 15-mm chain gun on the rear ramp and charged its ammunition feed. "All ready, boss!"

Grant gave him a thumbs-up and gazed out the rear ramp at what he was about to jump into.

It was utter devastation. The rainforest—what remained of it—was burned to the ground. There were thousands of smoldering heaps of vegetation from horizon to horizon.

Immediately to the rear of the dropship, about half a click away, was a more intense fire still blazing away, producing thick black smoke rising thousands of meters into the sky.

The ship's tail swung around until it faced a low black dome. For a moment, Grant was speechless. He'd become so used to Clinton's rugged and wild Carboniferous Period terrain that the dome was entirely out of place. It looked like a building.

He couldn't wrap his head around it. "Uh, you fellas get a good view of that dome? What is it?" he asked the pilots while glancing at Tom.

Tom just shook his head in return, totally in the zone.

The co-pilot responded, "We sure did. That's supposed to be the rocky monolith the crew is hiding inside, but it certainly looks like more than that. Should we radio this back to base?"

"No, sir, we need to get the crew out anyway, regardless of their digs. Stand by for my jump."

Grant took one last look at his landing zone, picked out his target, and then engaged his manpack lift. "Jumping now!"

He pushed himself forward with both feet out of the cabin because he was now weightless. Using his neural implant to control the lift, he slowly descended to his target.

Grant had a 6.5-mm automatic carbine ready in case critters became unfriendly. He commanded the lift to yaw in a slow circle during his descent to quickly sweep the entire zone.

"Touch down!" he cried over the radio as he made contact with the ground, disengaging his lift. As the total weight of his body and all his gear settled down on him, he used the momentum to roll over his left knee and position himself just to the left of where he'd landed.

There was a flash of bright yellow and chattering. A giant megapede struck up out of some nearby debris toward the ground where he had just been standing. "Contact!" Grant swung his weapon onto the monster and opened up. Too close for Tom to engage without possibly hitting Grant.

Emptying half a clip of explosive, semi-armor-piercing rounds into the megapede left it in a gory heap.

There was a loud *bam, bam, bam* overhead as Tom opened up with the chain gun. *Bam, bam, bam*, then something died over close to the dome. The way was clear. Grant scrambled the three meters of ground between him and the cliff face at the western end of the dome.

Bam, bam, bam, bam, bam.

"Sir, there are megapedes all over springing from the ground, closing on your position!" Tom cried over the tactical radio.

Bam, bam, bam, bam.

Bam, bam.

"Keep the fire away from the dome!" Grant yelled. They had been ordered to keep their distance. He didn't want to know what would happen if they unintentionally damaged the dome.

He held his head down, protecting it from the concussion and shrapnel of the chain gun's explosive shells.

Then he heard an unusual *thunk* from the hovering armored dropship as if somebody had just hit it dead-center with a large boulder.

"We're taking fire! We're taking fire!" the pilot screamed on the radio. The dropship dipped away from Grant and gained speed. They were fleeing.

The pilot punched his rocket torch to full throttle, and Grant felt heat waves engulf him as the radioactive plume barely missed him.

Tom was firing continuously at something above and behind Grant toward the dome's center. He mentally plotted the impact point based on the shell tracers he saw. Tom was firing *at* the dome.

Bam, bam, bam—

"Hold your fire, dammit!" Grant screamed.

—bam, bam, bam, bam, bam, bam, bam

A blinding streak of light flashed ten times brighter than the sun, a hundred times brighter. Connecting the dome and the dropship as if god had joined them with lightning.

The world exploded.

Benton heard over the radio, "Clinton Base, Clinton Base, this is Archangel Two. We are under fire! I repeat we are under—" It was suddenly silent.

"Archangel Two, this is Clinton Base, say again," Silvestre said in response.

"Archangel Two, this is Clinton Base. Come in," he said again.

"What just happened?" Kennedy Kauffmann, the Clinton Base director of operations, said.

"I don't know," Silvestre said. "Their transmission just cut out. I've also lost the telemetry stream from their dropship." He pointed to a box on his console display indicating *Loss of Signal* status flags. "Hold on. The satellite imagery is about to be updated."

A high-resolution satellite image of the terrain around the monolith was displayed on the large wall display at the front of the Ops Center. It flickered as it refreshed with a new photograph.

A new smoke plume bloomed about 1km south of the dome. Southwest of what they believed to be a reactor containment fire from *C195*.

"Please tell me we didn't just lose the dropship and its crew," Kauffmann said in a trembling voice.

Silence in the Ops Center.

Kauffmann's face was flushed. He cursed and pounded Silvestre's table with his fist. "What am I going to tell the Executive Committee? That this monolith has now cost us two ships and seven employees?"

"I recommend we halt all visits to this monolith until further notice," Benton said with a heavy heart, thinking of Grant, his friend's son.

"Damn right we will!" screamed Kauffmann.

"What if somebody survived?" asked Silvestre.

"We can't risk it. We need to send a small drone ship. Unpiloted. And find out what the hell is going on!"

"Do we have that capability?" Benton said.

"No," Kauffmann said, "we need to order it from corporate headquarters on Earth. It'll probably take a couple weeks."

"Can't we just do an overflight and see if somebody is alive?" Silvestre said.

"No! I won't lose another crew and ship, not on my watch. But I think we've answered the question about whether that monolith deserves more study. Yes, but we need the correct tools."

"I'll discuss it with the Executive Committee," Benton said.

Benton had many, many questions. There was more to this monolith than just a high level of radiation. The dropship pilots had been convinced somebody was firing at them. Could it be pirates? Had *C195* stumbled onto a secret pirate base?

Part Two

Marooned

13

Belle was startled out of sleep by what sounded like distant rolling thunder. She lay there in her blanket, listening for a minute, until she heard it again. *That's a fission rocket! They're here!*

She stuffed her right foot into its regular boot, the other into its medical boot, then raced out of the one-person shelter toward the sealed door of the foyer chamber. Through the one-meter-thick stone, she could hear the sounds of a circling aircraft, a dropship by the sound of it.

She had to get the door open but hadn't figured that out yet. Stepping back from the wall, she began looking for an access panel like she'd seen on the exterior wall. *There it is.* Just to the left of the door. That seemed to be the convention, to inlay a hexagonal panel in a tile to the left of, but not on, the door itself. She started pushing and prodding it, but nothing happened.

The roar became louder and more constant, then cut off. *Have they landed?*

Sounds like firecrackers came through the door.

A muffled series of more resounding bangs. Then more cracks and the roar of a rocket motor sounded again. *This doesn't sound right. Is somebody firing a gun?*

Something sounded like rocks dropping onto the roof above her.

Then there was a sudden almighty *bang* that shook the entire structure. Dust was shaken loose from overhead and raining down. For over a minute, smaller *bangs* and *cracks* outside the door sounded like small explosions. *What happened?*

Belle placed both hands on the panel, pushing with all her might, and in her head, called out, *Please let me out. My friends are in trouble! Please help me!*

With a *clunk*, the structure unlocked the door, and it rolled backward on its rails. As it cleared the wall and moved to the side, thick clouds of smoke and dust spilled into the chamber.

She realized she didn't have her mask and ran to get it. Remembering her earlier troubles, she also grabbed the first-aid kit, metal spike, and scraper.

Belle sprinted for the door, exiting the dome into a cloud of billowing dust and smoke that enveloped her. Only about one meter of visibility. *Great.*

Off to the west, she was hearing small irregular explosions. The terrain before the door was swept clean like a giant had waved a broom over it.

She found her emergency beacon, a smashed ruin against the wall. There were corpses of megapedes all around.

She walked the base of the cliff, trying to find signs of the dropship, which she could no longer hear.

She walked carefully, looking for the likely megapede hiding places. A leg stuck out under a pile of dead branches. *That's a human foot!* She pulled debris off the figure and found a wounded man.

Alive but unconscious and bleeding from somewhere. He

might be a soldier. Loaded with gear. An assault rifle was strapped to his right shoulder.

They couldn't stay here. She grabbed a convenient handle at the top of his backpack, just behind his head, and dragged him on his back toward the foyer door. *He must weigh one hundred fifty kilos!*

The door had closed again. What if she couldn't get back in?

Belle stood before the panel and pushed on it. She probed and pried for several minutes, but to no avail.

The smoke began to clear. A new smoke plume was visible to the west, about one kilometer. Her stomach sank in recognizing the remains of the dropship and her rescuers.

There was a scurrying sound behind her. A small megapede appeared, probing toward her. Grasping her spike, she impaled it through the head, then flung it four meters away.

Other smaller megapede corpses lay around her. She tossed them in the same general direction, hoping to lure the beasts away from her to buy some time.

What had happened the last two times the door had opened for her? What had she been doing each time?

The first time she pressed her head against it. The second, she pressed her hand. She had an urgent need to enter, a specific intent that motivated her and that she had called out in her thoughts.

Placing her hand on the panel, Belle expressed what she needed and intended to do. *My friend is hurt, and we need safety; I want to protect him and myself. Shelter us until we can be rescued!*

A welcoming *clunk* came from inside the structure, and the door receded, letting them pass.

She gently lowered the man to the floor one meter below the ground. Dragged him inside. As soon as they cleared it, the door sealed itself again.

How had she done that? Belle was convinced that her thoughts were the key to the doorway, but that seemed to fly in the face of everything she knew about science and engineering.

There would be time to experiment later, but she needed to tend to this soldier right now.

Pulling him the rest of the way to her shelter, she took stock of what she had dragged into the ruin.

He was covered head to foot in shredded and bloody combat fatigues, a loaded equipment webbing, something that looked like a miniature gravinegator lift, and a full-face armored helmet.

She needed to remove some of this before she could evaluate his wounds. On the upper right chest of his fatigues was embroidered the name *STEWART*.

"Hey, Stewart, if you can hear me, my name is Belle Machado, and I need to remove your helmet and equipment. You're injured and need first aid."

She started with his harness and combat webbing. The harness was heavy! He must be lugging around 50kg of equipment on his body.

A piece of shrapnel stuck out of his right thigh. She didn't dare touch it. Back in the academy, her first-aid instruction had taught her that protruding objects should be left in place if possible.

He could have also suffered a head or neck injury, so she called out to him again.

"Stewart, I'm here to help you. You're safe. I need to remove your helmet. Please respond if you can hear me."

"Mmmggh," the man said. His right hand motioned toward the latch of his helmet, but that was all.

That was good enough for her. Fumbling with the

unfamiliar latch, she finally got it to open fully.

Carefully bracing his head and stabilizing his neck with some ration packs, she slid the helmet upward off his head, taking great care in case he had a neck injury.

A handsome face appeared, a man about thirty years old. He was clean-shaven, had brown skin, a broad nose, and jet-black hair in a military buzz cut. Perhaps of Filipino descent. He was bleeding from the nose and ears.

Belle grabbed her first-aid medical computer and brought it closer to Stewart, hoping it would interface with whatever neural implants were in his head. The display printed: `Schedule II implant detected, some access restricted`.

The gentleman had military-grade hardware in his head.

Cycling through options, she selected `Quick Diagnostic` from the menu and waited while it did its business. About ten seconds later, a rather lengthy list appeared: `Concussion, puncture wound, internal bleeding, pain, ruptured ear drums`.

"Stewart!" she said. "I need to treat you; you have injuries. Do you understand me?"

His eyes fluttered open and seemed to focus for a second. He looked at her, raised a hand toward her as if in disbelief, then fell unconscious again.

Belle followed the instructions on the medical display as best she could, trusting it knew what to do, and the soldier's nanites—surely he had them—would also be doing their best to heal his injuries.

After about an hour of effort, the medical display finally instructed her to wrap him in a blanket and let him rest. Belle carefully dragged him to her shelter, slid him inside, wrapped him in the blanket from her survival kit, then resealed the shelter.

She was not alone anymore, though in decidedly worse

conditions than before. Now there were two of them, one seriously injured. Her emergency radio beacon had been destroyed, and she was pretty sure the burning wreckage outside was the remains of a rescue dropship.

Two ships had been destroyed in proximity to the ruin. This structure was active. Was it trying to protect itself? If so, then why had it let her enter? The answer wouldn't change the fact that the ruin was dangerous. To have any hope of rescue, she needed to find out in what way.

14

With Stewart occupying her bed and shelter, Belle decided to explore more. She needed to understand how the doors of this structure functioned so she could get deeper into the building. They were somehow connected to her touch and her thoughts, which was bizarre. What kind of a security system was that? And regardless, how could it read her thoughts?

She didn't want to experiment with the exterior doors, because she was afraid she would get them stuck open or herself shut outside. However, the foyer door was the only one she had succeeded in using so far.

She decided to try some of the doors in the foyer passage, where she had found the room full of stores and the other locked doors. She walked to the small passage with the three locked doors across from the open storeroom.

At the first door, she placed her hand on the tile panel to the left of the door. Nothing happened, which is what she expected would be the case. She brought thoughts to her head.

Open.
Let me in.

Help me!

Nothing happened. Then she tried some random thoughts, whatever popped into her head.

My oldest sister's name is Consuela.

My favorite color is turquoise.

I need food.

Suddenly, the door slid open.

This wall was much thinner than the exterior wall, and the door was only one meter high, so it opened quickly, swishing behind it.

Through it was a small room two meters deep and four wide. Lined up against the wall was a rack stacked with strange-looking metal boxes.

Approaching them, she felt waves of heat. She got a visual alarm in her optical nerve from her implant, reporting elevated levels of alpha radiation and advising her to exercise caution.

She left immediately, seeing nothing else in the room but the strange radioactive boxes. The door slid shut behind her.

Belle placed her hand on the panel again and thought to herself, *I need food.* The door slid open again.

If she stepped back and didn't enter, the door would slide shut again after about thirty seconds. If she entered, then it would remain open until she exited.

She performed the experiment again three times, and each time it would behave the same way. She also did it with different parts of her body touching the panel. It didn't seem to care, but it would not respond if she didn't touch it.

Also, touching it through thick objects didn't work either. For example, it wouldn't work through her boot, but would work through a thin cloth.

Touch was important, but there were lots of human artifacts that were also engaged using touch. What was strange was the key. Her thoughts! *How creepy is that?* What kind of technology enabled the reading of thoughts?

Belle went to the next door in the hallway and used the same approach but couldn't get it to open. She tried other thoughts:

The cheese is old and moldy.
The lawn needs water.
I need medical help.
I need light.
The ceilings are very short here.

Nothing she tried would work.

She had an idea. She went back to the storeroom door, the one that remained open. She was a little worried about shutting it and being unable to open it again, but she had an inkling about how the doors worked.

Standing in the small passageway, slightly hunched over, she pressed her hand to the panel to the left of the open doorway and expressed the thought. *I don't need anything.*

The door slid to a close. Okay, that result supported her hypothesis. *Let's check if I can get it back open.*

Touching the panel with her hand, she expressed, *I need to drink.* Nothing happened.

She tried, *I need water.* The door slid open! The cistern of water was stored here!

She commanded it closed again, but this time using the thought, *I am done*, and that also worked. Remembering the objects that looked like pressure vessels, she next tried, *I need air*, but nothing happened. She tried picturing a pressure vessel in her head, but that didn't work either.

Then she tried, *I need instructions*, and the door opened. Maybe those tablets of symbols were some kind of instructional documentation.

The doors somehow knew what was stored behind them

and would respond by the expressed wish of the person attempting to enter.

It wasn't a secure system because couldn't any thief walk into a locked room? There had to be more to this system than just thoughts.

She truly was hungry and thirsty, so Belle returned to the campsite, checked on Stewart—who was sound asleep or unconscious but otherwise okay—then sat on the floor at the short table, ate a ration pack, and drank some water.

She giggled to herself for feeling a little like an amateur archaeologist or anthropologist trying to decipher the writings of ancient people. The brief moment of happiness and satisfaction lifted her sore spirits.

Belle sat meditatively for some time, thinking about her family and her desires and letting her mind wander. She let herself be in the moment. Forgot the concerns about the structure, her career, and her losses. Allowed her nervous and limbic systems a chance to rest.

Sometime later, maybe an hour, sounds of movement arose from the shelter. Her guest was awake.

15

Grant's eyes opened to blackness. He felt trapped, tied up. No, that was wrong. His arms and hands were free. He just had a blanket tightly snugged around his torso. However, his legs were immobile, and his right thigh had a deep, throbbing ache. He also had a splitting headache, a ringing in his ears, and his chest felt like an elephant had used it as a chair.

His last memory was of a beautiful woman looking into his eyes and intently telling him something, but he didn't remember it. Something about his helmet.

Where was all his gear? And his weapon!

Everything came back in a rush. His planning with Tom, the drop into the rescue site, the fighting, and the final explosion. He'd lost consciousness right about then. Was his friend okay? The pilots? He was sure the woman was friendly but hadn't a clue who she was.

Grant slowly pushed the blanket off and felt around. He could feel thick fabric against his hands, all around him, with just a small open space around his head. He heard a portable pump, and the air smelled of canned and recycled oxygen. Still not knowing where he was, he began rubbing his hands around the fabric, looking for some kind of opening.

Somebody opened it and knelt next to him. A woman. "How're you feeling? Can you hear me?"

Through the ringing in his ears and the brain fog, he heard the distant voice asking how he was. "Yes, I hear you. I'm awake. Who are you, and where am I?" he croaked from a sore throat.

"I am pilot-candidate Belle Machado, and you are safe at my encampment. There has been a terrible accident. You are injured. Please stay still while I check your vital signs."

"Yes, ma'am." He lay back while she brought an instrument near him, which looked like a tiny medical diagnostic computer from a survival pack first-aid kit. *Oh Lord, what has this lady been doing to me?* He recognized her now. She was the same angel-faced woman who had been looking at him the last time he was briefly awake.

The computer beeped, and she pressed some buttons. With some doubt in her eyes, Pilot Machado explained, "This computer says you are okay to move around, but carefully. You have a bad wound in your leg." He couldn't place her accent. It was slight, but maybe South American?

"Thank you, and my regards to the computer, but I'll decide what I can and can't do."

Belle was silent.

"I'm Grant Stewart, a member of the Special Missions team. Here to rescue you." His little speech started with bravado, but he finished with a soft voice, realizing who had done the rescuing here. "Um, thanks for saving me."

"Grant, you're welcome to the help, and you're also welcome to take over the doctor job in this group. While you're at it, maybe you could look at my injuries." He hadn't intended to offend her.

"Are they serious? I could look at it immediately."

"No, that's okay," Belle said. "It's not urgent. A burn and a bite. The bite happened a day ago; a megapede bit my heel." She pointed at her foot. "I started to go into shock but got a shot of epinephrine in me soon enough. But I have painful swelling and can't get my boot on."

"What happened to the megapede?"

"I stuck it in the head with a spike that I scavenged from the wreckage of my ship. Why do you ask? Do you think I can't take care of myself?" She eyed him suspiciously.

Grant assessed her emotional state. She certainly wasn't helpless if she had fought off a megapede in hand-to-mandible combat and done it after being bitten. "What happened to your ship?"

"It burned to the ground. The other two crew members are dead."

"How did they die?"

"Is this an interrogation, or are you just the curious type?" Sighing, she said, "One of them died in the initial accident, and the other fell while escaping."

"Look, Ms. Machado"—he held a hand up in a calming gesture—"I need to know whether there are others alive and what other dangers are around. I'm not trying to make you look bad. I just need information."

"Call me Belle. It's not like it's going to help. You're stuck here with me now. I'll save the story for the mishap investigation if we make it back to base."

Grant was surprised by her defensiveness. There was something she didn't want to talk about.

"May I ask how you survived the fire?"

Belle recounted to him fleeing to the top of the dome, her harrowing survival of the firestorm, the fight with the megapede the next day, and then fleeing inside the dome. It was a remarkable survival story. She must be exhausted.

"Ops received your emergency beacon about twelve hours after your mishap," he said. "Or, rather, it was received by multiple nearby ships, who then forwarded it to Ops. They immediately contacted my team of rescue parajumpers to plan a rescue operation."

"That sounds about right. It took half a day for the fire to die down enough to where I could deploy the beacon."

Grant was amazed she had survived the wildfire. What an experience that must have been, like a real-life visit to the burning depths of hell.

"We were all set to rescue you within a couple hours of the beacon appearing," he said, shaking his head. "But then we received intel that the entire rescue site was engulfed by a wildfire and covered in smoke. Ops was considering canceling the mission, believing nobody could survive that fire—"

"Those cheap bastards," she exclaimed.

Good thing she didn't know that it was he who had called it off. No need to tell her that. It wouldn't help her, and he'd had no choice in the matter.

"But then you updated your beacon, so we all knew you were still alive. We got the go-ahead to retrieve you at first light, weather permitting, which we attempted. I picked my teammate and friend—" He had a catch in his throat and had to pause for a second. "My friend Tom to accompany me because he is—was—my best medic."

"I'm sorry for your loss. I also lost two crewmates."

"Belle, something destroyed the dropship! I only survived because I dropped first to secure the drop site." He shook his fists. "Tom was covering me with a chain gun, and the two pilots were holding in a hover. Then, *kapow!*" He slapped his hands together. "Out of nowhere, this arc of light vaporized it, and all three persons onboard, right before my eyes! I'm sure it came from that structure."

"You mean the one we're inside?" she said, holding her arms out wide, catching Grant by surprise. He finally took a chance to look around.

He was in a large rectangular room with a tall ceiling. 10cm hexagonal tiles covered the walls and floor. There were stacks of stone tiles and boxes scattered around the floor.

"So that's where we are. I was expecting something more like a cave. This looks like a building." He noticed a hexagonal door to the passageway. "Though a strange one."

"I think it is a ruined building. A thick layer of moss completely covered it. The fire burned that off."

She sat there looking at him with wide eyes. "There's something strange about this ruin. I've managed to enter several other rooms." She told him about the rooms she had entered and the little automaton creatures she had seen.

Just then, one entered the room through a ceiling vent and leisurely made its way across the ceiling, hanging upside down six meters above their heads. Grant was looking for his gun, which wasn't on him.

Grant couldn't take his eyes off it. "Nobody at base knows about this place. Our briefing said you were hiding inside a rock monolith, like in a cave or something." He pointed at the starfish. "Who made it?"

She shook her head. They sat there watching it until it exited the room.

Grant was still half inside the shelter, with his torso exposed and Belle kneeling beside him. "Let me take a look at myself," he said. "Where is all my gear?"

Belle pointed to the nearby wall. "I stacked it all over there. What do you need?"

"First, help me out of this tent."

She helped him extricate himself from the tent and slide on his behind next to the table.

"Can I have my canteen first, please?" he asked.

She handed it to him.

"Thanks." Grant took a long drink of water. "There's a large green bag with a red cross on the outside. Can you please give it to me?"

She did, and he took out a headlamp, put it on his head, then found a bottle of powerful pain medication and ingested a couple pills with more water. He looked over his body.

"Are you some kind of doctor?" she asked.

"Rescue parajumper. A pararescueman."

"What's that?"

"I'm a glorified medic who knows how to shoot a gun and fly."

Belle had splinted his entire right leg and wrapped a bandage around it together with the left, immobilizing his lower body. Grant unwrapped his legs and got a first view of the shrapnel wound.

A jagged piece of sheet metal about eight centimeters long had embedded itself in his right thigh, in the meaty part. His fatigue pants were shredded but had done their job of absorbing most of the shrapnel, protecting him from thousands of tiny missiles. But this large piece had penetrated.

He looked at Belle. "This is a good bandaging job."

"Thanks."

"You didn't have much to work with, but you did it correctly, leaving that metal in."

"I remembered from my training that removing objects from puncture wounds could cause even more harm." This was correct when the person doing the first aid didn't know what to look for.

"I think removing it will be okay, but you chose good."

"What about arteries?"

"This one probably missed anything vital. I have a portable ultrasound imager, and I'm going to have a look inside, but I bet I can remove it." He took the imager out of his medic's bag and scanned the flesh around the wound.

The part of the metal under the skin was visible. It was straight-edged and smaller than the piece outside. If he slid it out just so, he maybe could do it without slicing anything. There were no nearby significant arteries or nerves or other sensitive tissue.

He cleaned around the wound as best he could with an antiseptic and injected a local anesthetic to numb the flesh.

Then he grasped the piece of metal with forceps, spread the wound opening slightly with the fingers of one hand, and grasping the forceps with his other, he slid it out of his flesh.

It came away cleanly, followed by a large blood clot and bleeding. He cleaned it some more.

Next, he used a suturing kit to stitch up the wound, grateful for the numbing he had applied. A deep thigh wound like this would hurt a lot after the numbing wore off.

He bandaged the wound, then used safety pins to close his torn and bloody fatigue bottoms. At least now he was reasonably presentable.

When the dropship had exploded, an overpressure wave hit Grant. His helmet and fatigues protected him from the worst, but even so, his eardrums ruptured, and he'd suffered some internal damage to his sinuses, eyes, and lungs.

His nanites had managed to repair most of that, though

he would have a ringing in his ears for a while, and his eye sclera was bloody.

He would be okay, though he would walk with a limp for a while.

As a last measure, he injected himself with a broadspectrum antibiotic and removed a collapsible crutch from his medical bag to help him take the weight off his leg.

Looking over Belle, he said, "I can look at your injuries now, if you'd like."

She sat on the floor and removed the medical boot she was wearing on her left foot and the flight boot on her right. Belle had a deep second-degree burn on her right calf. Some large blisters had formed. The best he could do was clean it, apply burn ointment, and cover it with a protective bandage.

The heel of her left foot was swollen to almost twice its normal size and looked inflamed and painful. There were two large puncture wounds where the megapede had bitten her and a little bit of tissue necrosis.

He told her to numb her foot. Then he removed the dead tissue, making it bleed, and cleaned the wound again.

He also injected her with an antibiotic and injected the site of the wound with medication to help bring the swelling down. But she'd be using that medical boot for a while longer.

"Are we both ship-shape now?" she asked him.

"Definitely ready to hike out of here!" Grant smiled.

"Thank you for saving my life," he said, looking into her eyes.

"You're welcome."

"I would have died if you'd left me out there. With your injuries and everything you've gone through over the last couple days, most people would be a slobbering emotional wreck about now. Maybe we won't get out of this, but I am truly grateful for what you did."

She blushed, looked away, and shrugged. "You would have done the same for me, I'm sure. I'm glad I could be useful."

"Now, is there any water in this place? I want to refill my canteen."

Belle took his canteen. "Yes, that's something I can help with." She limped away toward the odd six-sided doorway in the rear wall. "I found a cistern. Be right back."

16

Belle limped slowly out of the foyer, grasping Grant's canteen to her chest. Her heel stung where he had cut away the dead tissue. It had been necessary to prevent infection, but the extra pain added to her anxiety.

She couldn't numb the foot with her implant because her body wouldn't heal properly if the nerve endings were interfered with. She had considered asking for some pain medication but decided against it because she wanted a sharp mind. So, she sucked up the pain. *Mama suffered worse than this, bringing me into the world. This is nothing.* Memories of her mother made her sad; she wondered if she would ever see her family again.

She was finally not alone anymore. There was a person to talk to, to lean on for help if it came to that. She didn't have to sit for hours and hours, wondering if she would die alone.

How much should she tell Grant about what she'd found? Would he believe her? The most important priority was to determine if the structure was dangerous. He'd said the structure shot down the dropship. She would have to be open with him on her own suspicions.

The passage outside the foyer was the same as she last

saw it. She'd left the door to the supply room shut this time because she wanted to test if something else would open it and leave it that way, but it was still shut when she arrived. Pressing her hand to the control plate, she said in her mind, *I need water.*

The door did not open. She tried again, putting her will behind the desire, but the door wouldn't open. *So much for deterministic behavior.* What had changed?

She went over to the door of the room with the radioactive boxes, put her hand on the panel, and thought, *I need food.* Nothing happened either. Where once this door had opened at the slightest expression of a desire for sustenance, now it did nothing.

Belle wondered about the strange behavior of the ruin's doors. Their locking mechanism seemed to be keyed to the thoughts of whoever was touching the control plate. Could any creature enter if they expressed the same thought? For example, if a megapede was thirsty and thinking about it when it walked over a control plate, would that cause the door to cycle?

Belle wasn't actually thirsty or hungry because she'd eaten a meal not all that long ago. She put her hand on the panel outside the storeroom again and thought, *Grant needs water.* The door slid open.

She went to the cistern, dipped in his canteen until it was full, then walked out. Pressing her hand to the panel, she projected, *I am done,* and the door closed. Then, *Grant needs water,* and the door opened again.

She returned to the foyer. *I suppose he does need water because I'm holding his canteen.*

The doors were more sophisticated devices than just reading thoughts and dumbly responding. Could it be that they were lie detectors? How would that work? And how could a machine, not designed by humans, interpret human physiology and body language?

Back at their campsite, Grant had pulled himself to the short table and sat sideways, resting one arm on top. She handed him the canteen.

He thanked her and took a long, satisfying drink from it. Afterward, he offered it to her, but she refused.

Belle sat at the table across from him.

He said, "This is a strange table. I examined its construction while you were gone and noticed it is a single piece. Woven together using some composite material, like carbon fiber, but not assembled from individual pieces." He placed his face up close to its surface. "It's like it was 3D-printed, but if so, using a better process than I've ever seen. I see no evidence of layer buildup."

"It gets stranger than that," Belle said. "This table wasn't here when I first entered the building. I went out exploring rooms for an hour or two, and when I returned, the table had appeared." Belle held empty hands out. "Was it built in place or carried in here? If the latter, then who did it? Because those little caretaker creatures aren't big enough to carry it alone." She tried to imagine a starfish robot ten times larger but didn't like the conclusions that led to.

"Maybe more than one of them carried it in."

"Could be. Who knows how many of those starfish there are. Could be just one, and we keep seeing the same one doing its rounds, or there could be dozens of them." She rested her arms on the table. "There are identifying marks on their bodies in infrared, though I haven't gotten a close-up view of one yet."

"Have you tried catching one?"

Was he nuts? They weren't on a safari.

"No, and it hasn't occurred to me to try. I feel like a guest and don't want to offend the host."

"A *guest?*"

"Yes. I haven't told you the full story of how I got into this ruin." Belle told Grant about having to use thoughts to instruct the opening and closing of doors and that, for most doors, she hadn't yet succeeded in finding the key.

He looked at her skeptically. "I doubt it can read your thoughts. Humankind has been trying for centuries to create some form of telepathy, and it's just impossible. You must subconsciously be doing something with your body, and that makes the doors open."

She rolled her eyes and sighed. How was she supposed to convince the scientists back at base if she couldn't convince Grant? "Well, you're welcome to try it yourself when you feel up to it."

"Okay, I'll try later, but we must discuss our situation." He pointed his finger back and forth between them. He was avoiding the subject of the strange door behavior. It was annoying that he changed the subject.

"I don't think the dropship pilots got a call out to Clinton Base before they were killed," Grant said. "Operations probably don't know what happened, though we'll have been reported as missing by now. Is your beacon still up and transmitting?"

"No, it was destroyed in the blast. The radio was smashed to pieces when it impacted the cliff face." She'd looked at it closely and saw no obvious way it could be repaired. Its power cell was damaged, and its circuit boards were snapped in half.

"What do you have as far as rations and water?"

"I have ten days of rations remaining, but for one person. Water is probably unlimited if that water cistern stays full constantly."

Grant looked through his gear and reported, "I have just two days of rations and the water in my canteen. So, between the two of us, we have six days of food for both, which we could stretch to two weeks if we begin rationing now." He began tallying on his hand. "We're good on water, shelter, and safety."

Belle shook her head. They weren't safe. It might be safer than being outside in the jungle, but the structure could kill them just as quickly as it killed their ships.

"Though both injured," Grant said, "I think we qualify as walking wounded, and unless one of us develops an infection or gets hurt again, we're probably also good on the medical side of things."

"You think you'll be okay?" Belle said. He was noticeably favoring the injured thigh. She'd seen how deep that shrapnel penetrated. Maybe he had better nanites than she did, but it would take him a few days to heal for sure.

"Yes. In short, we have two important unsatisfied needs: food and communications. Without both of those, I think we won't be surviving this. I suppose if we had an unlimited supply of food, we could live here indefinitely, but that would feel too much like a prison."

Imagine being stuck in here forever.

"And our headlamps and computers probably only have enough juice in their power cells to last a few months."

Belle gazed intently at him as he made this assessment. "I don't believe we're safe here. Perhaps at the moment, but you said the ruin did something to the dropship, which destroyed it."

"Yes, from where I was watching, it looked like the structure projected an energy beam of some kind, which destroyed the ship."

He'd arrived at the same conclusion as Belle.

"Listen, I suspect the structure also destroyed my ship too. Perhaps in not such dramatic fashion, but everything was going fine until I started drilling into the cliff face."

"Go on."

"The task Mission Ops gave me was to collect physical samples of this structure. At the time, they thought it was a rock monolith emitting anomalously high radiation levels. It certainly looked that way from the air." Maybe Ops knew more than they were letting on. Maybe somebody there knew this was a structure, not a monolith. "The dome was covered by many layers of gray-blue moss, which gave it an irregular surface."

"So, it didn't look like a dome when you first saw it?" Grant said.

"Not at all. Just a big dumb moss-covered rock. A monolith. I subjected it to a rotating rock grinder to remove moss and exterior weathering, so I could get a spectrometer reading and cut out a sample." She held up a finger. "However, as soon as the grinder bit touched the wall, I saw radiation levels rise rapidly. That continued even after I stopped the grinder." Levels should have dropped quickly. Had she overlooked something or made a mistake that led to the meltdown? "My reactor suffered a core dump not even fifteen seconds after the bit touched the rock surface."

"Yes, I understand how that is too much of a coincidence. Reactor accidents these days are so rare. A core meltdown seems impossible. What do you think did it?"

Grant was correct. Fission reactor accidents were almost unheard of these days. Modern power plants had multiple safety features designed into them, making it nearly impossible to cause a malfunction, even intentionally.

"The day after the accident, I analyzed my blood nanite history and noticed some patterns that would only be possible if I had been hit with a powerful pulse of neutron radiation."

"But you survived it."

Indeed, she had survived it, but only because of the blood nanites. However, a pulse powerful enough to put the reactor into a critical state would have killed her instantly. That's why she was sure it must have been a beam.

"It's possible that, if that pulse were a focused beam directed at the reactor core, the sudden increase in neutron flux would have caused the core to go critical suddenly and melt down. That's my working hypothesis."

"Well, I don't know anything about nuclear power plants, so I'll just have to take your word for it, but what you say makes sense. How would one create such a beam?"

"Short of a nuclear weapon, I don't know how to generate a pulse that strong." She wasn't exaggerating. A monumental neutron flux was required to put the reactor into a critical state.

"But you think it came from this structure?"

"Yes," Belle said. It had to be a beam. That's why Borya never evacuated. The neutron beam incapacitated him when he was caught in it. Belle and Phil only caught its edges.

"This structure destroyed both of our ships after we damaged it. And now we're inside the thing." Grant looked around the room with haunted eyes.

"It seemed the safest place to go. The jungle was going to kill me." Belle was willing to go almost anywhere if it wasn't in the jungle with the megapedes. It was a choice of the lesser of two dangers.

"What's to stop it from killing us inside here? Like we're some kind of germs."

That was a good question. But why was the building

allowing her to enter rooms? Was it because it hadn't recognized her as a threat? Just as the correct thought allowed her to enter certain rooms, was there an equivalent incorrect thought that would get her instantly killed? "We need to be careful with our minds," Belle said. "If we have thoughts about damaging the structure, maybe it will kill us instead of letting us through doors."

"Or maybe we just haven't met whoever lives here," Grant said. "And when we do, they'll panic and kill us."

"Kepler management must be having a fit right now after losing two expensive ships and seven employees in two days." There would be political fallout. A mad CYA scramble at Clinton Base, and Belle would become the scapegoat.

"To summarize," Grant said, "we have problems with food, communications, and safety. And possibly with our employment, if we manage to get ourselves out of this one."

"I'm most concerned about our safety in this structure. We need to find out more. Or get rescued," Belle said.

17

Grant considered everything he had heard from Belle so far. It was a fantastical story, one he would have a hard time believing if he hadn't seen some of it firsthand. A hidden building shooting down spaceships, thought-controlled doors, and starfish robots.

And then there was Belle Machado. In some ways, she was the greater enigma. Covered with dirt, her coveralls blackened, her hair in singed disarray, and her eyes tired and bloodshot. Yet there was a beautiful woman under all the grime. Flawless light brown skin, oval face, full lips, and a silky alto voice. Confident, resourceful, courageous, and independent. So unlike his own needy and domineering mother.

He felt a need to protect her and get her to safety, more than just because it was his job. He wanted her and him to survive so he would have the opportunity to know her in the ordinary world.

Her insights about the dangers of the structure were valid. If it could read their thoughts to decide whether to open a door, then it could just as quickly read them to decide to exterminate them. They had to tread lightly around here.

Belle explained her plan for re-establishing communications with Clinton Base. "The way I see it, of our four problems, the easiest to address immediately is the communications problem." She pointed at the exterior wall. "I propose we construct an SOS marker that can be seen by satellite. Do you think your tactical radio has enough range to contact anyone?"

"My comms are on VHF," said Grant. "Only line-of-site, max 30km range. I can try it; maybe we'll get lucky, and a satellite will pick it up." He shrugged. "But I wouldn't hold my breath. However, I think your plan for the marker is an excellent idea, and we should do it now before it gets dark."

"What can we use as markers? They must be big enough to see from kilometers away, but also a contrasting color against the ground."

Grant stood with his collapsible cane and flexed his injured leg experimentally a few times. It hurt, but he'd manage. The sutures were tight, biting into his flesh.

"The burned soil is a light brown," said Grant, "but many of the burned trees are pitch black. We keep collecting dead burned wood until we have enough to construct the sign. We build it just outside the entrance to the dome, with an arrow pointing at it."

Belle hesitated, then said, "I'm worried about the megapedes. They like to burrow under dead stumps and debris, then ambush whatever walks nearby."

Megapedes were only a problem if you didn't understand their behavior. They were burrowing ambush predators. He needed to calm her nerves.

Grant patted his 6.5-mm carbine, which he began cleaning while they talked. "That's what this is for. I have about one hundred fifty rounds of ammunition left, so we'll have to make each shot count, but I think it will be enough."

What else was he going to shoot at with it? It likely wouldn't be any help if the structure attacked them.

"I also think we should fashion some snake boots out of those empty containers in the corner," Grant said. He pointed to the boxes.

"You mean those knee-high boots with thick sides that snakes can't bite through?"

"Exactly. See, the megapedes like to bite down low. The fact you got bit in the heel is no coincidence. That's their favorite target." He pulled out his combat knife. "I'll use this to cut those containers down so they wrap around our legs and feet, then use some of the rope you have to tie it all down. It will be uncomfortable, but I think we have to assume that at least some of the megapedes will get past my gun and get a bite."

"You don't think they'll be able to bite through that material?"

He picked up one of the boxes and slammed his knife down point-first. It didn't penetrate. "Resistant to puncture. We only have my gun, so I'm on guard duty by default."

She pointed to herself. "So *I'm* going to have to collect all the dead wood myself?" Her eyes were wide. Maybe he was making things worse.

Grant raised a calming hand. "You're nervous, I understand. I would be too if I had gone through what you have, but we need somebody on overwatch. The only way we do this safely is if I stand guard while you scavenge for wood." To emphasize his words, he held his carbine to his shoulder. "We'll do it as quickly as possible, and if at any moment it gets to be too much, just tell me, and we'll retreat and try again later. But I'll be there right next to you the entire time."

She breathed deeply, closed her eyes, and said, "Okay,

let's get this over with."

Brave girl. He'd known a few scientists who'd survived megapede attacks. Most of them refused to return to the jungle, even after receiving treatment for post-attack trauma.

They both went to work on the containers. They had extremely high tensile strength but could be weakened if continuously bent back and forth along a seam. They managed to cut the bottoms off, then slice them up one side, making a long sheet.

Grant wrapped one around Belle's leg, forming a protective tube, and tied a rope around it. Then he fashioned a wide cone with an opening in one end to insert her foot. There wasn't any easy way to form it on her foot, so they had to make a cone to cover it. The soles of their boots would be in contact with the ground, but that should be fine if they walked with a shuffling motion, keeping their feet hidden under the cones.

After assembling Belle's boots, he repeated the process for himself.

They looked slightly ridiculous, a bit like the Tin Man from *The Wizard of Oz*. But Grant had to admit he felt much safer.

Belle put on her oxygen mask to protect herself from dust and smoke. She armed herself with her scavenged spike.

Grant put on his full-face combat helmet and grabbed his carbine, extra ammunition, and a large canteen for them both to share. He also carried his medic's bag in case the worst happened. Finally, just before exiting, he took a mild narcotic pain medication to help with the pain in his thigh. The next hour would be crucially important. He offered some to Belle, but she declined.

They went to the exterior door, she put her hand on the

plate, and a second later, the door opened. Since he had been unconscious when she brought him here, it was his first time seeing the door in operation.

They had to help each other up the one meter to ground level in their injured state. Despite the pain meds, his thigh hurt like the devil.

The smoke and air had cleared significantly since that morning, and the reactor core fire five hundred meters to the south was clearly visible. A still-smoking debris field lay one kilometer to the west: all that remained of the dropship and its occupants.

They started on the accessible sources of wood first, collecting burned branches that had blown up against the side of the dome. Then they both waddled out into the open to the west of the dome and began clearing an area of about five-by-eight meters of debris.

From the branches they had collected already, Belle selected a particularly long and sturdy one, about three meters long, and used it to probe the ground and debris in front of her before advancing. Grant stood to her left, about two meters away, where she was undefended by the spike she held in her right hand.

They encountered several small megapede specimens that he didn't even bother to shoot. He just squashed them with his boot heel, then tossed them as far away as he could from their position.

They soon had enough wood to construct the first S.

Next, they began collecting wood in a widening arc toward the west. It was slow work because the need to defend themselves forced them to keep one hand free at all times. They had to make about twenty trips back and forth between the marker and the burned forest.

Grant shot about a dozen megapedes, and Belle managed

to kill two that were too close for him to shoot.

One of them, an especially large two-meter beast, got past her, wrapped itself around her boot, and tried to bite through it. Belle yelled out in panic, and Grant began pulling his knife as he watched the megapede's mandibles slipping and sliding over the tough woven material. Then Belle shoved her spike into the creature's head.

It uncoiled, she flung it off, and for good measure, Grant put two bullets into it. A green gelatinous fluid covered Belle's snake boots, and he supposed it was the megapede's venom.

After two hours, they finished the SOS sign, with five-meter-tall letters and an arrow pointing toward the dome's entrance. It would be easy to see from the air, though they both wondered what would happen when it rained. They'd worry about that problem if it became one.

Exhausted, they made their way back to the entrance. Before going in, Grant sent out a couple transmissions on his tactical radio requesting help, but got no reply.

Belle touched the door panel, and a second later, it opened.

The campsite was changed. First, there was now a second of the short tables, though the new one was slightly larger, as if the maker was accounting for Grant's larger size.

Second, every single one of the empty containers they had used for constructing their snake boots—or 'pede boots, as they'd started calling them—had been replaced with an identical copy. All of this happened within the last two hours.

It was a mystery, but one fact was for sure: they were being spied on.

"Somebody is watching us," said Belle.

Grant had to agree with her. He felt eyes looking at him

from the walls.

18

Grant helped Belle remove her 'pede boots. Then she helped him with the same. The low tables were a good height for use as a bench, so they each sat at "their" respective piece and rested for a bit, sharing sips of water out of Grant's water canteen. They also split an emergency ration pack. It was time to go on half rations.

"Belle," Grant said, "tell me a little about yourself, if you don't mind. How long have you been with Kepler?"

Belle nodded, finished chewing, and washed it down with some water. It tasted like a sweet lemon bar—all the ration bars tasted like that. She was already sick of them. "One year and four months. I completed my one-year probationary copilot apprenticeship under Phil Curtis one month ago. My status was changed to pilot-candidate." With sorrowful eyes, she said, "This mission was my check-ride to qualify for promotion to pilot-commander."

"What's a check-ride?"

"It's an examination, but done in an actual operational context. I was taking the final exam to qualify for pilot-commander."

Grant nodded.

"My first three months with Kepler were spent in pilot simulator training, competing for one of the apprenticeship slots. I was hired after graduating from the University of Nuevo Peru pilot academy. Nuevo Peru is my home planet. I was born and raised there." Pointing at Grant with her chin, she asked, "How about yourself? How long have you been here?"

"One year. I left the military about fifteen months ago, and my father helped me line up this job with Kepler. He and Chief Scientist Valero go way back, roommates in their university days."

He had inside connections.

"There was an opening for a search and rescue specialist on the Special Missions team, and I had the qualifications. Pay and benefits are twice what I was earning in the service."

Didn't have to earn his position like Belle had. Just fell in his lap.

"About three months ago," Grant said, "the company decided to form a second search and rescue team, and I was promoted to team leader."

I bet Dr. Valero had a hand in that promotion as well.

"Before this, I spent eight years in UAAN Special Operations Command as a special forces spaceborne pararescueman. I spent two years in college but didn't like it. Decided to enlist in the military and see some excitement. Sort of regret that decision now; I wish I had finished school, but I don't regret my time in the service."

"You can still go back to school and finish that degree. Why don't you?" She never could understand why somebody would get bored with school and drop out. Belle loved to learn.

"I enjoy the work I do. It's fulfilling. Nearly every day I go to work, there's something I do that has an immediate positive impact on somebody. I didn't experience that in school, and I need it. It's what keeps me motivated. My regrets have more to do with opportunities. My lack of a college degree has closed some doors. Plus, it was a disappointment to my parents when I dropped out. My mother is a professor of English Literature and had just assumed I would have a similar outlook on life as she does."

"How many siblings?"

"Zero," he said emphatically. "My parents didn't want to have me. But when Mom became pregnant, Dad convinced her to keep me."

He was a pampered only child.

"They actually told you that?"

"Sure, my parents don't keep anything from me. I hear it all, both good and bad. That's why I live on the outskirts of human civilization." He grinned knowingly at her.

She couldn't imagine not wanting to be near her family. What an empty existence.

"That's too bad you feel that way. I miss my family," reminisced Belle. "I haven't seen them since I graduated, and we only talk for a few minutes once a month."

"Why is that?"

Should she tell him the truth? Make him feel guilty?

"My family are ranchers in Nuevo Peru and don't have much money. We've always been poor. I have a solid job now—or at least I did. We'll see what happens in the coming days—but new pilots earn peanuts, and I have student loans I had to begin paying off as soon as I started earning a salary."

"I'm sorry, that's hard."

You have no idea.

"Yes, there have been hard times, but my family is

everything to me. I am the youngest of six children and the fifth daughter. My elder siblings began working at young ages to help the farm survive, and most of them didn't finish secondary school. As the youngest, I didn't have to do that, and my parents forced me to do well in school."

Belle bit into the last of her ration bar.

"I hated school at the time," she said, "but now, I see they were correct. I earned a scholarship to the academy, and now my opportunities are, in theory, limitless. My mother said to me, '*Our eldest are preserving our ranch, but you are preserving our future.*'" Belle felt her eyes watering and had to pause for a second. "Now I've gone and thrown it all away on my check-ride! In my profession, losing your command is not easily forgiven, no matter who was at fault."

Grant said, "I'm sure it will be okay. I admire the courage and tenacity you've shown in how you responded to this emergency. Certainly the company will recognize your worth and keep you on."

If she had connections like Grant, then maybe. But she'd lost her only mentor, Phil Curtis, in the accident.

"The loss of my ship goes into my permanent log as an annotated incident. It's the first thing pilot recruiters look at when scanning resumes. It'll take me twenty years of commanding a barge, without incident, to get somebody to overlook that."

"That sounds unfair. Is it really like that?"

"If your goal is to become a starship captain, then yes, it often is this way. Too many qualified pilots and not enough command positions. Maddeningly, the industry values credentials and a spotless record more than they value experience."

Belle felt crushed by the mountain she was expected to climb to achieve her goals. She knew several students from the academy who were much less capable than herself but had gotten sweet positions in large starlines because of family connections. The only thing she had going for herself were her credentials. They had to be spotless if she hoped to compete with her well-connected peers.

"Is that your ultimate goal, to become a starship captain?"

Their conversation had suddenly become intimate. Why was she sharing her dreams with this man? He put her at ease with his handsome smile and optimistic attitude. *I bet he always sees the best in people.* She decided to tell him. Maybe he was a pampered brat of wealthy parents, but it didn't seem to have gone to his head.

"Yes, it's been my dream since I was a little girl, and it would make my family so proud. To visit the stars and faraway exotic places. I also enjoy people, and a captain gets to work closely with all sorts of people. And senior starship crews are allowed to take their family with them on journeys. Someday, I want to have children of my own and continue the legacy of the Machado family. This life"—she spread her arms wide—"is no place for raising a family."

There, she'd told him. What would he think of her traditional desires? She sounded old-fashioned. But ambition burned in Belle's heart. An ambition not fueled by ego or want of riches, but by a desire to honor her family and make the world a better place.

Grant said, "That's a beautiful dream. I hope you find it."

They were gathering moss sitting here talking. Belle wanted, needed, to find out if this structure was dangerous. She wanted to find proof of a neutron beam source.

"Come." She beckoned to him. "Let me show you how the doors work in this place."

19

"Now, in your mind, you must express what it is you need, but it must be a true need. Try thinking you need information," she explained slowly to Grant.

They had spent the last thirty minutes trying to get Grant to open the door to the supply room but without success. Belle could reliably open the door by expressing a need for information, but not Grant.

"I'm trying! I swear on my lucky socks, I am doing everything you say." Despite his evident frustration, he once again touched the plate and concentrated.

For about a minute, she watched his eyebrows and facial expression as he tried to muster some connection, but nothing happened.

"Darn it, I don't understand how it can be so easy for you, Belle." Was there something fundamentally different about his brain? He was a man. That was a possibility.

"Give it a rest for now. We can try again some other time. Until then, I want to try some of the other doors that haven't worked so far." She had shown him the contents of the supply room and the hot-box room, and he was intrigued by the possibilities of other treasures to be discovered. "If you need to rest, you can return to the camp. I can continue by myself."

"It's okay. We think this place is dangerous, so we should stay together." Wherever he went in the dome, Grant always had his automatic carbine slung on one shoulder and his medic's bag on the other. He carried them so naturally, like appendages to his body.

"That's fine, as long as you're not too tired or in pain." She was provoking him intentionally.

"Me too tired, ha! Who's the special forces operator here?"

She grinned back. "Okay, good, now stay quiet for a few minutes. I need to think."

"Yes, ma'am!" He gave her a mock salute.

Belle had been thinking about the logic used by the dome when deciding whether a door should be unlocked. She had already determined that expressing a desire for a known object behind the doors was insufficient. One must have a need and not lie about it.

Making things triply complicated, one must know what to ask for, but she didn't know what was behind these doors. There were symbols above all the ones she had seen, in a mysterious language she assumed described what was behind them. Of course, that was no help to them.

If I lived here for years and years, what sorts of things would I need? She tried to put herself in the shoes of the inhabitants, aware of the fact that she couldn't possibly guess what the driving desire of an alien being might be.

She and Grant hobbled down the long passage to the door at the end of the stretch to the right of the foyer door. They were hunched down because of the low ceiling, and Grant looked none too comfortable, but he wasn't complaining.

Belle pressed her hand to the panel and thought, *We need peace and rest.* The door slid quietly open.

"What did you say to it?" Grant said.

"I said that we need peace and rest."

"Well, that's definitely true."

Belle wondered again at what the consequences would be if she expressed hostile intentions at the doors. She wasn't about to experiment, but how sensitive was it? Could she accidentally trigger an attack just because she was a little grumpy? Or did it take more blood-thirsty feelings?

Like all the rooms in the structure, the one they entered was dark. It was large, about the same size as the larger foyer, though with a lower ceiling about two meters high. They could both stand at their full height.

The room was full of tables similar to the ones they had been "gifted," all of the same style but varying sizes. There were about two dozen, and they were arranged somewhat haphazardly around the room.

Leading away from the room were three additional hexagonal doors. Besides the tables, there was nothing else in the room except for more symbols carved into walls at different places.

Belle briefly put on her mask and turned on the thermal view. The walls were painted with geometrical patterns. She turned it back off. The thermal imager drained the power cells rapidly, so she limited her use.

Then, out of a ceiling vent, a starfish walked out and headed in their general direction. Because of the lower ceiling, this was the first starfish they'd seen that would pass within reach.

"I'm going to try and grab it," Grant whispered to Belle.

"Are you sure about that? We might make somebody mad!" she hissed back at him.

"I'm not going to hurt it; I just want to examine it, see how much we can learn by looking at it close up."

Her nerves were on notice. This was just the sort of thing she was worried might trigger the ruin.

"Okay, but let me do it," said Belle. "The ruin may be more comfortable with me snooping around, and that's why it's letting me pass doors."

Grant nodded in assent. It was actually a good idea. She couldn't think of anything less threatening than handling one of the starfish for a few minutes.

They stood to the side of the starfish's path until it was nearly overhead.

Belle walked up to it, put her hand over its body, and pulled it off the ceiling.

The creature came away easily, the legs sticking to the stone slightly as she pulled it away. The six legs and delicate arms immediately began reaching around randomly.

Holding its body between two fingers, she projected: *Be still. We just want to study you. We will not harm you.*

The little starfish stopped moving. That was a good sign.

Belle and Grant looked at each other in stunned silence. Moving over to the nearest table, they sat on the floor next to it, set the starfish on the table, turned it over so it was right side up, and studied it.

The creature tried to walk away until Belle touched it with her finger and thought, *Be still. We are studying you.*

It halted, holding perfectly still.

Up close, the starfish was intricately detailed. Each arm was whip-like from a distance, but up close, the tip divided into smaller whips, and those into even smaller, and so on, like a fractal pattern. The end product looked like a fine cloud.

The body was composed of three hexagonal plates, ten centimeters in diameter and three high, one plate on top of another. From the bottom protruded six thick legs, and from the top, the six whip-like arms.

Below the bottom plate was an even smaller hexagonal plate. It was scorching, too hot to touch with bare hands. It looked like a miniature version of the hot boxes they had seen in the hot-box room.

On top of the upper plate were six prominent elliptical blisters that seemed to be sensors of some kind. They were constantly reorienting along their major axis and reshaping the blister.

They spent fifteen minutes studying it, but little could be learned without opening one. She wasn't about to attempt that.

She picked it up, turned it upside down, and pressed it back against the ceiling where she found it. To the creature, she sent, *We're done. You may go, thank you.*

The little automaton continued on its way as if it had never been interrupted.

"Do you think that was humanity's first contact with an alien species?" she asked Grant.

"I don't think so," Grant said. "I have the distinct impression that it is a drone of some sort, purely mechanical. Not all that intelligent."

"I think you're correct, but it sure is a cute little creature."

"Anything that radioactive is not cute."

While studying it, Belle had scanned it with her radiation detector. Levels were relatively high, especially close to that miniature hot box underneath its body. Mostly alpha radiation and a little neutron radiation.

"I think those hot boxes might be radioisotope power generators," Belle said.

"You do?" He looked at her in surprise.

"Yes, and I find it interesting, and indeed a little frightening, that it lets me in when I tell it I need food at the hot-box room. Is that their idea of a good meal? A bite out of a block of plutonium-238?"

"Now there's a thought."

Grant christened the new room the Commons Room. "Because it looks like a lounge or a lunchroom to me," he said.

They decided to keep exploring. At the far door from whence they entered, Belle could open it, thinking, *We need peace and rest.*

The door led to a long thirty-meter passageway, running east-west along the long axis of the ruin. On the south side were eight doors, spaced at regular intervals of about four meters. There were no doors on the north side. A matching door was at the end of the passage opposite where they entered.

On a hunch, Belle held her hand to the panel at the left of the first door in the row and thought, *We need peace and rest.*

The door slid open.

The room behind it was a square about four meters on a side, and the ceiling was 1.5 meters, almost high enough for her to stand up straight. There were no other doors.

In the room were three more of the curious hexagonal tables. Two of them were next to a larger table that was twice as tall, and the third table was next to one just as tall but smaller in diameter.

Along one wall were many shelves containing ringed tablets and small containers.

There were some featureless boxes in the room that didn't reveal what their purpose was. However, a small container dripped a slow trickle of water at the back wall. Somewhere behind it, she could hear a matching trickle that must be a drain.

The room had a domesticated feel like it was somebody's

home. "I'm naming this one the Apartment," said Belle.

Grant nodded at her choice. They tested the next door in the passage, and the same thought of peace and rest worked on it. Behind it was a matching room.

They tried all the doors in the passage, and all led to identical rooms. This was a hallway of apartments, Belle was certain of it.

"I bet those little tables they gave us are actually their version of chairs, and the taller tables we saw in the apartments are actual tables."

Grant paused. "Then where are their beds?"

"Maybe they don't need them. I don't know. Or maybe they sleep sitting. I think the ruin let us through the first two doors using the peace and rest thought because the rooms we needed were found deeper in the structure, and through those doors was the path."

"Makes sense," Grant said.

"If I'm correct, then we maybe could use this rule as a way to enter other passages. For example, if we wanted to find the control center—assuming there is something like that here—I could try that thought at each door until we find one that opens. Then, we continue this way until we find it."

After considering it, Grant responded, "Sounds like a good strategy to me. Now, how about we get some rest? My leg is beginning to ache something fierce, and I've noticed your limp is worse. We can try your theory out during our next expedition."

"Come on, let's go a little farther." He wanted to quit now, just when they'd had a breakthrough?

"Oh, it's nothing horrible, but I know if we keep at this without rest then it'll become a problem. We need to heal."

He was correct, of course.

They returned the way they'd come. Curiously, on the return trip, they managed to pass the doors again using the peace and rest thought, even though they were going in the reverse direction. Or at least Belle was. Grant still failed to control any doors.

They sat back and rested at the campsite, eating another half of a ration bar each.

"We should set a watch," Grant said. "One of us awake and alert while the other sleeps."

"I'll take the first watch," Belle said. Grant looked beat.

"Okay, wake me in four hours, then we'll swap."

Grant checked and cleaned both of their wounds, then went to the tent and curled up inside.

In a few minutes, there was soft snoring coming from the tent.

Wish I could fall asleep like that!

Grant had given Belle his carbine, "just in case." Though she wouldn't know what to do with it if she needed it. She shoved one of the benches next to a wall near the tent and sat on it with her back resting against it.

Approximately every thirty minutes, one of the starfish would enter the room, walk around for about five minutes, then leave. It never walked the same path as the previous starfish.

From time to time, deep rumbles arose from inside the structure. Those always made her nervous. Was something waking up? Had they just been found out?

It was hard to keep her eyes open, but the starfish and rumbles would awaken her if she started to doze off.

After four hours, Belle approached the tent and shook Grant awake. He woke but didn't say anything. Just nodded at her, got up, took the carbine from her, then began pacing around the room.

Belle curled up and tried to sleep. It was difficult. Both legs hurt, and she was anxious about the dome. It was so large. Somehow, their success at penetrating deeper had made it all the more real. Where were the inhabitants? Did she really want to know the answer?

20

Belle woke after five hours. She felt refreshed and rested. The swelling in her heel had reduced significantly. "You didn't wake me," she said to Grant.

He was awake, reading something on a tablet computer. When he saw her sitting up out of the shelter, he called out, "Hello, Ms. Belle, a bright and cheery morning to you!" and gave her a warm smile. "I decided to give you a little more rest."

She smiled back and said, "How're you feeling?"

"Greatly improved. My nanites are doing wonderful things. Hearing is almost back to normal, and the pain in my thigh is just a dull ache. I've stopped taking the pain pills."

"Good for you. Now check my legs for me, please. I want to get rid of this medical boot." She sat in front of him, facing him, and stuck her legs out for him to examine.

He looked at her burn first and said it looked improved but put more ointment on it and bandaged it back up.

Her left leg, the one that was bitten, was almost healed. The swelling was way down, almost to normal size, and the puncture wounds were just small black dots surrounded by scabs from the tissue he'd cut away.

"That looks really nice. Sorry about your burn. Our nanite technology still can't do much with damaged skin and connective tissue. Not enough blood flow. But your bite wound looks better. I bet it feels that way too."

"It does. Can I use my normal boot?" Belle asked.

"Try it. If it bothers you, then keep using the medical boot for another day."

"Okay, Doc, thanks."

They shared a small ration bar for breakfast and drank water. Then they armed themselves and scouted the dome entrance to check the status of their SOS marker.

It was untouched, though it was raining a slow drizzle and it was overcast. Most of the fires were out, but the reactor fire continued to burn to the south and would probably continue like that for months, if not years.

Already new life sprang out of the burned ground. Green shoots were visible all over, as if brushed on by an artist painting the landscape. *Where there is a way, life will find it.* In a few months, this would all be verdant again, though it would take years for the trees to grow back to their former height.

Grant tried calling on his radio a few more times without success. Then they entered again.

This time, the door worked for Grant. Belle was correct that he had a stubborn personality that didn't like to quit, and he wanted to try again. He placed his hand on the designated panel, concentrated briefly, and opened the door.

They both stood back with wide-open eyes and looked at each other.

"What did you say to it?" she asked him.

"Please let us in. We need peace and rest."

Which is more or less what she had been saying

whenever she needed access to general-purpose rooms and passages. "And that's what you were trying yesterday?"

"Yes, I swear!" said Grant.

"Okay, one time is not a trend. Let's go inside and try the storage room."

They did that, and it also worked for Grant when he used the *We need information* thought. The hot-box room also opened.

She stood in front of him and looked him up and down. "What's changed since the last time we tried?"

"There are only two things I can think of. I was in a lot of pain yesterday and drugged up on pain pills."

"I don't think it was the pain. When I first gained entry into the dome, I was in excruciating pain. Literally on my knees, begging to be allowed entry, and it worked. Give me a dose of those pain pills."

He understood where she was going with this and gave her a large pill of something he said was strong but wouldn't make her helpless. They sat around for a bit while they waited for it to take effect.

Oh boy, was she feeling good! A feeling of calmness and well-being flooded over her. With a smile on her face, Belle walked over to Grant and wrapped him in a hug.

"I'm so glad you are here with me, Grant. This is right. You are a good man! What is it that you gave me anyway?"

"Don't worry about it." He unwrapped her arms from around him and patted her on the shoulders. "Feels good, doesn't it?"

She nodded.

"Yeah? That's how people get addicted to that stuff, so I'm not telling you what it is. If I have my way, you won't need another in your lifetime."

"Oh, stop it, don't be such a drag." She gave him a creepy

smile. Wow! She felt excellent but was acting way out of character. Though the pain in her legs was completely gone.

Grant grabbed her arm and led her to the foyer doorway. They walked to the supply room, and he told her to try and open it.

It wouldn't work. Nothing she could put into her mind would allow her to pass. Neither would the hot-box room.

Without waiting for him, she walked to the foyer exterior door. Belle put her hand on it, thinking, *I am done.* No success.

Not a door in the building that formerly worked for her would still allow it. She suddenly felt scared that she might get trapped inside or out.

"Belle, don't worry about it. I'm sure in about five hours the effect will wear off, and you'll be able to use the doors again. In the meantime, they all seem to be working for me."

Which was true. So, Grant took the lead in their explorations.

They returned to the Hall of Apartments and went straight to the door at the end of the long passage.

Grant said, "I'm going to try your idea from yesterday and search for a control room." He placed his hand over the door panel, and a few seconds later, it slid open. "I told it, *We need the control room*, and look!"

Through the door, they found a strange room. It was a large hexagon floor plan, about eight meters in diameter, and through the six sides, there were six doors, one of which they had just entered.

A small hexagonal atrium occupied the center of the room, only about two meters in diameter. More like a vertical tunnel than an atrium, but that's what it would be called in human architecture. It ran twenty meters up. In the light of their lamps, they could just make out what must be the roof. The atrium also ran down, plunging into the darkness, with no bottom that their lamps could illuminate.

Through the atrium, there were more floors visible like the one they were on. Three more above them, and at least three more below, though there were likely more. The atrium was also not an empty volume but filled with a latticework that at first looked like some kind of decorative feature. Like a modern art display.

"It's a stairwell!" she cried out.

She ran toward the atrium, looking at it in fascination. Grant ran right behind her and pulled her back from the threshold. She must not be using good judgment. She patted his hand and said she was fine.

"I think you may be right. But an *alien* stairwell," he replied.

The latticework was formed into something like a double helix and zigzagged from level to level. It would be hard to fall straight down, but it still looked dangerous. Not optimized for four-limbed humans, especially if they were carrying items in their hands.

Grant said, "I wonder if the builders of this place have the same body plan as the starfish we've seen. A stairwell like this doesn't make sense for a bipedal species, but it does if one has lots of extra limbs. Like a spider."

Belle's flesh crawled. "This place was not built for or by humans. This entire structure is an alien artifact."

The implications of that statement were difficult to imagine. Humanity was not alone in the universe. As bizarre as the structure was, in many ways it was also familiar. There were rooms, hallways, doorways. Even a stairway. Whoever built this had to deal with similar practical problems as humans. That means they could be communicated with. They'd seen the symbols. Those must be a written language.

If Grant and Belle discovered the aliens, that would make them the humans who made First Contact. They would be famous. Could Belle somehow use this to her advantage? To save her career? This discovery had to count for something.

She weighed this against the dangers of the structure. It had destroyed two spaceships and killed five humans. It had also saved Grant's and her lives. But was that intentional? Or was the structure's automation just following a program? Were Grant and Belle welcome visitors hosted by the grace of whoever lived here? Or were they nothing more than parasites exploiting a loophole in the security, destined to be exterminated as soon as they were discovered?

Grant tested each of the five unopened doors on this level, but none would open to the control room query.

"Let's go to the next level up," said Belle, feeling braver.

"I think we should wait," said Grant.

"Why?"

"I'm worried the drugs you're on affect your judgment and coordination."

"You were taking pills and still doing things, like shooting guns." She pointed at his carbine.

"But I wasn't climbing a rickety structure inside a bottomless bit." He pointed to the atrium.

"Look, my balance and coordination are fine." Belle spun in a circle a few times. "If you're worried about me, then you go first, and I'll follow."

"I don't know about that." He was shaking his head.

"We may not have much remaining time to explore the structure. I want us to use this time efficiently. Maybe we can find an alien?" There, she'd said it.

"All right, we'll try, but I want you right behind me. If you scare me again, I'm aborting, and we're returning to the campsite."

Belle agreed. At this point, she would do anything he said if it meant pressing on.

He checked his and her equipment to make sure everything was tied down on their bodies and that their hands and feet were unencumbered. Then, he stepped out onto the alien stairway and scaled it the three meters to the next level.

Stepping off the stairway, he waited until Belle stood beside him on the landing.

Grant went to the nearest door and touched the panel, but it didn't open. He went to the next door, and the next, and the next. Finally, the second to last door, one facing northwest, opened.

"I told them all the same thing," he said. "*We need the control room*. But this is the only one that opened."

They stepped through.

Belle gasped.

Grant said, "Jackpot."

They stood in a large chamber, about fifteen-by-fifteen meters square and ten tall. Its ceiling went all the way to the roof. Alien chairs were scattered around the room, including some around two large alien tables.

There were lights visible on several mystery box shapes, though too dim to be for illumination purposes. Maybe they were indicator lights. But why not infrared? Perhaps they unintentionally shone in human visible wavelengths.

What had astonished them was the opposite wall. It looked like smooth black stone, like obsidian.

Belle put on her mask and turned on the thermal imager.

The display was covered by thousands upon thousands of symbols. Slowly changing, about twice a second. There was also an image on it, though Belle couldn't understand it.

"Does your helmet have a thermal imager in it?" Belle said to Grant.

"Yes." He put on his helmet. A moment later, it was his turn to gasp.

The display occupied almost the entire wall, nearly fourteen meters across its diagonal.

"Is this their version of a wall display, you think?" Grant said.

"I think so," she responded. "Replace those infrared pixels with illuminated colors, and make it all move about ten times faster, then you have a video display. But look at the resolution and texture. Tens of gigabytes of information must be updated on each display refresh!"

This settled it. A display like this used a lot of energy. It wouldn't be running if there was nobody present. This was an alien structure, and it must have been inhabited. Whoever lived here was shy. Is it from this room where they shot down their ships?

Some of the chairs were situated in front of featureless boxes that could be control interfaces of some sort, but there were no visible means of manipulation. No input/output tools. She was looking for the alien analog of keyboard, mouse, trackball, touchscreen, wheel-and-lever, etc. But the tops of the boxes were featureless flat black surfaces made of the woven composite material. Their surfaces were hot to the touch.

After about two hours of wandering around the room, they finally gave up trying to interpret what they found and journeyed back to their campsite. They had been gone nearly four hours and were ready for food and a rest break.

They made it back down the stairwell without incident. On the last door in the Commons Room, Belle tried the door herself and found, to her relief, that it was working for her again.

"Curious thing how drugs seem to affect the use of the doors," she said.

"Yup," commented Grant. "I don't imagine the builders have too many problems with junkies. Can you imagine getting locked out of your house because you had one too many drinks?"

"Hey, I could actually predict some good outcomes from such a practice."

Coming off the drugs, she walked down the final passage stooped over. By the time she reached the foyer, Belle had a headache. However, upon entering their encampment, she forgot all about it.

Both halted in stunned silence.

Something new had appeared again while they were gone.

Correction, *somebody*.

21

Belle froze just inside the foyer doorway. Grant crouched halfway through, looking past her left arm.

In the middle of their campsite was a giant starfish. Just standing there. It had a hexaradial symmetry, making it difficult to discern where it faced. Maybe facing wasn't a concept it understood.

The creature superficially looked like one of the walking starfish. Like the latter, it consisted of stacked hexagonal plates, though much thicker and not as regular. These looked like circles trying to be hexagons, with rounded corners and edges.

This was it, an inhabitant of the ruin. They were looking at a real live alien. Not a robot. But was it intelligent? Adrenaline coursed through her arteries, making Belle hyper-vigilant, aware of every tiny detail in the visitor's body.

The lower section was more like a hexagonal prism than a plate, being about twenty centimeters tall and fifty in diameter. Attached to its six sides were legs, which were complex multi-jointed affairs, each ending in a padded foot. The legs held the bottom prism about thirty centimeters above the floor.

Had the being noticed them enter? Should they back out of the foyer and return down the corridor? Belle's heartbeat thudded, her hands were sweaty, and she was dizzy. Maybe starting to hyperventilate. *Calm down. It doesn't look threatening.* But looks could be deceiving.

Above the leg body section, the center section was another hexagonal prism of slightly narrower diameter. About forty centimeters and twenty thick.

The top body section was the same dimensions as the bottom, and to it were attached six spindly, whip-like arms, each about a meter long, ending in a small, clawed pincer.

Around the upper perimeter of the upper section, located directly above each arm, was a sensor blister on a stalk. It was difficult to tell what was being sensed, but the blisters constantly flitted around in all directions. Eyes?

The pincers looked sharp and pointed. Probably dangerous. All the arms, legs, and eye stalks created a nightmare of appendages. Belle suddenly wanted to run. Maybe standing here wasn't a good idea. But strangely, her eyes continued to capture the details of the creature. Despite how disturbing all those limbs were, the creature's body was beautifully symmetric. Their motion was smooth like a dancer, never still, yet also not rapid. Like flowing water in a gentle stream, gradually transitioning from one pose to another.

A high-pitched whine arose at the upper limit of her hearing, fading in and out. At the center of the being's head —if that's what the top section could be called—was a single pliable, dome-like organ.

Except for the dome organ, the rest of the being was covered in a rigid metallic or crystalline surface. It was a polished dark gray. Maybe an exoskeleton.

When standing, it was just one meter tall and eighty centimeters wide, including protrusion of the legs. But whereas the starfish looked like machines, this being looked organic. The hexagonal body appeared grown.

Grant and she had unwisely not discussed what they would do if they encountered one of the aliens. But she would not run. This was it. First Contact.

"Do you have any way to record this?" she asked Grant.

"No. Be careful," Grant said.

Of course she was being careful.

"I bet every one of them has a unique appearance," she whispered. "See how the legs attach to the body, the pattern it makes in the exoskeleton surface?"

Grant had moved up to Belle's left and stood frozen in place, looking like he was on a hair trigger, holding his carbine at the ready. She reached out a hand and patted his back. "Don't make any threatening gestures."

He only nodded, keeping his eyes on the being.

When Belle and Grant entered, the being hadn't turned but scooted over on its legs to put the benches between it and them. Its steps were almost silent. Its padded feet were shod in some kind of fabric or rubber.

The being's arms were in constant motion, touching objects nearby, moving to the next, touching the ground, and waving around in the air. They might be used for more than just manipulating objects. Like a spider's legs, they might be sensitive to sound and smells.

It had sensed Belle and Grant, no doubt, as evidenced by its movement to interpose objects. Was it scared? Had they cornered it?

There were objects hanging from its body, tools and what could only be called instruments. Nothing that looked like an obvious weapon, but this whole structure was probably a weapon. For all they knew, all the being needed to do was speak a command and a gun would appear out of a wall and shoot Belle and Grant.

"Grant," she spoke in a normal voice, "speak in your normal tone. Maybe we unintentionally cornered it, and it might feel threatened. How about we move away from the doorway and give it an escape route."

"Good idea," he said, never taking his eye off it.

They walked slowly to the left side of the room, giving the creature plenty of space. Treating it like a wild, unpredictable animal.

They moved together toward the exterior wall, creating an obvious path of retreat for the being, back to the interior spaces of the dome.

As they made these movements, the visitor moved toward the door but did not exit. One could argue that now she and Grant were the ones trapped. However, that had been the case from the moment she entered the ruin.

Belle said loudly, "Thank you for helping us. Thank you for letting us stay in your home." She motioned with her hands open and visible, in humanity's universal sign of peaceful intentions. What if she was instead signaling hostility? She hadn't a clue what she was doing.

"What should we do?" she said.

"I don't know, but keep doing what you're doing."

Great. So it was up to her to think through this. She tried to remember the First Contact protocols but had only read them once about three years ago. Back at the academy, during an elective class she'd taken in xenology. She would have paid closer attention if she'd known she'd actually need the knowledge someday.

She sat cross-legged on the floor and invited Grant to do the same.

He lowered himself also, but only to one knee.

Every time she or Grant spoke a word, the being's arms would undulate in response, as if they were absorbing the meaning of the signals they heard.

They and the being stayed there staring at each other for some minutes. What must be passing through its alien mind? It must be intelligent because it carried technological artifacts on a belt or apron around its midsection. Clothing?

The alien's actions suggested caution and restrained curiosity. Perhaps Belle and Grant had just met the builder. Or, at least, the current inhabitant.

Then, to their shock, the being spoke in a deep, slow rumble, near the bottom frequencies a human could perceive. The sound emitted from the dome-shaped organ at the top of its head. "You speak, I understand." It spoke perfect English. Slowly, about one syllable per second.

And here she'd worried they would have to tap on the floor and exchange sign language until they figured out how to communicate. How convenient. How had it learned English?

Belle stretched her arms wide, bending at the elbows, slowly bringing both hands in to gesture at her chest, and said, "My name is Belle Machado. I am a human." She pointedly looked at Grant and raised her eyebrows.

Grant rolled his eyes, adjusted his carbine—which he had been gripping in both hands—so it was hanging from his shoulder, then made the same wide arm gesture and said in his deep voice, "My name is Grant Stewart. I am a human."

The visitor rotated its body and scooted over to the closest bench. Belle flinched. It only raised its body up slightly, then scooted some more until it was directly over the bench, and then lowered itself, relaxing the weight on its legs.

Now Belle understood the purpose of the benches. They were chairs, though optimized for a body design lacking a spine.

It said in its deep, slow voice, "My name is Zoogosghi Ixgogogh. I am an ighakan." The names sounded like boulders rubbing against each other. "You may call me Iron Seer."

Belle glanced at Grant, then looked again at the visitor sitting on the chair in a non-threatening manner. She moved slowly to the other chair, just a meter away, and sat down facing it. "Iron Seer, you may call me Belle. Is this structure your home?"

It didn't immediately answer but started waving its arms more rapidly. "Belle, touch your appendage to my body."

She hesitated.

Iron Seer said, "Do not fear. I will not harm you."

She reached out a hand and rested it on the upper surface of Iron Seer's top body section between two eye stalks. The surface was hot to the touch, almost too hot. Smooth, though, with irregular bumps and dips, like a rough stone that had been polished without first being leveled.

One of Iron Seer's arms whipped out and touched a sharp claw to her chest. She stood deathly still. "You are welcome here, Belle Machado.

"Now you, Grant Stewart, touch your appendage to my body."

Belle retracted her hand.

Grant, who had moved to a standing position a meter behind Belle, stepped forward and rested his hand in the same place as Belle.

"You may call me Grant," he said.

Now Iron Seer moved its claw to touch Grant and said,

"You are welcome here, Grant Stewart."

Belle didn't know what had just happened, but it looked like an important custom of some kind.

Iron Seer and Grant both withdrew their respective appendages, and Iron Seer spoke. "No, this is not my home, but it has been my dwelling for a long time."

"How do you know our language?" asked Grant.

"For some time, I have heard it spoken over radio waves on this planet. However, I did not know the source until I observed you inside this installation. What are you, and why are you here? And if this language is yours, then who are the large flying creatures who disturbed me?"

Belle answered, "Our name for our species is human. Grant and I are humans. We are from a different star system and are exploring this planet, which we call Clinton."

Iron Seer's arms waved in random patterns.

"The language we speak is called English," Belle said. "It is a common tongue among our species. We know of no large flying creatures, but two of our space vehicles were destroyed recently. We believe by this structure."

Grant spoke, his voice shaking, "Five humans died when our vehicles were destroyed."

Iron Seer's arms suddenly stilled and slowly slumped down low to the ground. It was silent for a long time. Belle and Grant looked back and forth at each other, wondering what they should do.

Then, after about two minutes of silence, Iron Seer spoke again. "The death of humans is regrettable. It was I who destroyed the vehicles. But I would not have done so if I had known they carried sentient beings. I thought you came from the Zyd. I have committed unjustified homicide and will be punished in due time. Until then, I can only offer my regrets and my assistance."

So the structure hadn't attacked the ships, it had been Iron Seer. But only because it felt threatened. Who were the Zyd? And why had it concluded Grant and she had come from them?

"You humans are in grave danger," Iron Seer said.

"From what?" Belle said.

Seer's arms all stood out erect momentarily. "From agents of the Zyd Hegemony. I know they are on this planet."

"Who are the Zyd Hegemony?" Belle asked.

"A confederation of alien civilizations, dominated by the nimat species. All other species in the confederation are clients of the nimat, subject to them."

"And they have agents on Clinton?"

"Yes, I sensed them as soon as humans arrived. You brought them with you. That is why I defended myself and destroyed your vessels. I thought the Zyd sent them."

Iron Seer concluded the Zyd were controlling Belle and her crew. That's why it lashed out. Yet even then, only after Belle had marked the ruin with the grinder. Maybe Iron Seer was friendly and avoided confrontation.

"Why are these agents dangerous?" Belle said.

"Zyd agents are nimats, who are masters of infiltration. They do not reveal themselves intentionally, preferring to manipulate beings through others."

An awful surprise if true, if they were among humans.

"I don't believe this," said Grant. "I've seen no evidence of an alien species manipulating people on Clinton. How could they hide?"

"I don't know their precise infiltration techniques. However, I detected their presence through their influence on the R-field. Do you humans know of synchronicity theory?"

Belle and Grant both replied in the negative.

"Synchronicity theory describes a universe-spanning, extra-dimensional, non-causal, reverse temporal field generated by the intentions of all lifeforms. Loosely translated into English, we call it the R-field. It lies outside the four space-time dimensions."

That was quite the earful. Belle was already lost.

"How do you measure this R-field?" asked Belle.

"Using a device called an R-field auger. I possess an auger on my person." Iron Seer pointed to a featureless black box on its belt. "When you touched me, I read your synchronous connection to the R-field, and your intentions are in good faith. Both of you. You are uncorrupted by the Zyd."

That was a relief to hear. One and one added together, and Belle got two. She suddenly understood. "Does this have anything to do with the doors in this building?"

"Yes. You are quite observant, Belle. I am pleased." Iron Seer twirled its arms in small circles. "All the doors contain small augers that measure the intentions of the being attempting entry. Those with wrong intentions are denied."

"I found that one must make physical contact with the door entry plates for them to function."

"Their augers are small, and you have not been trained to manipulate your influence upon the R-field."

"How can you detect the intentions of somebody on the other side of the planet?"

"This facility houses a large auger able to measure R-field emissions across the entire solar system. It is a listening post."

The ruin was not a ruin. It was an active structure. The entire monolith was a giant sensor intended to measure the intentions of living beings within the solar system.

The idea was mind-boggling. The amount of data that

must be processed every second. Every single living being on the planet and in orbit around it. Every single human being on Clinton.

"Great, so they can read our minds," concluded Grant, looking at Belle.

"Not at all," said Iron Seer. "We sometimes can read intentions, which are deeper than thoughts. And not everybody can do so. It takes special training, and the trainee must have a certain mindset and ethical philosophy. If not, their own intentions will interfere with R-field readings."

Something occurred to Belle. "You say intentions of living creatures. So that means you understand the intentions of lower lifeforms, like megapedes."

"If by megapedes, you are referring to the giant multi-segmented arthropods common to Clinton's rainforests, then yes, even they have intentions manifested in the R-field. Indeed, the simpler the lifeform, the easier to read their intentions."

Iron Seer extended its legs and relaxed them again.

"High intelligence tends to disrupt the R-field," it said, "because personal agency is a strong influence. Mental impairments are also more common in the intelligent, further blurring the field."

"Are you special because you use an auger?"

"All members of my species can read the R-field to a certain degree."

"How long have these Zyd been infiltrating humanity?" Grant said.

"I do not know, for you were already infiltrated when the first humans arrived on this planet. Some humans have the imprint of Zyd manipulation in their R-field emissions."

"These Zyd, what do they want with humans?"

"To play the Grand Game. Zyd clans compete for influence over alien civilizations. They cause internal strife and instability because of the Grand Game, steal your knowledge and manipulate you for the sake of entertainment. And to use you to help them destroy my people, whom they hate. My motivation in helping you is that it will also help the Quynh."

This was stunning knowledge. Humans, pawns in a game? Where was the proof? And yet, somehow, Belle knew it was true. Had she been manipulated into probing the monolith? What about the human presence on Clinton? Was that a result of manipulation? Humanity's free will was threatened. The fruits of her commerce were stolen.

"So we might have traitorous humans who have sided with these Zyd?" said Grant.

"Those humans under the influence of the Zyd will not likely know it. The Zyd corrupts others by corrupting the information they have access to. They are master manipulators and infiltrators and will never reveal themselves unless dominance is assured."

The Zyd would be difficult to detect. Anybody on Clinton could be under their influence. But Iron Seer had said that neither Belle nor Grant was under Zyd influence.

"How can we reveal the Zyd agents on Clinton? How do we fight them?" Belle asked.

"A human must learn to use the augur. I cannot do it for you because I must maintain a presence at my post in this facility."

A human could learn to use an auger. Maybe this was how Belle could save her reputation and career. Atone for her errors, at least in the eyes of those who would hold her at fault. The shroud of helplessness she'd felt since the mishap lifted ever so slightly. Also knowing she was unquestionably not at fault strengthened her self-confidence. Would Iron Seer testify on her behalf, even if it was self-incriminating? Would Belle be correct in asking them to testify?

"What is your purpose here?" Grant asked.

"This facility is a Quynh auger listening post. It's part of a picket on our borders to detect Zyd activities and anticipate their future actions. Interfering in Zyd operations is expressly contrary to my directive, for through their detected operations, we learned their government's intentions. However, I can still help, but you humans alone must act to rid yourselves of Zyd infiltration."

"Your facility feels vacant, like it was built for dozens of your people," Belle said.

"Yes, Belle, it is currently at a reduced state of operational readiness. I am the caretaker and sole Quynh currently present. I have notified my superiors of the detected increase in Zyd activity and hope staffing will be augmented in the near future."

They continued speaking for hours with Iron Seer. It was slow because of Iron Seer's ponderous speech.

Iron Seer told them about their people. Their species was called the ighakan, and they consisted of a loose federation of independent planets called the Quynh Federation.

An ighakan body was based on a hybrid silicon and carbon biochemistry. Their preferred planets were hot, low gravity, and rocky. Like humans, they reproduced through sexual reproduction. Iron Seer was a female because she could produce clutches of unfertilized eggs, which a male ighakan fertilized with his genetic code.

Ighakan metabolism was much slower than humans. Consequently, they had long lifespans lasting over a thousand years. Iron Seer said she was approximately 351 years old by human timekeeping. This was considered a young adult among her people.

The Quynh Federation was at war with the Zyd Hegemony, though it was a proxy war. They were fighting the client species of the Hegemony that was dominated by the nimat.

Belle rubbed her hands on her knees. "We need to get back to our people to tell them what you've told us. We also need rescue. We're trapped here. Can you help Grant and me?"

"Yes, I will help you, but you must promise to limit the number of humans you tell of this facility. The Zyd must not find out about this facility. I will try and teach you to use an auger and allow you to take one on the condition you will give it to nobody."

"Okay, so we can't allow the Zyd to find out about you, and we can't give the auger to anybody. Correct?"

"Yes. If you agree to these conditions, and if one of you learns the auger, you can detect who you can trust."

"I agree," Belle said without hesitation.

"I'm uncertain," Grant said. "I want to first see an auger in operation."

"Of course. When would you like to begin?"

They agreed to meet again after a meal. Belle needed to consult with Grant.

22

Iron Seer left Belle and Grant to eat a small lunch. They agreed to meet afterward in the Commons Room.

Belle felt overwhelmed by the events with Iron Seer. Humanity had not yet made contact with an intelligent, sentient alien species. Now Belle and Grant had met one and heard of a confederation of multiple other species, and the latter were potentially hostile to humans.

"This is too big for us to handle on our own," said Belle to Grant. "We should be telling DPE about the First Contact and letting them take over."

"I agree completely," said Grant. "How do we even know if Iron Seer is telling the truth? Or perhaps she's honest but just mistaken. Belle, I'm worried. We're considering what could be construed as a conspiracy to hide details about a First Contact event."

"We wouldn't be permanently hiding the event. Only until we find the Zyd agent."

"But what if there is no Zyd agent? Or we can't find it? What then? I think we need to find the quickest and safest way to return home and immediately inform Kepler of the First Contact. Let them take over from there."

Belle's view of the universe had been completely altered. What if she and Grant mishandled their relationship with Iron Seer? It could have negative consequences for all of humanity. What if humanity refused to help her? Now that Iron Seer had revealed so much information about herself and this facility, would she still allow Belle and Grant to leave freely, as she'd promised, or might she change her mind?

Knowledge of Iron Seer and the listening post would drastically change Kepler's activities on Clinton. Certainly, DPE would revise its survey contract. There would be questions about who owned Clinton. Was it a Quynh possession? By aiding Iron Seer, were they implicitly aiding the Quynh in their war with the Zyd? Were the Zyd actually hostile or merely conducting low-level surveillance of a peer state?

"If we were in contact with them, I would agree. But we're not. We need to make a decision on our own, using the best information we have."

"Look," said Grant, "my responsibility is to return you safely to base. That priority overrides all others."

"What if the easiest and safest way to do that is with Iron Seer's help? And what if the only way to get that help is by agreeing to her conditions?"

"I suppose we're under duress. Let me avoid judgment until I see what this auger can do."

It's not like Grant had any alternative plans. They were stuck there, and Iron Seer offered to return them home. The condition was that they help her with the Zyd problem, but they would actually be helping the humans on Clinton also. To Belle, it was a win-win. On top of that, add the potential benefits to their careers from being the humans who made First Contact. She might still get promoted despite the loss of her ship and crew. To her, there was an obvious choice.

Grant would come around.

Iron Seer was waiting for them when they arrived at the Commons Room. "Follow me," she said.

Seer led them down the Hall of Apartments. Belle noticed that Iron Seer did not need to touch the panels before going through the doors and wondered if she could do the same.

They entered the stairwell and descended two floors using the double-helix stairs. Iron Seer made it look effortless but waited for them patiently at the landing. From there, they exited the landing to another passage and entered a room connected to it.

Like all the rooms in the ruin, it was illuminated with infrared lighting. There were several chairs and tables and a couple featureless black boxes.

Iron Seer asked Grant to sit in a particular chair, then waved a tool that looked like a black paddle around his head and upper torso. She simultaneously looked at one of the black boxes, and Belle noticed one of its surfaces was slowly undulating in infrared, like a miniature version of the giant display they'd seen in the Control Room.

"I am imaging your brain. You possess extensive brain hardware not natural to your body."

"Yes," Grant answered, "that's correct. Those are neural implants installed in my head eight years ago. They provide supplemental computing and additional interfaces to external devices."

"These would be useful for interfacing the auger. However, I detect the presence of significant anti-tampering security mechanisms. It would be unsafe to attempt interfacing your implant to the auger."

Grant nodded but didn't seem disappointed. He didn't

seem enthusiastic about the auger.

Seer gestured toward Belle, and she switched places with Grant. Iron Seer waved the paddle around Belle's head and upper body. A strange sensation presented in her senses, especially her taste and smell. As if she could taste a flavor but couldn't quite put a name to what it was. The smell of something from an old forgotten memory. There was also a moment when auras of color appeared around objects.

After a few minutes, Iron said, "You also have neural implants, but these I can modify safely to accept an interface with an auger. They are much less sophisticated than those of Grant, and the anti-tampering features will be easy to bypass."

"Well, that makes me feel really safe," Belle said sarcastically. The implants had cost her the equivalent of three months of her current salary, and she was still paying them off. "I suppose we're about to void the warranty."

"What is a warranty?" asked Iron.

"Don't worry about it. What does this auger look like, and how will it interface with my implant?"

"This is it." Iron showed them a disk about five centimeters in diameter and one thick. She let them hold it. It weighed perhaps one hundred grams. "We must attach this somewhere to your body. You will need to recharge its power cell about once every fifty days."

"It doesn't need to go inside my implant? How will it interface?"

"I will add a small wireless transceiver to your implant that will be the interface. This facility's computer must add software to your implant to translate signals into senses you can learn to associate with emissions from the R-field."

"What does the transceiver look like?" She was nervous about Iron Seer poking around in her implant. Especially if there were hardware modifications.

"I am designing an expansion card that will plug into one of your implant's expansion slots."

Wow, that was fast. Ighakans must be incredible engineers.

"What will it feel like?"

"When I scanned your brain, you may have felt odd sensations. If so, that was the computer mapping your nervous system. I recommend tapping into your senses of taste and smell as these appear to have a suitably high dynamic range."

"How will I control the device?"

"The software modifications will include implant commands for enabling or disabling its features and adjusting sensitivity parameters. Also, note that it will have anti-tamper routines of its own. If it detects unauthorized attempts to reverse engineer or modify the software, interface, or the auger itself, it will erase the software and render all of it unusable."

"Would that damage my implant?"

"No, that should not happen, but I would suggest you check with me before attempting any modifications or upgrades to your implant. I can safely remove it if needed."

"Okay, that sounds fine, I think." What was she thinking when she'd agreed to this? She had second thoughts but didn't want to back out now. "Does the auger need to touch somebody or something to operate?"

"Not normally. Close proximity is usually enough, though physical contact can increase sensitivity slightly. The auger may be placed anywhere on your body and remain useful."

"What if we attach it to a wristband?" Grant said. "Then you could wear it like a watch. It would look exactly like one, I think."

"That's a good idea, Grant. Let's try that," Belle answered.

"Belle, would you like me to proceed with the modifications? We can do them now," said Iron.

"Already? Don't you need to make the interface card for my implant?"

"It's already complete." She picked up a small card from inside a drawer in a nearby black box. That was amazingly fast. It took minutes to do what would have taken humans at least hours, if not days.

"What if something goes wrong during the upgrade?" Belle asked.

"I am making no modifications to your hardware. I am also not modifying your software, though I will install modular application drivers into your implant to control the auger. If there's a malfunction, your implant's operating system will isolate them and disable the interface card. In short, the worst thing that could happen is the auger will simply not function."

"Okay, let's do this."

Iron Seer asked Belle to sit on a chair at a different table and lean her body over it to expose the back of her head. Her neural implant's external interfaces were located behind her left ear.

Belle gave the unlock command to her implant and authorized the installation of a new interface. Iron Seer gave Belle the wireless card, and she slid it into an existing expansion slot and told her implant to re-lock itself.

Next, they performed the software installation. Belle received a notification in her implant that another device was attempting to connect. She gave it permission, then was notified that the device was attempting to install new software. She verified the checksum calculated from the info provided by Iron Seer, and then gave permission for it to proceed.

"It's complete, and I can see four new commands for the auger. May I sit up?" Belle said.

"Yes, my computer says the installation has been completed successfully. Now, let me show you how the auger works. It will take extensive training before you can benefit from its full capabilities, but there are some simple exercises we can try right now."

Iron gave the auger to Belle and told her to turn it upside down. She gestured with one of her six arms to a switch on the side and a small hatch on the rear.

Iron Seer said, "Moving the switch position to the side with the bump next to it will power it on. Moving it back powers it off. So, as you can see, it is currently off. The power cell port is behind that panel on the rear. I have modified it to accept one of your standard charging cables. You may power it on when you are ready."

Belle flipped the switch to the *On* position. "Nothing is happening."

"You must also command your implant to accept it and enable it."

She did as Iron instructed, selecting the *Enable* command in her implant's new auger control menu.

Belle smelled baked bread. It made her stomach rumble. "I smell baked bread. This is bizarre."

"Good," Iron Seer said. "I cannot interpret your senses for you nor your implant. All it can do is convert the auger's signals into something your brain recognizes, which are these smells you speak of. You will have to train your brain to associate these senses with what the auger is actually measuring. Do you understand?"

"I think it makes sense to me," Grant said. "It's kind of like people who are born deaf, then receive an implant that allows them to hear. But their brain hasn't been trained to interpret the signals, so it can take many years for them to build the brain capacity."

"Is it going to take years to learn how to use this thing?" Belle asked with her eyebrows raised.

"Possibly," Iron Seer said, "but the reason I had the computer program it to use existing senses is to reduce the time your brain needs to interpret the signals. Of course, it also means that using the auger at the same time as those senses are being used for their normal purpose could lead to some problematic outcomes."

"Great, so I can't use the auger when I'm eating."

"I cannot say for certain. Only experience will determine how well you can separate the auger signals from those of your natural senses."

"How do I pick a target? Or does it sense everything around me all the time?"

"The auger has a directional sensor array that is electronically steered. I have slaved the sensor beam to your eyes. The point of maximum detection sensitivity will follow where your eyes are focused. Try moving your eyes around and test how it affects what you sense."

Belle had been holding the auger in her hand in front of her chest as she sat at the table. At Iron's direction, she pivoted toward Grant and looked at him. The smell of baked bread changed to lilacs. Then she looked back at Iron and smelled the baked bread again, though a little stronger. "You're the one who smells like baked bread." She pointed to Iron. "And you smell like lilacs." She pointed to Grant, who smiled back at her.

She swept her vision gradually back to Grant until she could smell lilacs again. "Whatever you're thinking right now, stop and think about something completely different." After a few seconds, the smell of lilacs changed to cinnamon. "What were you thinking about?"

"That I need food. And it's true; I'm hungry."

"You smelled like cinnamon. You're not thirsty right now, correct? Good. Try thinking that you're thirsty."

After a second, she smelled nutmeg combined with a sour taste in her mouth. She started smacking her lips.

"You smelled like nutmeg, but at the same time, I got a taste of sourness in my mouth. It was kind of gross. We'll try it again next time you're thirsty."

Suddenly the taste changed to something like warm chocolate chip cookies, and her mouth had an ever-so-slightly sweet taste. "What are you thinking about right now?" she asked him.

"I'm not going to say." He smiled and winked at her.

She punched him playfully in the shoulder. "You clown."

He just smiled back, and the taste in her mouth became sweeter. *Hmm, that's interesting.* She could get additional information by scanning her senses while interacting with a target of interest.

"Iron Seer, how do you suggest I go about training to use this more effectively?"

"Just as you've been doing right now. Ighakan younglings learn how to use an auger at a young age and do it in much the same way. By playing guessing games with their companions and schoolmates. I recommend you practice with Grant and perhaps with some of the wildlife. Also, the automatons in this facility."

"But doesn't the creature have to be alive?"

"The automatons are live creatures. They are bioengineered animals based on a domestic pet from my home planet of Ghatti.

"Belle, your auger has one other important feature. You should see a defense mode in your new implant interface. When enabled, you cannot detect the R-field, but the defense mode will protect you from coercion."

Belle looked at her implant control menu and saw a command labeled *Defend*.

If the auger had a defense mode, then it was intended to defend against a threat. That must be the Zyd. But Iron Seer had told them ighakans were immune to nimat coercion. Why had they created a defense mode? And were the Zyd really that dangerous a foe?

23

Iron Seer watched the two humans. Such fragile creatures with their soft outsides, little redundancy in their limbs and organs, but efficient bodies. Aliens, yet sentient beings, exotic bodies, but familiar minds.

Iron was grateful for their company. She mourned the humans she had killed in her ignorance. Believing Zyd forces had discovered her and were assaulting her, she'd done her duty and defended the installation. The deaths were a case of mistaken identity. She would atone for her error by giving Belle and Grant all the help she could.

It had been almost one Turn since she had seen another ighakan. A tenth of the lifetime of a human. She missed her husbands. Her egg clutch was full. It itched. Soon, she must return to her husbands to lay and fertilize her eggs. Maybe they would be fortunate this time. Perhaps the ancestors would bless them with a child.

Zyd nimats infested the humans. Though the only humans the Quynh had met were the ones on Clinton, the symptoms of infestation were there. And should she be surprised? The Zyd were everywhere in the galaxy.

The Quynh Federation would do its best to help

humanity, as they had always done for other races since the time they'd encountered the Zyd over thirty Turns ago. Yet the Zyd destroyed anything they failed to corrupt. They would not allow a race to exist if they could not control them. The entire nimat species was afflicted with racial psychopathy. All because of their sacred entertainment, the Grand Game.

Iron remembered the ogark race. An alien civilization that the Quynh had encountered eleven Turns ago. They had already been infested by Zyd infiltration and corruption, though not completely under their control. Much like the humans' current situation.

The ogark were six-limbed amphibians. Highly intelligent. They had recently discovered FTL jump drive technology and established several fledgling colonies in star systems near their homeworld.

The ogark civilization was marred by internal conflict and wars. Divided into nations that competed against one another for resources and political power. This caused widespread suffering and stalled progress.

Despite their problems, ogark society was resilient. Their homeworld's population numbered in excess of fifty billion ogarks. It was a beautiful world that they'd tried to preserve and care for.

When the ogarks and ighakans met, the ighakans revealed the Zyd corruption hidden within their population. The Zyd Hegemony was like a parasite feeding on other civilizations. Consuming their scientific knowledge and information about the galaxy. Playing the Grand Game to the detriment of the host species.

The ighakans taught the ogarks about synchronicity theory. They shared their auger technology with them. Helped them develop auger defensive capabilities. Though not masters of the R-field, the ogark proved competent enough that they completely eradicated Zyd influence within two Turns.

After the eradication, the ogark civilization entered a golden age of progress and political unity. Freed of the Game's corrupting shadow, they began to realize their full racial potential.

Iron remembered what happened next. She had been there in the ogark home system to witness it.

At that time, she'd still belonged to the Universal Faction and was a young line officer in the Quynh Space Force.

The nimats of the Zyd were a jealous species. To them, the Grand Game was everything. To be denied the chance to play the Game with another species was tantamount to violating their most basic natural rights.

They took the termination of their influence over the ogark as a personal offense. In their eyes, the ogarks, who now possessed augers that gave them *de facto* immunity against the nimat, were irredeemable. They were marked for extermination.

The Zyd attacked ogark exoplanet colonies, completely destroying them. Hundreds of millions of ogarks died.

The ogark consolidated their defenses at their homeworld, Atlan. They called upon the Quynh for assistance.

The Quynh had planned to send three battle fleets to help the ogarks, but interference from the Quynh Ancestral Faction reduced it to only one battle fleet reinforced with an extra battle squadron. Less than half what was recommended by Space Force Command.

Iron had been a junior officer on an escort in that fleet, crewed by 150 ighakans. Their gallant ship *Zapper* was a screening vessel designed to stop small enemy vessels from closing the distance with the giant Quynh battleships.

Armed with thousands of AI-controlled short-range missiles, *Zapper* was death to skirmishers, missile carriers, and attack ships.

The ogark space navy was numerous, but their technology was utterly inferior to the Zyd. They'd never stood a chance. In truth, the fight was between the Quynh and the Zyd.

Not long after the last ogark colony went silent, the Zyd invaded Atlan and its solar system. The Zyd initially launched a relativistic bombardment of Atlan, accelerating rocks up to ninety-nine percent the speed of light and smashing them into Atlan. Any one rock could have wiped out the planet. But Quynh space-time traps orbiting Atlan intercepted every one of them with ease.

Then the Zyd battle fleets moved in. Quynh warships were superior to Zyd warships, but the Zyd fleet outnumbered them ten-to-one.

A Quynh battle squadron blunted the first Zyd incursion into the inner system. Then the Zyd were pushed back by a counterattack from two other battle squadrons on its flanks. *Zapper* was part of one of those flank attacks. They'd cut through the panicked, fleeing Zyd battle line. *Zapper* destroyed dozens of skirmishers and missile boats and was instrumental in crippling a Zyd railgun battleship when one of *Zapper's* close range missile volleys disabled the battleship's propulsion.

The Quynh suffered almost no losses, while the Zyd lost a third of their fleet. But the Zyd were nothing but persistent. And jealous.

After their disastrous defeat, the Zyd fleet switched to a hit-and-run strategy, sending out large fleets in concentrated sorties against single points on the Quynh defensive lines. The Quynh had an entire system to defend. The Zyd controlled the outer system and used deception, so the Quynh never knew exactly where they were.

The Zyd began to achieve a small degree of success. For each Quynh ship they destroyed, they would lose four. But the Zyd had far more ships and were replacing them quicker, while the Quynh Space Force had difficulty getting support from the Ancestral-controlled Ighakan Assembly to send reinforcements.

Over the course of one Turn, the Quynh battle fleet was winnowed down to half its strength. And those who remained were battered and war weary. *Zapper's* crew was demoralized, Iron exhausted.

Then the Zyd attacked the inner system again as they had in their first disastrous battle. The spearhead was blunted. But this time, the Quynh lacked the reserves to mount a counterattack.

The Quynh battle line held for a while. Then it broke.

All Quynh battleships were destroyed or escaped after being severely damaged. Their escorts were decimated. Those who remained were ordered to retreat.

Zapper, being one of the swiftest and toughest ships in the Quynh fleet, was ordered to remain behind to monitor the aftermath of the Zyd invasion from a distance. Iron saw the atrocities that followed.

The inadequate ogark fleet mounted a last-ditch counterattack. Their ships' weaponry was impotent in the face of Zyd armor and shields. Nonetheless, they made suicidal charges on the Zyd's battleships, ramming them when they could, knowing they were all that stood between the Zyd and beautiful Atlan.

The brave ogark caused no small losses to the Zyd, but they were never going to stop them. The ogark fleet was annihilated in their first and only engagement.

The Zyd fleet first destroyed the now undefended space-time traps. Then they restarted the relativistic bombardment.

Rocks impacted Atlan's atmosphere at relativistic velocities, instantly vaporizing and creating huge gamma-ray bursts. In a matter of hours, the entire planet's surface was sterilized of life. The atmosphere was pushed into a runaway greenhouse cycle that rendered it permanently uninhabitable.

The balance of the Zyd fleet spent a Duodeciturn systematically destroying every known habitat and remaining inhabited ogark station, ship, and colony in the ogark home system. No ship was too small to pursue. A mere hundred ogark survived in the universe. Refugees living in a small habitat orbiting the ighakan homeworld of Ghatti. Denied the privilege of stepping foot on sacred Ghatti by the xenophobic Ancestral Faction.

Iron Seer had witnessed the death of over fifty billion sentient beings. A species with so much promise, destroyed merely because they refused to allow the Zyd to play the Grand Game. The Quynh gave the ogark the means to refuse to play but failed to protect them from the consequences.

After the horrors of Atlan, Iron Seer switched factions. She left the Universal Faction and the Quynh Space Force. She adopted the Reformist Faction and became a Listener to ensure a tragedy like Atlan never fell upon another species.

The Quynh would help humanity throw off the Zyd Game, and Iron would do her best to see they were also protected. But the humans still might suffer the same fate as the ogark.

Belle and Grant could not fathom the dilemma their civilization faced.

24

Iron Seer explained to Belle and Grant the basics of synchronicity theory and the origins of the R-field.

"The ability to observe and creatively manipulate the environment defines life. We ighakan discovered that all living things are tied into a universe-spanning information network. Information feeds back to lifeforms, enabling them to accurately navigate decision trees leading to optimal outcomes under criteria defined by individual expressed intentions. For example, the primitive, unicellular microorganism uses this mechanism to exploit feeding opportunities, while the advanced, intelligent, sentient macroorganism uses the same to profit from social opportunities.

"A forcefield known as the R-field describes this feedback information. It is a non-causal, extradimensional forcefield located outside the four-dimensional space-time forcefields; information flows backward from the distant future to the beginning of time."

"From what future?" asked Belle.

"All possible futures. They are potential futures that have not yet happened. A specific intention increases the probability of some future occurring while decreasing that of others. A simplified description of the R-field is that it represents a mixture of those probabilities' influence over the present."

"You said all living organisms. What about bacteria?"

"All living organisms, through their expressed intentions, create a small but measurable influence on the R-field, independent of the physical, space-time configuration of the universe. Consequently, that relationship is non-causal, which is why seemingly impossible coincidences—so-called synchronicities—in reality become commonplace.

"More advanced creatures possess nervous systems that amplify connectivity into the R-field. Belle, your brain has one hundred trillion synapses, each mapped onto the R-field. Compare this to a single-cell microorganism, whose entire body maps to only a single point on the R-field, and a weak mapping because it cannot specialize for R-field interfacing."

"So you're saying that the human and ighakan brains are specially evolved to efficiently interface with the R-field?"

"Correct. This auger now permits you to read the R-field. Whenever enabled, the detection sensitivity will be most substantial in whichever direction you view."

"And I'll see what my brain sees?"

"Approximately. It is more complex than that. The human brain is unusual," Iron said, whose arm tips were twirling in circles. "Perhaps the most malleable brain of any creature I know of. It takes arbitrary sensor inputs and recognizes patterns. This means I can modify your neural implant to accept electrical signals from the auger. Then the implant will stimulate your brain, which can read the R-field with proper training. This ability is remarkable. For any other creature, we would have to redesign the auger specifically for their nervous systems to accept, and this would take ages."

"I'm glad it was easy," said Belle.

"The Quynh must implant augers in ighakans during their childhood and customize them to their unique nervous system. It is a long and arduous process, and few become proficient in using the auger. But I believe Belle's brain can adapt rapidly, as an adult no less."

Belle remembered the phenomenon called projective synesthesia. The human brain sometimes could interpret senses with other brain parts not originally adapted to accept them. Sometimes, one could hear colors or smell sounds. For most humans, it was experienced only when the brain was subjected to certain types of psychedelic pharmaceuticals. It projected sensory input to brain parts not normally exposed to such inputs. Projective synesthesia was the root cause of hallucinations.

"I think I understand. I'm going to taste and smell hallucinations, but those are real hallucinations. If that is understandable. They're from the auger."

Iron Seer was quiet momentarily, then continued. "Belle, that roughly describes how I am interfacing the auger into your brain. Your neural implant will accept electrical signals from the auger; then, the software will project those signals into conventional sensory input. I have decided to project R-field amplitude measurements onto your olfactory nerves and R-field frequency measurements onto your taste nerves. This is because those all have high dynamic ranges, and projecting either into your optical or auditory nerves would be disorienting."

"Can you tell me anything about what you mean by frequency measurements?"

"There are four distinct types of R-field frequencies you

can distinguish through taste. Sincere intentions, deceptive intentions, corrupted intentions, and coerced intentions. Most non-sentient lifeforms emit exclusively sincere intentions. Among less intelligent lifeforms, you will sometimes encounter corrupted intentions in those with a sickness affecting their nervous system. However, corrupted intentions are most often seen in sentient lifeforms."

"Like mental illness?"

"Yes. Mental illness or from somebody who has been manipulated into believing a lie. From their perspective, they act sincerely, but the whole of the R-field is unsettled by the corrupted intentions that conflict with intentions expressed by lifeforms following the truth.

"Deceptive intentions are outwardly expressed intentions that mask contrary true intentions. With practice, you could easily detect false intentions of lifeforms because they cannot hide those from being reflected back to the R-field. Deceptive intentions are almost exclusively from sentient lifeforms because most non-sentient life cannot express a lie."

"What about coerced intentions?" Belle asked.

"Coerced intentions are rare, but the most reliable way to detect Zyd agents. This is their preferred method of infiltration. To coerce a victim into doing their bidding. It differs from deceptive and corrupted intentions because the victim has no control over their own intentions, which the master has superseded. A coerced intention is the intention of the master, modulated by the victim's ineffectual intentions."

Belle's eyes were glazing over and beginning to wander around the room. This was a lot of information. She brought them back to Iron Seer. "How will each of these types of intentions taste?"

"I'm unable to tell you because I do not understand the human sense of taste. You must learn their taste through experience. You and Grant should spend more time practicing with the auger to give your brain training."

Belle and Grant were outside the ruin, standing in front of the exterior door to the small foyer. "Here I go, enabling the auger." She flipped the switch of the auger, then loaded the software drivers in her implant. Her mind was flooded with an overwhelming number of new scents and all accompanied by a sweet taste in her mouth.

"You don't look so well," said Grant, as her stomach did a few lurches.

She closed her eyes and leaned a hand on Grant's shoulder to maintain her balance. She was experiencing sensory overload and needed to calm down and try to focus her attention on specific senses. She opened her eyes again and saw a large pseudo-dragonfly making its way past them about eight meters away. She focused her vision on it, keeping it at the center of her visual field, and noticed it was easier to control the number of items she sensed.

She smelled flowers and tasted sweetness, though the sensation weakened as the dragonfly flew away from them.

Next, she focused on a distant beetle-looking arthropod standing stationary on a burned stump about ten meters away. It was huge, about thirty centimeters long, and unmoving. She could smell honeysuckle and taste sweetness, though they were slight. She wondered if the creature was sleeping, so she asked Grant to try and startle it with something.

Grant picked up a short branch and tossed it in the direction of the beetle. When it landed about a meter away, the crash startled the beetle, and it took flight. Belle kept her vision focused on it; the taste of its R-field became much sweeter, and the smell changed to strong cinnamon. "Thanks, that was interesting. Got a much stronger response from the auger."

They spent the next hour experimenting with a number of creatures. In almost all cases, the taste from the auger was sweet, but smells were all over the spectrum, though tending toward simple perfume and spice scents.

One exception was a megapede that looked horribly wounded, missing the back half of its body. The taste was mostly sweet, but there was some bitterness there also. She wondered if the megapede had a damaged nervous system and she was sensing corrupted intentions.

They re-entered the foyer, and Belle practiced using the auger to detect Grant's intentions. They designed what they hoped was a decent controlled series of experiments, with Grant acting as the subject.

She got to where she could easily detect when Grant was being deceptive; indeed, he said he had used techniques he'd learned in special forces training for capture evasion and deception, yet she'd still easily detect his deceptions. Those gave a distinctly sour taste in her mouth.

Practicing to detect corruption and coercion was more difficult, and despite their best attempts, they couldn't replicate any sensory output that was distinctly different from the sweet and sour tastes that Belle had experienced up to that point. She still didn't know how to recognize corrupted or coerced intentions.

Then Grant told her to wait a moment. He went to his medic's bag, took out a pill, and consumed it. "Wait a few minutes until it begins to take effect."

After about ten minutes, she detected a mildly bitter taste whenever she looked at Grant. "The taste of your R-field changed. It tastes bitter. What did you take?"

"A mild opioid painkiller. I was using the same kind for pain, similar to what I gave you, when the doors wouldn't work for us. The drug is influencing my mind. Maybe this causes the corrupted intentions Iron Seer was explaining."

"So that's why the doors stayed locked," said Belle. "They detected corrupted intentions. How interesting. It isn't a sharp taste, but it's definitely there."

Grant sighed, looked down at his feet, then straight at Belle. He said, "I'm convinced now that Iron Seer knows what she's talking about. I've seen firsthand what you've done with the auger and how it's affected you. Especially the way you could see through my evasions."

"Then you'll agree to Iron Seer's conditions?" Belle asked.

"It's the only way we currently have to get you home safely and timely. And if there really is a Zyd agent, and they are hostile to humans, then I'm willing to take the risk of being wrong."

"Thank you. My gut says you're making the correct decision."

Belle secretly celebrated. Things were looking up. She had solid evidence that the mishap was not her fault. She'd discovered the true nature of the monolith. Had taken part in a historical event, making First Contact with the ighakan. And she was likely to play an important role in helping the humans on Clinton with the Zyd problem. There was no way anybody could sideline her career now.

"Belle," Grant said, "we need to discuss with Iron Seer the details of how we're going to get back to Clinton Base."

Part Three

Homeword Bound

25

Grant, Belle, and Iron Seer were meeting about how to reinsert Grant and Belle back into Clinton Base. The trick was to do it without revealing the ruin's true nature or Iron Seer's existence until the Zyd agent was eliminated. She was not against humanity knowing these facts, but unwilling to risk that knowledge becoming known to the Zyd Hegemony. They needed to proceed with extreme caution until they had identified, exposed, and eliminated the Zyd influence on Clinton.

The first problem to solve, though, was transportation. So far, they'd seen no signs of further rescuers looking for them at the site, not since the loss of the dropship. Perhaps Kepler management had decided everybody was likely dead and would work to recover bodies and materials later.

Belle and Grant were low on food, and both needed medical care. Iron Seer was not equipped to help with either problem. Ighakan biology was distinctly different from human and Clintonian biology. Whatever Iron Seer ate, it wasn't edible by humans, and Grant had expressed a suspicion that the crystal-encased alien's species didn't eat in the conventional sense.

Iron Seer said in her slow and deep voice, "This facility possesses air transport capable of carrying both of you anywhere you need to go. It is in storage because human sensors will easily detect any use of it. But if it were to follow a low-speed path close to the ground, you could escape discovery."

Grant said, "There's a remote outpost about fifty kilometers from here, located in some low mountains at the edge of this rainforest. Normally, it is unstaffed and used as a staging location for supplies. It's equipped with emergency shelter and supplies. Most importantly, it has radio communications. I've been thinking that if Iron Seer can help us reach it, we could call Clinton Base from there and ask to be picked up."

"Wouldn't that look suspicious?" Belle asked. They would appear out of the blue at this outpost days after being marooned in the jungle.

"It would raise some suspicions but should be plausible. It's well known that I'm trained for jungle survival, so if the two of us make it to the outpost, we could concoct a story about spending several days hiking through the jungle to get there."

Belle certainly couldn't survive out in the jungle, even for a few hours.

"Would that be believable in my case?"

"That's where I come in, like I said. I've been thinking about this anyway, wondering how we might self-rescue ourselves. That is, until I heard about Iron Seer's offer of transport. Yes, it would be a dangerous hike. However, I think it makes a great cover story."

"When's the soonest we could leave?"

"If we leave tomorrow, it will have been three days since the dropship was lost. That's enough time for two people moving fast to make it to that outpost. I think we can make the story work."

"Iron Seer," said Belle, "can your transport be ready to carry us tomorrow?"

"Yes. I must remove it from storage and recharge its power cells, but it can be ready in less than twelve hours. Where is this outpost located?"

Grant brought up a map on his tablet computer to show Iron Seer.

Iron Seer said, "I am sorry, Grant Stewart, but I cannot interface with your electronics. You must speak to me the coordinates in a geocentric non-rotational reference. I can translate your human standard latitude, longitude, and altitude coordinates."

Grant read the coordinates, which were long sequences of numbers.

Iron Seer didn't appear to have any means of recording them, but she said, "Thank you, that is sufficient."

About ten seconds later, she said, "I calculate the transport can deliver you in about three hours, following a path and speed that minimizes chances of discovery. Shall we plan on you departing at sunrise tomorrow?"

Grant nodded. "Yes, let's plan on that. Will you be piloting the transport?"

"No, the transport is fully autonomous but will follow my instructions. You will also have limited control, in case you must stop for some reason. I will also order the transport to wait until you command it to return in case something happens and you must abort the insertion."

"That sounds like a wise decision. Thank you. We're grateful for your help."

The three of them discussed what would happen after returning to Clinton Base.

"There will be at least two mishap investigations," said Belle, "and I'll be grounded while mine is being conducted. This is potentially a good outcome because it gives me an excuse to stay at Clinton Base and poke my nose around to see what I can discover regarding this Zyd agent. Iron Seer, what can you tell us about this being?"

"About the agent themselves, I unfortunately have little information. We know they are from a race called the nimat, who are experts in coercion, infiltration, and disguise.

"Ighakans are immune to nimat coercion, and because of this, the nimat avoid direct contact with us, preferring to work instead through other species. No ighakan I know of has ever seen a nimat in the flesh and reported it, so their exact physical nature is unclear.

"But with the auger, I believe you will easily detect the Zyd agent once they are located; even from my distant outpost here, I can sense the influence of a nimat agent of the Zyd Hegemony upon the humans here at Clinton. But it will be up to you to find them and eliminate their influence."

"When that is accomplished, how will we contact you?" Grant asked.

"I will contact Belle Machado through her neural implant as soon as I sense the loss of Zyd coercion."

"Grant," Belle said, "I think we'll need help to do this investigation. Do you have any suggestions?"

"I think we should inform Chief Scientist Benton Valero," Grant said. "He's been a friend to my family for many years, and as chief scientist at Clinton Base, he has a lot of influence. I trust him.

"Iron Seer, do we have your permission to tell this person what's happened to us and about you?"

"If you feel their assistance is necessary, but the more persons you inform, the more likely the Zyd agent will discover us."

Grant and Belle agreed that after returning to Clinton Base, they would meet with Benton Valero and bring him into their scheme with Iron Seer. *If* he first passed screening with Belle's auger.

After that, Belle would focus her efforts on using the auger to scan people in secret. Grant would do background investigations of anybody they felt needed additional attention. They would ask Benton to use his resources within the corporation to find out how the monolith had become a target of direct sampling.

"Iron Seer." Belle looked at the alien. "Once the Zyd agent is located, how will we eliminate it?"

"It depends on who the nimat has brought under its influence and the nature of that relationship. By themselves, they are cowards. Our limited past interactions with them suggest they are helpless when isolated and threatened.

"If their influence or resources are small, then I believe the agent will attempt to flee. It likely has a ship hidden away somewhere on Clinton. On the other hand, it's just as likely the agent could use its resources to eliminate you and your team. You must proceed with caution."

Grant asked, "What types of weapons would be most effective if we need to attack the agent?"

"I do not know, but the nimat by itself is probably helpless. Your biggest threat will be from whatever beings it is influencing. Because that is one or more humans, you should prepare for combat against others like yourself. If it comes to that."

Belle released a heavy sigh. "What happens if we capture the nimat? Would that be a valuable outcome?"

Iron Seer was quiet for so long that Belle was about to repeat the question. She finally responded, "I believe that is unlikely. To my knowledge, a nimat has never been captured, dead or alive. That is why we know so little about their physical characteristics.

"It would be extraordinarily good fortune if you captured the agent, and I would insist you surrender it to the Quynh Federation. But I believe it more likely that it will escape or destroy itself to avoid capture."

Belle and Grant agreed. Belle was surprised and a little troubled by how little Iron Seer knew about the nimat. The Quynh Federation and the Zyd Hegemony were mortal enemies. So why did they possess so little knowledge of the threat they were facing?

26

The Quynh transport was tiny, built to carry bodies half the size of humans. Belle and Grant had to slide into the cargo compartment and remain sitting on the floor. At least Belle could sit up comfortably, but Grant's tall torso forced him to lie on his back with his knees up, or lie on his side in a relaxed fetal position. Nevertheless, they made do and loaded up all their remaining equipment.

Belle could feel the weight and pressure of the auger strapped to her left wrist. She now kept it on most of the time, only switching it off when eating or sleeping, and even then only to avoid sensory overload and let her brain rest. She was trying to get as much practice time as she could.

It was soon after sunrise on the next day, and sitting in the back of the transport, she sensed the intentions of it. "This little ship is a living creature also," she commented to Grant. She could smell the simple, fresh air smell of anticipation of a journey and intent to do it efficiently and simply, and the strong sweet taste in her mouth indicated the transport's intentions were true and sincere.

So far, all simple creatures Belle had tested with the auger gave that sweet taste in her mouth. Even the monstrous megapedes. She was beginning to associate the auger taste with life and evidence of a living being that was sincerely trying to live life to the fullest purpose they could. In that context, even the megapedes seemed less monstrous than they once had.

The only sourness she had tasted was from Grant and herself. It was the taste of deceit. Because this journey was being made under false pretenses.

Yes, she could taste her deception when carrying the auger. Her R-field was always firmly in the background, and she was learning one of the tricks to use the auger effectively: clear her mind of intentions and plans and be her true self in the moment.

The only distinct bitterness she had tasted from the auger was after Grant consumed the pain pill and from that severely injured megapede they'd seen.

Smells she had sensed were categorized into three types: hot objects, usually from intelligent beings, like humans or ighakan (smells of cooked food were common, and burning wood, plastic, etc.).

Perfumes were simple but strong smells, and she associated them with intentions based on animal instinct (like the smell of fresh air emanating from the transport).

Chemicals, like the smell of gasoline or bleach or unscented soap. These were also associated with intelligent beings when they were exercising free will and personal agency. Especially when countering base instincts.

As Grant was moving around, trying to find a comfortable position, she sensed sweet acid from him. His right thigh was bothering him, and the contortions weren't helping, but he wasn't complaining.

"How's your thigh feeling?" Belle asked.

"Never been better," he mumbled at her.

The taste went sour in her mouth. *That little liar!* She smiled to herself. *Men, they always think they have to show a stoic face.* She reached out and squeezed his hand twice. "We'll be home soon, and you'll get to stretch out in your own bed again."

He just looked at her for a moment with a flat stare and said, "We'll see that when we see it."

Iron Seer stood inside the large foyer of the facility, just behind the cargo compartment, watching them get arranged. "Remember, you have a three-hour journey ahead of you. This transport must go slowly and stay low to the ground to avoid detection. If you need to stop for any reason, express your intentions to it, and it will listen if it is safe to do so."

"Okay, Iron Seer," Belle said, "thank you for everything you've done for us. We'll do our best to return the favor and track down the Zyd agents."

"You're welcome, Belle Machado. In helping you, I know that I'm helping myself and the Quynh Federation. Be you well. I'll be in contact with you soon, let's hope."

"Yes, indeed. Goodbye, Iron Seer," Grant said.

"Goodbye, friend," Belle said.

"Fair you well, and be safe." The transport's rear hatch closed, shutting them into near-complete blackness.

Belle found a small viewport on her side of the transport and slid it open, revealing a small window to the outside world, transparent to human vision. They were still in the foyer. Sunlight streamed in when the exterior door opened. It must be larger than the small foyer's door. Otherwise, how would this ship exit?

They felt a rocking motion, and the transport lunged up and forward. Then they were in the clear, and as the transport made a slow turn to the north, the domed monolith receded into the distance behind them.

Grant had also found a viewport on the rear door, opened it, and was looking outside.

The ship was low to the ground, sometimes almost touching, and moving only about five meters per second. If they went too fast or high, they would be detected by orbiting satellites carrying moving-target-indicator, ground-scanning radars. They would be seen instantly.

The craft flew at about the speed of Clinton's largest flying fauna, but it was worth it. It was bypassing all the rough terrain and dangerous animals between them and their destination and saving their still-healing limbs from the hike.

Despite the erratic winding path, the ride was smooth. Soon, Belle drifted off to sleep and dreamed about riding horses back at her family's ranch.

She was gently shaken awake by Grant. "Belle, I think we've arrived." The transport was stopped and resting on the ground. He paused while she collected herself, then said, "Are you ready?"

She nodded.

Grant instructed the transport to open the rear door.

He was all business. He kept his automatic carbine at the ready and swept the touchdown zone. They were in a clearing among some of Clinton's giant coniferous tree-analogs. It smelled of sap and a cool mountain breeze.

"I don't see the outpost," Grant said, "but my INS says it's just over this ridge here."

"Good," Belle said. "I'll tell the transport to hold here in case we have to abort."

He nodded, walked slowly, and crouched about thirty meters away at the top of the ridge.

Belle trailed him by about two meters and tried to copy

his movements.

At the top of the ridge, he knelt behind a tree and peeked around it with a pair of small binoculars. He stayed still for about a minute, just watching.

He looked in her direction. "Somebody's here. Good thing that little ship dropped us where we can't be seen."

"That outpost is supposed to be unstaffed!" she said softly to him. "Who is it? What are they doing?"

"Looks like a resupply ship and maintenance staff. Definitely Kepler folks though. Looks like innocent activities. This is a complication, but look at it this way—this saves us from having to figure out a way to call in to base."

"How much longer do you think they'll be here?"

"Hard to say. I see a utility ship landed on the pad, and I just saw a pilot walk from it and enter the outpost. They were kind of casual about it, like they've been here for a little while."

She belly-crawled up next to him and waved for the binoculars. She studied the ship. "That vehicle is rated for a pilot and co-pilot, so there are at least two people. They may also be carrying technicians if they're doing some kind of special maintenance." She handed the binoculars back to him. "Should we just walk up there and say, 'Hi, watcha all doin?'"

"Actually, yes, basically that."

She looked at him with a raised eyebrow. How would the crew likely react to them walking out of the jungle? Maybe they were on the lookout for them because they were missing. On the other hand, they might be presumed dead. They were going to get a shock in a few minutes.

"All we need to do is get our story straight," Grant whispered. "We've just finished a three-day hike through the wilderness from the monolith. We both look like it, mostly, but get some dirt and rub it on your face and hands. Good," he said as she gave herself a quick dirt bath. He did the same. "Make sure and act tired and worn out when we meet them."

"That won't be difficult. Remember, we're undernourished and injured."

"Right. I'll take the lead, and we'll just walk down there. Let me do the talking."

She nodded at him, then they walked back to the transport, got the rest of their stuff out, and loaded it onto their backs. Belle touched the transport and instructed it to stay put until the other ship departed.

Grant grabbed dead branches and laid them on top of the transport, enough to break up its straight lines. He looked at her. "You ready?"

She nodded.

Grant walked off at a slow, steady pace. She could tell he was trying to get into the act, walking like he was on a long hike. She did the same.

Curious, she enabled the auger and searched for Grant's R-field. She pulled the oxygen mask tight over her face to cover the scent of the forest.

At first, it was difficult because there was so much life surrounding them, but then she smelled a complex mixture of wet earth mixed with acid and a sour taste. Belle also tasted sour. They both had deceitful intentions, and it manifested in the R-field.

Grant continued his steady walk around the base of the hill instead of over the ridge. She stayed three meters back.

After about five minutes, they broke out into the clearing where the outpost was constructed and stopped behind a two-meter fence. Rather than scale it, Grant halted and waved her to a stop. He brought a hand to his mouth and yelled, "Hello there, may we enter?"

About ten seconds later, a woman peeked out from around a corner of the building with a surprised look. Like she was seeing ghosts.

Rather than respond, she disappeared, but about ten seconds later, she appeared again with a large man walking in front of her. They both wore Kepler's orange flight suits.

Belle didn't recognize them but wasn't surprised because Kepler had hundreds of pilots. She just hadn't been employed that long.

The two stopped about two meters away—still on the other side of the fence—and the woman spoke. "Tell me who the hell you are and what you're doing here."

Grant answered, "I am Grant Stewart of Kepler's Special Missions SAR Team." Gesturing to Belle, he continued, "This is Pilot Belle Machado, a Kepler survey tender pilot. Our vehicles are down, we need rescue, and hiked to this outpost. Thank goodness somebody was here!" he said with relief, and she sensed it was halfway genuine.

"Belle?" said the tall man.

Closer up, Belle recognized him.

"Isaac? Isaac Altimari, correct?"

"Yes, ma'am. I didn't recognize you because of the mask."

She realized it was still on her face. "Sorry, this thing saved my life. Forgot I still had it on." She slid the mask up on top of her head.

Isaac Altimari was an acquaintance of hers. He had been in the same new-pilot cohort with her when she joined the company, and they went through training together, though she didn't know him well. Hadn't seen him in a while, in fact. Looked like he was still a co-pilot, but that could be because he had no interest in piloting the smaller craft.

All four of them just stood there looking at each other

awkwardly for a few seconds, then the lady said, "Um, hello, I'm Pilot-commander Jordana Sharrow, and this is my co-pilot, Isaac Altimari. Who, I guess, you already know," she said, gesturing to Belle. "I suppose you'd like to enter the perimeter. Walk over in this direction." She pointed to a spot on a different side of the fence. "There's a gate we can let you through."

They both made their way to the gate and, upon entering, were both given hearty handshakes by the two pilots. Isaac rested his hand on Belle's shoulder while shaking her hand. "Everybody thinks you're dead! Both of you!"

"You know what happened to us?" Belle asked.

"Of course! For the last five days, each of our daily flight briefings has included instructions to keep an eye out for any information about your whereabouts. Golly gee! Everybody in the company knows you're missing!"

"Where's the rest of your rescue team?" said Jordana, looking at Grant.

"They unfortunately didn't make it. I'm the only survivor from the rescue dropship."

Jordana was taken aback. "I knew both the pilots. What a loss. Belle, what about your crew?"

"They didn't make it either." The questions opened wounds that had begun to heal.

"I knew Phil for many years," Jordana said. "Everybody in the company did. What a tragic loss." For a moment, she looked like she was going to cry. Had she been close to Phil?

They all stood in an unplanned moment of silence, remembering their dead. Belle hoped that the plan they were carrying out would lead to the best outcome for everybody. Including her chances to stay at Kepler.

"Though extremely surprised to see you," Jordana said, "I'm happy. I need to report this to base immediately, but first, do you need anything right now?"

"Food, please," Grant said.

"Food!" Belle said almost simultaneously.

Isaac led them into the little outpost and showed them where to find food while Jordana walked to the landed ship, probably to call back to base. They heated a meal of packaged and reconstituted pasta, vegetables, and meat in the outpost's small oven and dug into the food with relish.

"I never thought field rations like this would taste so good. We've been on short rations for three days," Belle said to Isaac out the side of her mouth as she ate.

"You said you've been hiking for three days? How far?" Isaac said.

"About fifty clicks," Grant said. "The first thirty was fairly easy because the rainforest had burned down to the ground. But we've been in these hills since yesterday, and it's been a little slower. Really glad to be done with that trek."

"Tell me what happened to your ships."

Just then, Jordana walked into the room. "Stop, don't answer that." She looked at Isaac. "We've been instructed not to talk with either of them about anything related to the mishaps."

Then she looked at Grant and Belle. "And you are ordered not to speak with each other about them. They even went so far as recommending that I separate you, but I think that's silly. You've been together for days already, and I can see you've gone through great hardship." Jordana was looking over their torn, dirty, burned, and bloody clothing. "Just keep the conversation to small talk, okay?"

"Yes, ma'am," Grant said respectfully.

Belle nodded at her. *The debriefing procedures have begun.*

27

About twenty minutes later, the pilot, Jordana Sharrow, told them it was time to load up and return to base.

"Already? What about the other delivery?" Isaac Altimari asked Jordana.

"Not today. Ops wants these two returned ASAP." She smiled sympathetically at Grant and Belle. She knew what was in store for them. Now that they were recovered, Kepler would immediately initiate a mishap investigation. And because there had been deaths and loss of ships, the DPE's inspector general would become involved.

They loaded into the utility ship, and Isaac showed them where two unused acceleration couches were behind the cockpit. The liftoff under the gravinegator was much easier on Belle's stomach than it had been with *C195*. This was a much larger craft, and the lift field was more uniform, creating fewer physiological side effects for the passengers.

It was a ninety-minute uneventful flight back to base. Belle used some of the time to scan the two pilots with the auger. It was difficult to get a good reading because they were focused on the flight, but during a pause in the middle of the flight, she noticed Jordana Sharrow leaning back and relaxing for a few minutes and decided to try it then.

Jordana's R-field tasted bitter and smelled of rubbing alcohol. Belle wondered what it could mean. Jordana looked unhappy and stressed. Was it because of Phil's death?

Upon landing, there were medical staff and corporate middle management waiting for them. She and Grant were separated and taken individually to medical facilities to be treated for their injuries.

Belle hoped to understand how she would be treated, but nobody would talk with her, other than the briefest exchanges. Management didn't want the witnesses to be contaminated.

The woman physician treating Belle was respectful but insisted she undressed completely and submit to a thorough examination. She kept detailed notes, completing paperwork required by the mishap review board which would be filed into her permanent flight record.

Belle explained that none of her injuries were due to losing her ship but were caused afterward during the wildfire and encounters with wildlife.

The physician patched her up but didn't really do much more than what Grant had already treated her with. Her heel bite was almost completely healed, and the burned area on her right calf had started peeling.

While the examination was underway, a Kepler representative stopped by and informed Belle she had a debriefing at fourteen-hundred hours at the base's corporate offices.

When the examination was completed, Belle said her thank yous and put her torn and dirty clothes back on. They were the only things she had with her. Then she walked the half mile to her base quarters. It was twelve-thirty hours, and she had enough time to clean up and eat.

Her small room was one of numerous in a prefab building of modular studio apartments. Down a dark hallway with broken lights, three flights of stairs, and another dim hallway. Her room was as she had left it.

Belle arrived at the debriefing early, showered and wearing a fresh flight suit. She was told by an office assistant to take a seat in the waiting room.

While waiting, Belle considered the potential outcome of this meeting. She would present her story as evidence. Because she was the only survivor, and the ship was a complete loss, without even a flight data recorder surviving, much of their investigation would focus on Belle's testimony. This could be a make-or-break moment in her career. She wished she could share all the amazing things she'd learned about the monolith, Iron Seer, and the Zyd threat. Instead, she had to lie. It was not her nature to lie. Belle had always despised liars. She felt she had a justifiable reason to do so now, but she didn't like how it left her feeling.

Twenty minutes later, the conference room door opened, and the Kepler employee who had spoken to her at the clinic stepped out and called her in to meet with the mishap investigation committee.

Besides this employee—who it turned out was the committee's recorder—there were three other Kepler employees in the room, none of whom she recognized. There was the committee chair, the recorder, an engineer, and a safety officer.

After some brief introductions, the chair, Hodel Vroomen, asked her to describe in her own words what had transpired between the time she left on her mission and the moment she landed back at Clinton Base.

She did so but left out Iron Seer, the R-field auger, and the nature of the monolith. It took her about thirty minutes to summarize what had happened. The committee politely listened, never interrupting with a question, though they scribbled notes at several points.

Though this mishap investigation was focused on the loss of *C195*, she also told them what she knew about the loss of the dropship. Grant Stewart was responsible for her rescue, and she generously praised him for his bravery and skill.

While telling her story, she reached out with the auger strapped to her left wrist and sampled each of the committee members. The safety officer and recorder tasted sweet, but Hodel Vroomen and the engineer, Brit Corti, tasted bitter. Brit Corti, in particular, was emitting a strongly bitter taste.

Belle finished her story.

Vroomen said, "Ms. Machado, I'd like to talk about the order in which events occurred leading up to the explosion of *C195*."

He was reading from his notes, then said, "Is it true that radiation levels increased as you approached the cliff, and this happened before you extended the external arm?"

"Yes," said Belle. "Each time we came closer to the monolith, radiation levels increased."

There was a moment of silence as Vroomen wrote notes, then he continued, "Is it true that your co-pilot, Borya Utkin, was not in the cockpit while you were operating the external arm?"

"Yes, Mr. Utkin was in the drone maintenance workshop," said Belle.

"And he was in the drone workshop when the reactor was dumped?"

"Yes."

"Why was Mr. Utkin not in the cockpit?"

"He was responsible for maintaining our complement of drones. In order to begin sampling the monolith while there was still daylight, we packed up at our previous site before he could finish." Belle was sitting rigidly, wondering where this questioning was going. "He chose to complete those tasks while I performed the sampling."

No regulation said that Borya had to remain in his seat when the external arm was used and they were secured for ground operations.

"Given that detected radiation levels continued to rise, would it not have been wise to keep him in the cockpit?"

Belle folded her arms. "Sir, though rising, levels were initially quite low. Certainly too low to be of any danger to life or equipment."

Vroomen continued to write and made a *humming* sound.

"And yet, you believe that a neutron radiation pulse is what caused the reactor to melt down. Might that have been avoided if Mr. Utkin had been in the cockpit monitoring vehicle systems?"

That was preposterous! There was nothing that Borya could have done, or any of them, to stop the chain of events once they began.

"I strongly doubt it," Belle said. "Immediately before the explosion, the rise became so rapid that there was little time to react. Besides, the reactor was on standby mode. There was nothing anyone could have done to make it safer than it already was."

Vroomen's face was blank in response to her conclusion.

"Next question," said Vroomen. "Is it true that you did not immediately order vehicle evacuation after the explosion?"

Completely false. She couldn't order evacuation until the evacuation checklist was completed. The only delay was caused by the time needed to assess and run through the checklist. She'd actually flown through it rapidly, almost recklessly. Belle didn't like where these questions were going.

"I ordered the evacuation about one minute after the explosion. After completing the evacuation checklist."

"Why did it take so long?"

"It took time first to assess the situation, second, search for Mr. Utkin, and third, perform the evacuation checklist. Given the circumstances, I feel that we actually evacuated quite rapidly."

"Hmm, but if Mr. Utkin had been in the cockpit, you wouldn't have had to search for him, correct?"

"Yes, sir."

"Is it true that you used an unapproved method of evacuation when you chose to use the external arm to reach the ground?"

Was this man intending to make this her fault by fabricating some special circumstances?

"Yes, other escape routes were blocked by fire."

"And your instructor, Phil Curtis, died as a result of falling from the arm when he failed to jump to it, correct?"

"Yes." Belle felt a tightness in her chest.

"If you had evacuated quicker, couldn't you have used an approved evacuation method?"

"Yes."

"That's all I have," said Vroomen. "Anyone else?" He looked at the rest of the room.

Belle was furious at the accusatory questions from Vroomen. He made it look like she'd been negligent when she'd allowed Borya to enter the workshop while the sampling was underway. As committee chairman, Vroomen held her career in his hands at this precise moment. Even if the explosion was proven not to be Belle's fault, if he successfully blamed her for the deaths of her crewmates, then it wouldn't matter that she was innocent of the explosion. Causing the death of her colleagues through negligence would sink her career. She would likely never fly again.

She hadn't foreseen this line of reasoning that Vroomen was using. Suddenly, she felt her renewed sense of hope unraveling.

Brit Corti asked, "The increase in radiation you detected right before the reactor overheated. From where do you believe that originated?"

Belle needed to get her flustered mind under control and consider her answer carefully. "I don't know. Perhaps from the reactor itself, though it was in standby mode then. It's unclear whether the radiation spike preceded the reactor core dump or was caused by it."

The engineer asked a few more technical questions—all specific to the reactor—and Belle answered as best she could.

Unfortunately, she was still mystified about what caused the incident and hadn't gotten a response from Iron Seer when she'd attempted to quiz her. Though she had admitted to being the cause of both vehicle losses, she wouldn't explain what weapons were used.

The safety officer asked her a series of additional questions about her crew's evacuation from *C195* and their use of the survival kit. He sounded critical of the fact that it contained no protections against Clinton wildlife. Not Belle's fault.

Two hours after the meeting began, Vroomen concluded,

thanked Belle for participating, and told her there would likely be some follow-up interviews later, depending on what other information they learned.

The recorder also informed her she was grounded until the committee released its preliminary findings and recommendations in roughly two weeks' time.

Belle was given orders to report to Operations for desk work the following day, as soon as medical cleared her to return to duty.

Belle left the building with crushed hopes. Vroomen's accusations—and that's precisely what his questions were intended to be—were based on a false premise that regulations required Borya to be in the cockpit when the reactor was secured and they were conducting ground operations. No such regulation existed. Yet he was clearly trying to make it stick. Probably so Kepler could blame the mishap on her instead of on their own organization's decisions.

She checked her messages and saw one from Grant. *Benton Valero agreed to meet with us and invited us to his quarters for dinner at nineteen hundred. —Grant*

She sent a quick reply of confirmation, though she suddenly didn't feel like going. Belle wanted to go to her quarters, curl up in her bed, and cry. But she wouldn't. She wasn't going to give up. She still had promises to keep. Made with Iron Seer. And if she could bring to light all that happened, Kepler would *have* to exonerate her.

Wouldn't they?

The key to this strategy was to reveal the truth as quickly as possible, which meant eliminating the Zyd agent ASAP.

28

Belle knocked on Benton Valero's door promptly at nineteen-hundred. She wore casual cotton slacks and a modest blouse, with her flight jacket over it. Though she had some unhealed but minor cuts, scratches, and burns on her face and hands that showed, all the other more visible injuries were covered.

The door was answered by Benton, who she had never met. Before her stood a short, dark-skinned man of about sixty, with short gray hair neatly combed, wearing jeans and a khaki shirt. "You must be Belle!"

They shook hands.

"Welcome! Please come in. Grant arrived a few minutes ago."

"Thank you, and it's nice to finally meet you, Dr. Valero."

She followed him into a hallway that led into a spacious living and dining space. "Please, call me Benton." He took her jacket and hung it in a coat closet, and she thanked him. "How are you feeling?"

"Considering I spent a week in the wilds of Clinton, I think I am doing stupendously. The base clinic gave me the all-clear to return to duty, though I won't be flying for at least two weeks. Not until the mishap committee gives me permission."

"I was so sorry to hear about Phil Curtis," said Benton. "I've known him for over twenty years. Had several opportunities to work closely with him during that time. His loss is a tragedy."

She nodded but didn't say anything. She was at a loss for words.

They walked into the living room, where Grant was seated in a chair. He stood and gave Belle a one-armed hug around the shoulders and a reassuring smile.

Benton invited them all to sit down and eat. The table was already prepared, and a simple dinner was laid out for the three. They began eating, and after a few minutes of additional small talk, Benton asked Belle to please tell the story of what had happened to her during the last seven days.

During the telling, she scanned Benton with the auger. His R-fields tasted sweet and smelled of a slight chlorine scent, which she had begun associating with somebody absorbing information.

Belle initially gave Benton almost the same story she had given the mishap committee, though instead of telling lies about Iron Seer, the ruin, and the return trip, she replaced those with vague descriptions. She and Grant had agreed beforehand that they would tell only truths to Benton but would share the entire, yet incomplete, story first before disclosing the full truth.

When she got to the part where Grant's rescue team arrived, she asked Grant to take over the rest of the telling. Grant didn't hold back and told the grim details of what happened to the dropship and the people still inside it when it blew up. He brushed over the next few days by saying,

"We found shelter in the monolith, then made our way to the outpost, arriving yesterday."

"You just hiked to the outpost," said Benton in amazement. "You're making that sound way too easy. I want to hear about the hike through the jungle."

But Grant managed to wave off his questions until the story was finished.

Belle sighed, looked at her feet, then at Grant, then finally at Benton on the other side of the table. Grant nodded to her.

"Benton, what you have heard is the story we've been telling the two mishap committees. But Grant and I were not completely honest about what happened during our stranding. Everything we've said to you so far about the facts surrounding the loss of the two ships is true. Events transpired exactly as we've described. But we've hidden some details—some important details—of what happened during the following days."

Benton looked to Grant with raised eyebrows. "Why would you do such a thing?"

Grant replied, "Because, Benton, it was necessary. Please listen to Belle. You'll soon learn why."

During this exchange, Belle again sensed Benton's R-field. It still tasted of sweet sincerity.

"Yes, indeed," said Belle, "and why don't I just cut to the chase? Grant and I made contact with an alien. An intelligent, sentient, and we believe benevolent being dwelling in the monolith. It—she—calls herself Iron Seer."

"A sentient alien! In the monolith?" Benton yelled.

"We did not hike across fifty kilometers of jungle to reach the outpost but were, instead, delivered there by Iron Seer's transport."

Benton's eyes and mouth were wide open.

"Furthermore," Grant said, "she has warned us of a

threat to humans on Clinton, and because of it, we need to keep Iron Seer's presence secret for as long as possible. But she allowed us to share this information with you, which is why we're having this conversation."

Benton held his hands to his head. "An *intelligent* alien species! Why wouldn't you tell us of this immediately? This needs to be reported to the DPE without delay!" He was visibly upset and was picking his phone up from the table.

"No, Benton!" cried out Grant. "Please, give her a chance to explain. This was not a decision we made ourselves but is the express wish of Iron Seer, who is trying to help us. It was a condition of her help with returning us to base."

Benton wasn't taking the news well. He likely felt torn between his duties to his profession as a scientist and his loyalty to Grant through his father. What would they do if Benton refused to cooperate?

Benton put his phone back down. "But…you must tell me about this Iron Seer." He stood from his chair and began pacing behind it. "You all know that humankind has not yet encountered sentient alien life, nothing remotely intelligent. What you are talking about is First Contact! This isn't the way it's supposed to work!" He was shaking his finger at both of them. "There are protocols to follow! If it's thought we were hiding information on a First Contact event, it could mean our careers. We could all go to jail!" Benton Valero was agitated, looking accusingly at Belle and Grant.

The First Contact protocols were part of the Xenology Accords, international treaties that were adopted when the first alien life was discovered about a century ago. Belle had learned about them in her xenology class back at the academy. The treaties were intended to protect xenological research and alien artifacts. Also to ensure knowledge of a newly discovered alien civilization was propagated as quickly as possible for the security of humanity. In reality, the treaties made criminals out of anybody making such a discovery and not making it known to the world.

This is why they needed Dr. Valero's help. So they could resolve all of this as quickly as possible.

"Dr. Valero, sir, I will explain, but please, sit down," Belle pleaded.

Finally, Benton took a deep breath, blew it out, and returned to his seat.

"First off," Belle said, "if not for Iron Seer, neither Grant nor I would be sitting here. She saved our lives, quite literally, by giving us shelter when she had every reason to ignore us. We owe her our lives."

Grant nodded in agreement.

"Second," she said, "she's shared a powerful technology with us that will, we believe, reveal a threat to both humans and her, but secrecy is key at this stage because we don't know who we can trust. While we've been sitting here talking, I've scanned you with it to confirm we can confidently talk to you, though Grant was already convinced we could trust you. You and Iron Seer are the only two persons we trust on Clinton now."

Grant nodded again.

"You scanned me without my permission?" Benton asked.

"I'm sorry, but I couldn't tell you about it until I determined you were trustworthy. And you are. Don't worry. It's a passive scan. No energy was directed at your person."

"What is this scanning technology?"

"First, I need your promise that you will keep this secret until we meet Iron Seer's conditions. Though I know how uncomfortable this request must make you feel."

"For now, you have mine," said Benton, "but I will withhold final judgment until I've heard the rest of this...

impossible story!"

Grant and Belle glanced at each other, and Grant gave her a nod.

"I suppose that's the best deal we're getting for right now, but we'll take it. We really do need your help."

Belle uncovered her left wrist, revealing the auger. "This is called an R-field auger." She let Benton handle her wrist. He appeared unimpressed by the featureless dark gray disk.

"Looks like just a piece of silicon crystal to me," said Benton. "And what is an R-field?"

"Iron Seer is a member of a race known as the ighakans, who form a polity called the Quynh Federation. They have knowledge of something called synchronicity theory—a new kind of physics probably only hypothesized by human scientists. They have the technology to detect the universe-spanning forcefield defined in synchronicity theory. This is called the R-field for the reverse temporal field."

"I've heard of synchronicity theory," Benton said. "Though I know little about it."

"Good. This device on my wrist is an R-field auger that detects the R-field generated by living beings. Iron Seer installed a modification into my neural implant, allowing me to interface with the auger and read the R-field." Belle launched into describing how it worked and its implications for everyday objects, such as doors and automation.

"So, what you have on your wrist is just a glorified lie detector," said Benton.

"It's both more and less than a lie detector. It measures intent. Whereas a lie detector requires somebody to actually tell a lie, the auger does not need that. It detects deceptive and corrupt intentions. At the same time, it lacks specificity. For example, it'll tell me somebody has a deceptive intention but not what is being hidden or from whom. At least, I haven't figured that out yet."

"And how is this *auger* supposed to help us with this threat you speak of?" asked Benton skeptically.

Grant said, "The Quynh Federation has an enemy known as the Zyd Hegemony—yet another alien civilization. Iron Seer claims that the Zyd has infiltrated human society. Their influence is present on Clinton. She believes an actual Zyd agent is here on Clinton right now."

"Have you also met an alien from the Zyd?" Benton asked. Probably made half in jest, but the man seemed to suffer from temporary intellectual shock.

"The Zyd want human knowledge and to manipulate us for some game they play. Iron Seer also says a Zyd agent on Clinton uses humans to seek out herself and her facility—the monolith—a Quynh Federation listening post."

Belle continued, "Because Iron Seer doesn't know who or where the agent is, she's requested we keep secret the knowledge of her and her facility until the immediate threat is eliminated. However, she hasn't left us defenseless. The auger—and the training on how to use it—is her way of helping us to help ourselves. We have an investigation to conduct, and quickly, before the Zyd agent learns of the Quynh facility, but it has to be done in secret. Grant and I need your help."

Benton was still skeptical and wanted proof of the auger's capabilities. She and Grant ran several experiments with him, like they had done with each other, to convince him that Belle could detect and sense their deepest intentions and deceptions. Benton became more agreeable at one point, but Belle noticed that his R-field taste had switched from sweet to sour. He was being deceptive.

As they finished the exercises, and everybody seemed to

be in agreement, Belle confronted Benton Valero. "Benton, you say you now believe us, but over the last thirty minutes, your R-field has changed from sincerity to deception. With all respect, I don't believe you when you say you believe our tale. Or, at least, I don't believe you are being completely open with us regarding your intentions going forward."

He eyed her for a moment and seemed to be considering. Then the taste of his R-field changed from sour to sweet once more. "It's okay. You have now convinced me. As a scientist, I needed to do a proper experiment. That is, to test a hypothesis. If I was to make a plan to betray you, then if everything you've been claiming is true, you would sense it.

"It was a little difficult because I had to convince myself the betrayal was the correct course of action. However, you just proved the hypothesis correct by detecting my deception. Please forgive me, but it was necessary, and I am convinced."

Belle laughed, then looked at Grant and said, "He's a brilliant man, isn't he?"

Grant just smiled and nodded.

"This Iron Seer lives in the monolith? And it's not a monolith, but an alien building?" Benton asked.

"That's correct," Grant said. "We lived inside the facility all the days we were missing. We've seen a small amount of the interior, but what we've seen was amazing. It's too bad we didn't have recording devices with us."

"How were the ships destroyed?"

"In error. Iron Seer concluded a Zyd threat was attacking her. She assumed this because of the Zyd activity she had detected. She defended herself. Only after she observed us inside the structure did she decide we weren't the true danger."

"Please, I have so many questions. I don't even know where to begin," Benton said. "Tell me how this marvelous auger works."

"Sure," Belle said, "I sensed the moment your intentions changed. As I've learned to use the auger, I've noticed that the most informative moments are usually when somebody's intentions change while I observe them. Your's was sharp."

"Incredible. I wouldn't believe it without seeing it in action. The physicists working on synchronicity theory are going to be blown away when they learn of this. How do you interface with it?"

"Iron Seer had to find the best way to interface it with my existing senses, otherwise it could have taken months or years for me to learn how to use it. She studied my brain and chose to translate its measurements into signals that could be detected and measured by my senses of taste and smell."

"And this was made through your neural implant?"

"Yes. Taste tells me something regarding the sincerity of a person's intentions. Smell tells me something about what type of intention they have."

"So you know what my intentions are just by smell?"

"In theory, but I've learned little about interpreting smells. Most remain a mystery. However, taste is becoming more clear. For example, a sincere person and almost all lower lifeforms exhibit a sweet taste. Deception, on the other hand, produces a sour taste. I've not yet found an animal lifeform that produced a sour taste. It seems that deception requires higher intelligence."

"What if you tasted bitter? What does that mean?"

"Three other persons I have found whose R-field exhibited a bitter taste—other than in an experiment Grant helped me with. But I don't completely understand its meaning yet. It could mean corruption. Iron Seer said that the auger would easily detect corrupted intentions, but she couldn't tell me how it would manifest. After all, how do you explain to somebody what bitter tastes like if they've never experienced it?"

"Looks to me like you need calibration targets for the auger," Benton said.

Belle nodded. "Indeed. I also haven't yet experienced a salty taste from anybody, and like the bitter, I wouldn't know how to interpret it."

"Who were the three people who were bitter?"

"A pilot named Jordana Sharrow, an engineer named Brit Corti, and Hodel Vroomen."

"I know all of them actually. All good people. I have a hard time believing they are somehow corrupted. Perhaps you are incorrect in your interpretation, or perhaps I just don't know any of them as well as I thought." He stood there shaking his head. "We should assume they are suspect until we have reason to know otherwise."

"I performed a cursory background check on all three this evening," said Grant. "Nothing too deep. Brit Corti has not been with the company long. Only about five years, and I couldn't find information on his activities before then.

"Benton, this is how we would like to propose we conduct the investigation."

Looking at Benton, he continued, "We would like you to look into the source of the monolith investigation. Given your seniority within the corporation and access to records we don't have, you would be more likely to find the truth."

He then gestured to Belle and himself. "In the meantime, Belle will continue scanning Kepler employees as much as she can, and I'll do follow-up investigations into suspicious targets, beginning with Brit Corti."

"I can help with the monolith investigation," Benton said. "I'm also puzzled. The direction to sample it came directly from the DPE as part of a Phase Two contract modification. I'm the one who ordered the sampling, but I was just following instructions. Now I want to know how it ended up in the updated contract. I'll follow the paper trail and see what I find."

"Good," Grant said.

Benton nodded. "Grant, you need to be circumspect. If management gets a whiff of you invading the private lives of its employees, they won't think twice about showing you the door and inviting law enforcement to handle you."

"I will be."

"There are so many aspects of what we're about to do that are probably illegal. Improper use of company proprietary information, invasion of privacy, improper use of personally identifiable information, violation of the Planetary Exploration Act, violation of the Xenology Accords, filing a false report, and so on."

"We'll be careful, we promise," said Belle.

They discussed when to meet again and decided on the evening in two days' time.

29

Early the next morning, Grant and Belle met for coffee at a base coffee shop. It was busy like a beehive, but they found a quiet corner in the back.

Grant felt drawn to Belle. Last night at dinner was the first time he had seen her cleaned up. She was even more beautiful than he had predicted. And he could feel there was mutual attraction. Not a definite thing, but like the gravitational potential between two physical bodies: given the correct initial conditions and impulses, they could eventually meet.

This hope for a thing that didn't yet exist had encouraged him to invite Belle for a coffee.

Grant said, "Thanks for coming. I just wanted to make sure we had a chance, at least once, to meet, the two of us, in normal circumstances."

"I'm glad," she said. "How is your mishap investigation going? You already started, right?"

"Yeah, the committee interviewed me yesterday. I told them everything I could, which wasn't much. I was trapped on the ground when it all happened. I suspect they'll want to interview you in the coming days."

"You're probably correct." She sipped her hot chocolate.

"How about you? Did your investigation begin?"

"Oh, yes, yesterday also. I was interviewed for about two hours in the afternoon. I don't think it went well."

"Why's that?" asked Grant.

"The committee chairman, Hodel Vroomen, asked some pointed questions that led to the conclusion I caused the deaths of my two crew members. He seems to think that my co-pilot should have been sitting in the cockpit monitoring the reactor, even though it had been put on standby mode."

She appeared low. Her eyes were sad, and she averted her sight while describing the meeting.

"You're upset about it."

"Yes, because the reactor went out of control so quickly there was no time to make well-thought decisions. He seems to think I had the luxury of hitting the pause button and analyzing the situation."

"What's the worst thing that could happen?"

"Probably be terminated by Kepler. If I'm found negligent, that's what they'll do, and my career as a pilot will be over."

"What would you do if that happened?" asked Grant.

Belle shook her head. "I don't know. I don't want to think about it. I need time to digest what is happening and come up with some contingency plans." She pounded on the table. "But I refuse to go down without a fight!"

"We're sitting on some good information that, if it comes to light, should help you with the mishap committee."

"You're right. And I'm holding onto that. I need for us to finish this thing. Thanks for being a trusting person."

Grant's face burned. He didn't think he was a trusting person at all. But he had a hard time saying no to Belle. And he didn't want to say no. He wanted her to be happy, and it had been a long time since he'd felt that so specifically for one person.

"Tell me," Belle said, "what is the most fulfilling job you've ever had? Not profession, but a specific job task."

"The most fulfilling job task...Why? You looking for recommendations?" He let her laugh at his joke while he took a moment to think through his happiest professional moments. "That's easy. Rescuing you!"

"No it isn't, you flatterer!" she laughed.

"No, really, it is. We're not done yet, it seems, but it's looking like this is my best moment." He was being honest with her.

"Okay then, what is the second best?" Again, he had to think about it. This was harder.

After a moment, he answered, "Rescuing miners and their families in the Primavera system."

"What happened?"

"There was a mining colony living in an asteroid habitat in the Primavera system. About two thousand civilians in total. They lived there and mined the asteroids in the surrounding belt.

"There was an accident where a mining ship lost control and collided with the habitat. Initially, it killed about two hundred people, but it also destroyed their life-support systems. The habitat became structurally unstable, and its rotation made it begin to disintegrate."

"So there were eighteen-hundred people trapped on a disintegrating asteroid?" Belle said. "And you had to rescue them?" She had wide eyes.

"Yes, my team got called in to do the rescue. It took two days with no sleep, but we rescued every single family and individual who was still alive.

"After we were done, I had a chance to walk around the

freighter where they had brought all the families to live temporarily. I remember being struck by how precious each moment in our lives is. Seeing fathers hugging their daughters, mothers hugging their sons, and friends greeting each other. Each of those moments would have been lost forever if my team and I hadn't been there to help them."

"That is quite the story," said Belle. "And you think rescuing me is somehow more positive?"

"It's a close competition, but we might be changing history right now. In fact, I know we are. What I'm waiting for is to know if it's a good thing for humanity. I think it is." He started to reach his hand out to hers but thought better of it and rested it on the table between them. "You made this happen. My part is small, but I'm helping smooth the path for you. Just trying to do my part in a history-making event."

"Your part is not small! It better not be because I can't do this without you."

He didn't say anything, but raised his hands and smiled at her.

Their cups were empty, and he knew they needed to go soon. He searched for an excuse to see her again. Should he just come right out and ask her to dinner?

"Hey, Belle, I was thinking maybe—"

"Grant!" he heard from behind him, and a woman grabbed his shoulders. It was Roxanne and a friend of her's whose name he didn't remember.

Oh, no! She had barged right into their table, had her arm around his shoulders, and was practically sitting in his lap. He'd gone on a few dates with Roxanne about six months ago. Knowing her, she'd probably seen him sitting with this beautiful woman and been jealous, felt the need to mark her territory. As if she had any!

Roxanne said, "I heard the craziest thing, that you were stranded in the jungle?"

"Yeah, just got back yesterday. Hey, I want to introduce you to my friend, Belle Machado."

They exchanged names, how-do-you-dos, and so on. Grant wished Roxanne and her friend would just go away.

"You'll have to take me out to dinner sometime and tell me all about it," Roxanne said to Grant.

"Sure, maybe." Not likely. "Nice seeing you again, Roxanne." Goodbye.

"Bye!" She gave Grant a peck on the cheek (still marking territory) and waved at Belle.

"Sorry about that," Grant said.

"Old girlfriend?" Belle asked with a smile.

His face was hot.

"No, just a friend. We haven't seen each other for a few months. She's...touchy-feely."

"I noticed that." Belle was collecting her items from the table.

"Hey, Belle, I was wondering if you would have dinner with me later this week. I've enjoyed our chats, and I'd like to get to know you better."

Belle had her arms crossed across her chest and was nodding but remained silent.

"Just as friends," said Grant, trying to reassure her. "Honestly, I just like talking to you."

Belle said, "Sure, I'd like that too. Let's wait and see how things play out over the next couple days. It would be nice to sit down with you for dinner once things calm down."

"Great! I look forward to it!" *Awesome, she said yes!*

"Good luck today."

"Yes, and may you have fair weather and blue skies also." He was in a good mood.

30

Belle watched Grant walk away to wherever he was headed. She had mixed feelings about meeting him for dinner. Belle couldn't remember the last time she had met one-on-one with a man her age in a social setting. A date. She'd always avoided them. Grant was helping her discover another side of her, needs she didn't know she had. Needs that conflicted with the life and dreams she'd been chasing for as long as she could remember. She wouldn't make good girlfriend material, and she didn't want to ruin a friendship she enjoyed.

She headed off to work. With medical's clearance, she'd been given some office work to keep her nominally busy during the day, but in reality it only occupied about half her time. She used the rest to scan as many Kepler employees as she could.

There were a couple of ways she did this. One was to park herself in a public location near a choke point, like the entrance to a shop or a security checkpoint, then simply scan each person she saw with the auger. One of her favorite locations became the base cafeteria. While not everybody ate there, and not every day, it was a sure bet at least a quarter of the base population passed through there during the lunch hour.

So, at lunchtime each day for the next two days, she found a table near the cafeteria's main entrance and brought a laptop computer and a book to give her props that made it look like she was doing something. Then she would watch people as they passed through the doors.

Another good place was the security checkpoint at the entrance to the main office building. Many of the corporate higher-ups didn't eat in the cafeteria, so this was the only way to snag them. Fortunately, there were some waiting benches outside the entrance, and she would sit there for ten to fifteen minutes at a time, watching people. But not any longer than that, because otherwise security might notice. She changed her clothing and hairstyle each time to reduce the likelihood of being noticed, and it seemed to work.

The third place she'd tried was the base commissary. She could stroll through its shopping aisles for hours, hidden by the crowd and scanning everybody. This approach had the advantage of lots of exposure, but the downside of being random and chaotic.

The fourth and last place she went was the mission operations center. The office work she'd been given was mostly to assist Operations, so she had a reason to be there. Also, all the incoming and outgoing pilots and maintenance crews had to check in at Ops before and after missions. She spent hours acting like she was working, when in reality she was scanning people as they came and went.

During the next two days, she scanned at least four hundred individuals, perhaps more. Some were possible duplicates, especially at the chaotic commissary and cafeteria. She also had the disadvantage of not knowing who most of the people were, because of being still somewhat of a new employee.

Regardless, it didn't matter most of the time. Most people had a sweet taste to their R-field. While discouraging for her investigation, at least it cheered her up to know most people were honest, sincere, and uncorrupted.

Twice she saw Brit Corti again, and once Jordana Sharrow. Both still exhibited that bitter taste.

There were many other people she saw multiple times, and occasionally they would have a bitter taste to them, or sometimes even the sour taste of deception, but not always.

Once, she was sitting outside the office building checkpoint and a man exited who was clearly distraught. His eyes were red and puffy as if he'd recently been weeping. The man's R-field was sharply bitter, but minutes before, he had entered the building looking calm and had tasted sweet.

At the commissary, there was a pub. She'd stopped by there a few times. Some of the customers became inebriated, and that also produced a bitter taste.

Belle believed that bitterness was a sign of corruption and emotional distress. When the mind was not completely rational, it would give off that bitter taste. However, it was probably a complicated mixture of things, so how was she supposed to separate the corruption of a Zyd agent from corruption caused by mental disorders, or temporary incapacitation due to things like drugs?

Brit Corti projected an incredibly strong bitter taste each time she'd seen him. Consistent. There was something there. She would find out from Grant this evening what he'd found.

One time, while in the operations center, the base director of operations, Kennedy Kauffmann, came in to talk to his assistant, Silvestre Jenkins. Belle noticed a subtle salty taste coming from Kauffmann's R-field, but she had just eaten lunch and wasn't sure if it could have been from that. When he left the building a little later, all she could taste was a subdued sweetness instead, so perhaps she'd mixed them up.

Interestingly, later that day Jenkins started tasting bitter. That was curious. She wondered if he had some kind of emotional stress in his life right now. He certainly hadn't looked happy at that moment.

After two days of scanning people, she had collected massive amounts of new data but not anything that gave her conclusive clues. She hoped the others were faring better.

31

Grant had been on PANNET databases all day yesterday, looking up all the information he could find on Brit Corti. With the unusual name, one would think there wouldn't be many matches, but that was a wrong assumption. He'd found dozens of Brit Cortis scattered on humanity's colonized worlds. Fortunately, one of them was definitely *their* Brit Corti. The problem was that his online persona just seemed to appear out of the blue only five years ago. How had he gotten through Kepler's background checks?

Grant called a lady friend who had been hitting on him for months, and he knew she had quite the crush. She also happened to work with Kepler's personnel records.

She was super happy to go on a date with him that night on short notice. During that, he made some hints about how happy he would be to know more about this guy named Brit Corti, who he was sure he'd met years ago, and oh, by the way, would she happen to know if there was a way to learn his middle name, birth date, and place of birth?

He was careful to drop her off at home that evening with a sense of promise that he would call on her again soon. He let her give him a chaste kiss on the cheek.

The next day, he found an email message from her with Brit's personal info. Oh boy! He couldn't believe she'd just sent that to him. They would both get fired if management ever found out, yet the girl hadn't made so much as a frown in objection to the request. *Definitely has fallen for me.*

But his thoughts were for Belle. It surprised him how much of an impression she had made on him, with her combination of a gentle soul combined with a spine made of titanium. And the head she had on her shoulders. *Beautiful, in more ways than one.*

He could contact an old friend in a law enforcement agency back on Earth with the information. He gave him a lie about needing to run a background check on a creepy guy at work who was hitting on a friend but didn't want to embarrass the friend by working it through company management.

His police friend just chuckled knowingly and asked for the guy's info. Grant gave him the name Brit Adalwolf Corti, birth date, and place of birth.

Not one hour later, he got a response back from his friend. He said the guy had been employed at Kepler Research Corporation for five years, but his record showed him living in a monastery on planet Zuwanda for the previous twenty years. He said that, given Zuwanda was sparsely populated by colonists who had sworn to return to a hunter-gatherer style of living, it had all kinds of red flags. His friend said it was likely a stolen identity, taken from somebody who'd died in Zuwanda five years ago. Grant thanked his friend, telling him he owed him one (and oh boy, he knew he would, too, next time he was on Earth).

Bingo!

Brit Adalwolf Corti was not who he claimed to be. Even without his police friend's hints, Grant would have guessed it anyway. He'd met a few people from Zuwanda, and they had thick French accents, if they even spoke English. He'd heard Brit speak enough to tell that dude had been raised in Midwestern USA.

Grant was supposed to meet with Belle and Benton again tonight, and he wanted to have news. He began planning a little operation to verify once and for all who Brit Corti was. Grant would break into his living quarters and have a looky-look.

He could find Brit's address in the base directory and walked over to the building it was in. Nice apartments: much better than the studio apartment he had. Brit was clearly better paid than he.

Brit's apartment was on the second floor, with a window looking out on a main walking path. Grant positioned himself under the shade of a tree where he could look through its leaves and see the window. Maybe that was a phone on the wall of what looked like a kitchen. Then he called the number from the directory. A light blinked on the phone, and the ringtone sounded—this was the correct place. However, nobody answered. He'd been hoping for this. It was the middle of the day, and Brit was probably working, perhaps even tasks on Belle's upcoming mishap report.

Grant remembered back to his days in training for close-quarters combat and building entry. He'd been taught basic lock-picking skills, and knowing how bad the locks were in these places, he was pretty sure he could pick the lock.

Brit's door was one of four in a quiet stretch of hallway. He double-checked the way was clear. He pulled out some simple tools he'd scrounged together when he realized he might have to break in and got to work. It didn't take long, and he unlocked the door and was inside.

Shutting the door behind him, he stepped carefully on the tile floor, making sure not to move anything inadvertently.

The one-bedroom apartment had a separate living room from the bedroom and a full bathroom. It was almost twice the size of Grant's place.

He rummaged around the kitchen and living room, looking for any identifiable information that would reveal who Brit really was. Both were pretty sparsely furnished and had few objects beyond the typical domestic decorations and comforts.

In the bathroom, he noticed several prescription medication bottles in the medicine cabinet. Grant looked at them. *Clozapine? Aripiprazole?* From his medical profession, he happened to know these were antipsychotics used for treating schizophrenia, among other things.

Grant heard the front door open, a person whistling a tune, and then the door shut again.

Uh oh…

He was in deep trouble. Standing in the middle of the bathroom, he had nowhere to hide.

Grant stepped out of the bathroom with a purpose in his posture. Brit Corti stood at the other end of the shared hallway, and on seeing Grant—who purposefully put an angry, knowing, and disgusted expression on his face—Brit looked like he might have messed his pants right there and then. He was speechless.

"Mr. Brit Adalwolf Corti, we've had our eye on you!" Grant bellowed.

"Wha—what are you talking about?" he squeaked out with wide eyes. He dropped the papers in his hands, which looked like something innocent from work.

Grant walked over aggressively, as if he had a right to be there, and snatched them up.

"Hmm, what have we here?" He looked accusingly at Brit.

"Nothing, I swear! Just some take-home work!"

Grant thumbed through it, acting interested. Complicated diagrams and mathematical equations. Engineering documents. Grant kept up his act anyway. "Are you authorized to remove these from the workplace?"

"Of course I am. As head of nuclear engineering at the base, it's my job to know our power systems inside and out!"

Probably true. He needed to change the subject before Brit's courage returned and he asked awkward questions—time for the jugular.

"Mr. Corti, recent information came to light that suggests you may not be who you say you are. Care to tell me the truth?"

Suddenly, Brit began to panic. Grant noted the moment when the anxiety peaked, and he decided between flight, fight, or freeze. He needed it to be a freeze. "Don't think you can run from this. We know everything! The false identity, the drugs." He held out the pill bottles in his face. "Everything!"

Brit was suddenly kneeling in the middle of the floor, bawling. Perhaps Grant had overdone it.

"I swear it's all innocent!" The poor guy could barely talk. Finally, he managed to get a breath in. "The base psychiatrist knows all about it. I told her everything, I swear! About the false identity and my paranoid hallucinations! You see...you see..."

Grant had to give Brit another moment to collect himself.

Brit continued, "I have hallucinations about being tracked and spied on by government agents, and the false identity was something I bought on impulse during one of my worst episodes. But I know I did wrong, and the doctor knows, and she's treating me with medication. That's what the drugs are for. I swear to god. It's all true!" The poor man was a slobbering mess on the floor.

Grant felt horrible, absolutely horrible. Not only had he suspected the wrong guy, violated his privacy, and broken into his apartment, but he now had made the guy think his paranoid hallucinations were real. That he was being tracked and spied on. He'd probably just destroyed whatever recent progress the man had made with his mental health care. What was he going to do?

"Thank you for telling me the truth. We already knew all this. This was just part of an internal security audit. I'm Agent Jason Woodrow with personnel security, and you never saw me. Do you understand?"

"Yes, sir, Agent Woodrow, sir!" he cried out in relief.

Grant set his medication on the table in the living room. "And, Mr. Corti, make sure to stay on your treatments and see your doctor. She doesn't know about this visit and doesn't need to, but we will. Goodbye, and enjoy the rest of your evening." He quietly opened the door, walked out, and left quickly.

Oh, what a story he would have for his partners in crime tonight. Oh boy, what a story...

32

Benton Valero studied Clinton's Phase One survey looking for evidence of the monolith. When it had been detected, with what types of sensors, and what had been the initial response. He also looked for any other similar anomalies detected during the Phase One survey and how those had been handled.

The survey was composed almost entirely of remote sensing data from satellites in polar orbit. There had been limited sampling of animal life on the ground. Over ninety-nine percent of the data had been collected via satellite.

The initial, planet-wide, digital elevation scan detected the monolith as a prominent rise in the local terrain in an otherwise flat landscape. But no specific annotations were made at that time.

The monolith was again detected during hyperspectral satellite imaging as an anomalously colored and unusually shaped terrain feature in an area of the nearly uniform jungle canopy.

It was detected a third time during measurements of background radiation levels, showing a localized rise in ionizing radiation.

Though easily visible in the data in all three instances, the monolith had not been annotated as an object of interest. Nor did it appear in the chapter of the survey's final report on targets and features recommended for further study. There were over fifty recommendations made, and as Kepler's chief scientist, he was familiar with many of them. Volcanoes, unusual fauna, and the dangerous tropical cyclones on Wordonia's southern coast were all subjects recommended for further study. Even a relatively minor cave system was one of the recommended targets, but the monolith did not appear on the list.

By itself, the omission was not surprising because the monolith was unremarkable based on Phase One remote sensing data. Merely an interesting local terrain feature. Even the elevated radiation levels were nothing special. The surfaces of young terrestrial planets like Clinton typically exhibited significant variation in background radiation levels, depending on what minerals were exposed on the outer crust.

No, what was interesting was the fact that the monolith had been called out for special attention in the first place. He'd been led to believe that the impetus from DPE for the sampling was based on the Phase One survey, but that was not the case.

Benton had received orders to perform the monolith sampling via an internal email from Clinton Base's local corporate executive committee. He still had the message and studied it more carefully. When he received it, he must have been busy that day because, at the time, he hadn't noticed attached to it a long email chain documenting the origin of the order. Benton opened it up.

The order to perform additional studies on the monolith came directly from the office of the secretary of the Department of Planetary Exploration and was directed to the base's executive committee chairman. The order was the last in a long chain of emails, and he traced those back in time over the course of about a week. Mostly jargon-filled short messages between mid-level DPE bureaucrats discussing the merits of the anomaly, whether further study fit within the scope of the contract DPE had with Kepler, and if it could be done within the current contract schedule.

However, in one of the chain's earliest emails, he noticed a Kepler employee's email address had been CC'd: Kennedy Kauffmann, Kepler's Clinton Base director of operations. *Why would Kauffmann be involved in this discussion at all?*

Reading through some of the later messages, he noticed a vague comment made by one person about being tipped off to the presence of the monolith from a member of Kepler's operations team.

The connection was tenuous but noteworthy for being present at all. It appeared that Kennedy Kauffmann, an important high-level manager at the base in charge of day-to-day operations, had directly contacted somebody at DPE to tell them about the monolith and perhaps requested further instructions. However, in doing so, Kauffmann went completely outside his chain of command and seemed to have done it without the knowledge of anybody at Kepler.

Moreover, Kauffmann's job duties did not encompass decisions on what should and should not be investigated. That was the science team's job, for whom Benton was the leader. Not only was this discovery notable for that fact, but Benton felt personally offended at the breach of protocol made by Kauffmann.

It was also uncharacteristic of Kennedy Kauffmann, who Benton knew quite well.

Kauffmann was a stickler for rules and regulations and ran an efficient operation. Going outside the chain of command to get some pet project approved was completely unlike the Kauffmann he knew. Furthermore, while having many good qualities, he was not known for being curious or creative, so why would he suddenly decide he needed some odd terrain feature investigated? And why hadn't he brought it to the attention of Benton and the science team?

It was precisely the sort of behind-the-scenes manipulation that Belle Machado was looking for.

Operations had a planning map based on Phase One survey data used for planning Phase Two operations. Perhaps it would have some additional evidence.

Benton opened the Operations database. There were hundreds of documents, but he found the copy of the Phase One data he was looking for.

He opened the digital elevation map and scrolled to the coordinates for the monolith.

A grayscale image appeared on his large display. Mostly the featureless gray of flat terrain, but in the northern half of the grid was the oval outline of the monolith, which was a lighter color than the rest of the map, indicating higher elevation.

There was an annotation attached to the monolith. Last edited by Kennedy Kauffmann, with a timestamp from about one month ago. That was four days *before* the first email in that chain. How revealing.

The annotation said, "Follow-up Required."

Benton pulled up the Operations planning calendar and saw where it had been modified to indicate that Belle Machado and her crew had been assigned a task to sample the monolith. He remembered that day. He'd watched Silvestre enter the task into the system.

But the annotation and its timestamp were clear evidence that Kauffmann took the initiative himself to have the monolith sampled, even though he hadn't gone through

Benton's office. He'd gone straight to the office of the secretary of the DPE. The DPE came back with instructions that eventually arrived at Benton's desk. A circuitous process that one would use only if one wanted to delay the process.

Or hide something.

He would bring this discovery to the attention of Grant and Belle at their meeting this evening.

33

Belle met with Grant and Benton in the evening at Benton's apartment. They discussed what they'd found over the last two days of their individual investigations.

Grant went first, explaining his misadventure investigating Brit Corti's background. While he'd been successful, his conclusion was that Brit, though a disturbed person suffering from mental illness, was not part of some secret plan to overthrow humanity. Grant was hanging his head down and seemed troubled by what had happened between him and Brit.

Belle reached out and patted Grant's knee. "Don't worry about it. Look on the bright side. You just helped me better understand what the bitter taste means when I sense it from the auger."

"How's that?" he asked.

"I saw Brit a couple times, and always his R-field tasted bitter. Strongly bitter, much more than other people I've scanned. I think I am convinced it's because of his schizophrenia and whatever that is doing to his mind. It means his intentions are corrupted, perhaps because he is not completely living a rational life."

"Remarkable!" said Benton. "You think we could use these augers to diagnose mental illness?"

"Possibly. It seems likely, yes," she responded.

Next, Belle reported on her findings. She hadn't had much luck discovering specific people but had learned a lot of potentially useful data. She told them about the interaction she observed between Kennedy Kauffmann and Silvestre Jenkins and her momentary salty taste from Kauffmann.

"That is fascinating," said Benton, "because Kauffmann came up in my investigation as well."

"Oh really? How so?"

Benton explained all he had found regarding the origination of the orders to sample the monolith. He was convinced that Kauffmann was acting suspiciously, though uncertain what his motives could be. Maybe it was just out of pure curiosity or his way of flexing his managerial muscles.

The three decided that Kennedy Kauffmann would be the next target of their continued investigation. That night, after their meeting concluded, Belle decided she would try to find a way to approach Kauffmann about it the next day. She was scheduled to do some work in the Operations offices and would possibly encounter him.

The next day when Belle got to work, she was immediately called into a meeting with her group manager, Danny Jephson. Danny was her direct administrative boss within Kepler.

Belle tested him with the auger. He tasted of corrupt intentions.

Belle took a seat facing him.

Danny said, "Belle, we need to talk about where to go

after this mishap investigation is completed."

She nodded.

Danny sighed. "There's good news and bad news."

He folded his hands. "The good news is that Phil Curtis' evaluation of your check-flight arrived before his unfortunate death. And it is glowing, one of the best evaluations I've seen during my time at Kepler. He gave you top marks for piloting, command, systems knowledge, and mission execution."

"Hurray! I'm so happy!" Belle clapped her hands. What a relief! And bless Phil for being such an efficient guy. That upload must have been his final report on her work.

"Don't get carried away." Danny made a calming gesture. "There's also bad news."

Uh oh.

Danny looked miserable. He shifted around in his chair and avoided her eyes. He sighed again. "Certain people believe you acted negligently in handling the reactor meltdown and that this led to the loss of your vehicle and your two crewmates."

Belle was dizzy. "Is it Hodel Vroomen? I met with his mishap committee three days ago. He got all hung up on how nobody would've died if Borya had been in the cockpit when I was doing the sampling."

Danny looked at his feet, then finally looked her in the eye. "I'm not supposed to say anything, so keep this between you and me. Yes, it sort of is Vroomen, but he reports to Kennedy Kauffmann. Kauffmann is making a big deal out of all this."

No, it couldn't be! Kauffmann's name again. *This can't be a coincidence. But why?* What advantage could Kauffmann gain by making these accusations against her?

"Danny, this is unfair to blame me for a freak accident.

We had less than a minute to evacuate before the whole vehicle was in flames."

"Frankly, I don't understand why he's making a big deal out of this. And I've told him so. Your survival is remarkable and is due to your skill and resourcefulness. He's not listening. He has an agenda. I'm working on the problem from my side, but you're stuck with his decision for now."

"And what's that?"

"It gets worse, unfortunately. You are grounded indefinitely, and your pilot's license is suspended."

"What?" she yelled. *How can this be happening?!* Belle stood and paced around Danny's office.

His office door opened, and two security officers entered. "Belle Machado?" the first said to her.

"Yes, can I help you?" she asked in confusion.

"Ms. Machado, you are being detained pending an investigation into the deaths of Borya Utkin and Phillip Curtis. You are coming with us."

"Danny! What is this?" she cried out. Her heart was pounding, and her chest hurt.

"I'm sorry, Belle, this is how they wanted to do it."

"Am I under arrest?" she asked the officers.

"Not at this time, but we have orders to detain and isolate you."

Belle decided there was nothing she could do at the moment. She gave Danny what she hoped was a look of betrayal, and he dropped his eyes.

The officers didn't restrain her but closely escorted her out of the building. The commotion brought people to their office doors. Belle felt embarrassed and ashamed. She was on a perp walk!

They put her in a car and brought her to a security building, where she was locked into a holding cell. Because she wasn't being arrested, they left her with her clothing, jewelry, and most of her possessions. They took her mobile electronics. The holding cell also had some sort of jamming device to block her neural implant from outside communications.

They were going to take the auger, but Belle convinced them it was jewelry. The lady processing her shrugged and let her keep it.

The holding cell was windowless except for a small window in a solid steel door with a food tray door near the bottom. The cell was three by two meters, had a small bed with a thin mattress, and a toilet and sink combo. There were two armored security cameras watching her.

They left her in the cell alone. She was effectively in jail, even though they used the euphemisms "detained" and "holding cell." No lawyer, no phone call, no legal rights read to her. This wasn't the way it was supposed to work.

She sat for hours in solitude, wondering how many people knew where she was. Did Grant know? If so, would he try and get her out? Could he even do anything? And why did she think of him first?

Somebody brought her lunch. A disgusting mix of beans, rice, and vegetables that tasted like they were all canned. But she ate it.

Evening approached, and still nobody came for her. Kepler was treating her like a criminal. Belle felt deeply depressed.

Things had been looking up. She'd passed her check-flight with outstanding marks. They were on track to discover the Zyd agent, she was convinced of it, but she couldn't find them from here. And if she couldn't find them, there was little hope of bringing to light the truth about how her crew was killed.

She had been so happy the other morning having coffee with Grant. When she was with him, she felt she could open up about her opinions and feelings and wouldn't be judged. She felt safe, supported, and peaceful.

Now she was in jail. Her job likely lost. Career ruined. Contact with friends lost. Zyd agent free.

34

Sometime in the middle of the night, Belle was awoken by a guard.

"Wake up, Machado, and follow me."

She stood up sleepily and asked, "Where are you taking me?"

"Somebody wants to talk to you."

Belle tried to clear the cobwebs from her mind. Who would want to talk to her in the middle of the night?

She wouldn't complain. At least someone had finally recognized her existence.

The building was quiet, most of the lights off. No other people except for the guard who woke Belle. She followed her to a different secure room with a small table and three office chairs.

"Sit," said the guard, pointing to one of the chairs. "Somebody will be with you shortly." She closed and locked the door.

Belle wondered if she would finally have a chance to ask for a lawyer.

About five minutes later, the door opened again. It was the guard, followed by Kennedy Kauffmann. What was he doing here?

"Take as long as you need," said the guard, who left and locked the door behind her.

Kauffmann was middle-aged and tall, blond-haired with a touch of male pattern baldness and sharp Nordic facial features. He walked in with a confident stride and sat in the chair across the table from where Belle sat.

Why was Kauffmann visiting her in jail? Belle was way below his pay grade. Didn't he have underlings to do this sort of thing?

Belle sampled him with the auger. He tasted of salt.

The taste of coerced intentions? Was Kauffmann under the control of the Zyd agent?

"Belle Machado, you are in quite the mess."

"Why are you here? And why am I being held in this jail?"

"You are under suspicion of gross negligence in the deaths of"—he looked at a notepad—"Borya Utkin and Phil Curtis. I knew Phil. Good employee. Quite the shame to lose him." Kauffmann was shaking his head. He didn't look sorry.

"Are you law enforcement of some kind? Come to arrest me?" Belle said.

Kauffmann laughed. "No, I'm not law enforcement. But I do have a lot of power. Kepler's survey charter under DPE delegates extensive law enforcement powers to us on Clinton. You are being held under my orders."

"I want a lawyer, and I want to go home."

"Unfortunately, neither is an option at the moment. The only lawyers on Clinton all work for Kepler. No court would allow them to represent you due to conflicts of interest. And we have the power to hold you as long as we deem necessary."

"That can't be possible. As a UAAN citizen, I have rights."

"You do, but good luck finding a court to hear your case. Look, we've gotten off on the wrong foot. Why don't we start over?"

"Okay, what do you want?"

"I can make all these accusations go away if you tell me the full truth about what you found at the monolith." He narrowed his eyes. "You're hiding something."

"Where is Grant Stewart?"

"Don't worry about Mr. Stewart. Let's talk about what you know."

She had to be careful what she told him. If they'd held Grant and had gotten him to talk, they would compare whatever he said with her story. How would Grant respond? Probably with the truth, but not all of it. He would hide details.

"Why are you so interested in that rock?"

"Who wouldn't be? You saw it. So out of place in the middle of that vast expanse of jungle. And emitting such high background radiation. You saw it, didn't you?"

"Yes, it was unusual."

"Unusual in what way?"

She decided to reveal more details. Anybody flying an aircraft nearby would see it was not a monolith but a building.

"After the fire burned off its covering of vegetation, I saw a strange dome. One end was flattened into a cliff, on which were carved many strange markings."

"Describe the markings," said Kauffmann, leaning forward with an intense look in his eyes. The taste of salt from the auger was overpowering.

"Difficult to describe. Like nothing I've ever seen before. Carved into the granite using power tools of some sort. Looked like writing, but not in a language I've seen."

"And was the cliff covered with hexagonal tiles?"

"Yes. Now, I've answered your questions. Let me go home, please!" Where was the Zyd nimat agent hiding? How was Kauffmann being manipulated? Was the nimat in the building?

"A few more questions, then we'll let you be on your way with all accusations dropped. You entered the monolith, didn't you?"

"Yes."

"What did you find?"

"Just some boring rooms with nothing in them. They were empty."

Kauffmann stood, looming over her. "You lie! Tell me the truth! What did you see?"

"Not unless you tell me why you want to know." Belle desperately considered how to get herself out of this situation.

"I see we're going to have to do things the hard way."

Kauffmann grabbed her arm, pulled her to a standing position, and shoved her against the wall. The impact of her head against the concrete dazed her. He was strong.

"Help! Help!" she yelled.

"Nobody is coming. Didn't you hear the nice guard? I can take as long as I want." His face was right in hers. His breath was putrid. A creepy smile exposed yellow teeth. His eyes darted around, taking in every detail of Belle's face. She felt violated.

Her mind flashed to a horrible night years ago. She'd been helpless. *Never again!*

Belle rammed her forehead into Kauffmann's nose. Briefly stunned, he released her, stumbling backward a few steps. She then delivered a vicious kick to his groin.

Kauffmann fell to his hands and knees, clutching his groin

and moaning, having trouble breathing.

He would be down only for a few seconds. The door was locked, and nobody was coming. Belle needed to ensure he stayed down, but she wasn't strong enough to disable him with her bare hands. The guy was twice her weight.

Belle picked up Kauffmann's chair, raised it over her head, and hammered it down on his back.

He bellowed out and collapsed to the floor, his arms and legs waving wildly, trying to catch her. She'd hurt him. His face was bright red, and drool dripped from his mouth.

Belle raised the chair again and smashed it down on Kauffmann's head.

He rolled over on his back, then began convulsing. Blood splattered onto the floor underneath him. She'd hurt him badly. Overdone it.

Belle jumped up and down in front of the room's security camera, trying to get somebody's attention. She pounded on the door and screamed, "Help! Help!"

Returning to Kauffmann on the floor, she looked him over. He'd stopped convulsing but, more worryingly, also stopped breathing. She hadn't intended to kill him. Even if she had wanted to, she still needed to find out where the Zyd agent was!

She mentally reviewed her CPR training. Belle checked for a pulse. Nothing. At the same time, she noticed the salty taste was gone, replaced by an incredibly sweet taste and the smell of decay, like month-old bananas.

But he's still alive at least.

Belle clamped down on her disgust and prepared to give him chest compressions, her two hands placed on his sternum.

She felt something warm and sticky touch the top of her hands. It was moving up her lower arms.

She recoiled across the floor onto her back, looking at her arms in the light. Something translucent white, like thick mucus, covered her hands and lower arms. It was gooey and seemed to be alive. *It's moving on its own!* Her hands felt numb, then involuntarily started to open and close, their muscles spasming.

The door to the room crashed open. It was the guard.

"Hands up!" she yelled. The woman stood in a shooting stance, with a stunner in two hands aimed at Belle.

"Help me!" Belle cried.

The guard looked in confusion at the scene. Kauffman, motionless on his back, blood staining the floor under his head. Belle, on the floor with her arms above her, covered with a gelatinous substance.

The door shut behind the guard.

The slime continued creeping up Belle's arms, past her shoulders. She had lost all feeling in her hands and arms.

The guard just stood there.

Now the goo was past her shoulders and at her throat. She felt tendrils of something touching her ears. Her arms and upper body were paralyzed.

This isn't correct. Something's not right here, her thoughts came dreamily.

Disoriented, she sampled the auger and got a taste of herself. She was salty! *This is the Zyd nimat agent!* She realized in terror.

It was too late. She was nearly paralyzed, and in seconds the nimat would invade her skull and nobody would be the wiser. She was about to become their new host!

The guard called on her radio for backup and paramedics. Too late.

Then Belle remembered the training she'd received from Iron Seer. The auger had a defense mechanism against coercion. Using her last conscious control over her brain, she scrolled through the short list of auger commands in her implant and executed the defense program.

Like lava flowing through her veins, feeling returned to her body. She let out a bloody scream, both in pain and at the horror of what was happening to her. The slime was past her hands and arms and pooled around her neck like a scarf, preparing to plunge into her brain stem through the back of her neck.

"Stay quiet. Help is on the way!" the guard said.

Still screaming, Belle pressed her fingers under the nimat blob, between the skin of her neck and their own gooey, sticky skin, wrapped her hands around them, and powered by adrenaline and disgust, she pulled them up and over her head like a grotesque necklace, and flung them at the wall in front of her. A *splat* sound, and they were squashed against the wall, unmoving for the moment.

The nimat suddenly shot out pseudopods at the guard. They grabbed her by the head, pulled the rest of their body off the wall, and jumped onto the guard. She fired her stunner, but missed and hit the opposite wall.

Belle was free. She stood on wobbly legs.

The guard had a silent scream frozen on her face. She remained in her shooter's stance. The nimat completely covered her head but then collected themselves into a blob behind her neck.

A tearing, popping sound arose from the guard. Like a whole chicken being butchered in the kitchen.

Belle stumbled back in horror against the table as the guard's body shook. The guard performed an odd uncoordinated dance. Dropping her hands to her sides, the stunner fell to the floor. Standing ramrod straight. Looking directly ahead.

The nimat disappeared. The skin around the guard's neck rippled, then was still.

The guard's eyes shot in Belle's direction. "That was unpleasant."

Belle sampled the guard with the auger. She tasted salt.

The nimat was a parasite! She'd just watched it leave one host—Kauffmann—and take another—the guard.

"This body will not do," the guard—the nimat—said. They looked with regret at Kauffmann's body. "But it's good enough for dealing with you." They held Belle with their gaze.

"You're the Zyd agent," Belle said.

The nimat stood with their arms crossed, watching Belle. "You just murdered Kauffmann. Yes, that's how I'll explain it. They'll be here soon. But I can't have you giving them a different story. This situation can still be salvaged."

Belle stepped away from the table, shoved it to the middle of the room, and stood behind it. Blocking the nimat.

"It's too bad," the nimat said. "I wanted to find out what you learned at the Quynh facility."

The nimat knew about the listening post.

"That's what I thought. You did find one," the nimat said. "Tell me, who did you meet? An ighakan?"

Belle said nothing.

"A disgusting, dangerous species. Primitive bodies and completely uncontrollable."

The nimat circled the table cautiously.

Belle moved to keep the table between them.

"Who are you?" she asked.

"You may call me Madhur."

"Madhur, what do you want with humans?"

They continued circling the room. The stunner was on the floor. Madhur forgot about it, or didn't know what it was.

"To know everything that you know. And to stop you from becoming friends with the Quynh Federation. We can't have the Quynh meddling in human affairs. You make such good playmates!" They smiled.

Belle was almost to the stunner.

"This is unfortunate," Madhur said. "You would be an ideal host. In taking you, I would learn everything you know. But the Quynh gave you an auger. Loathsome witchcraft."

"But effective," Belle said.

Madhur grimaced.

Belle picked up the stunner. Madhur looked at her, puzzled, then realized what she had. They leaped at Belle across the table surprisingly fast.

Belle successfully raised the weapon quickly and fired just as Madhur reached her.

They both collapsed in a heap on the floor.

Belle scrambled away and stood.

Madhur convulsed and screamed on the floor. There was another ripping and popping sound. Blood splattered on the floor underneath the guard's body.

Madhur's pseudopods sprang from the guard's neck to the wall, and Madhur jumped to the wall. They were still, their gooey body shaking fitfully. Hundreds of tiny pseudopods shot uncontrolled in and out of their body.

Belle must have injured it with the stunner.

Kauffmann's large coffee thermos sat by the door.

Belle grabbed it and emptied it onto the floor.

The nimat was beginning to move again, making its way up the wall to the ceiling. Belle moved a chair to the wall, then trusting her auger was still defending her, scooped Madhur into the thermos with one hand.

Immediately, dozens of tendrils of slime squirted out

between the edge of the open thermos and her hand. Madhur was panicking as they realized what was about to happen.

Belle screwed the lid on the thermos, trapping the nimat.

When she closed the trap, Belle noticed several globules of slime on the floor that got chopped off the central blob. They lay still and were beginning to turn a cloudy white.

Thirty seconds later, a man called out loudly. The door was thrown open, and two guards entered with weapons raised. "Hands in the air! Hands in the air!"

Belle set the thermos on the floor and raised her hands.

She was pushed to the floor and cuffed. One of the guards knelt on Belle's back. Breathing was difficult.

"What happened here?!" the guard said.

Everything that happened was recorded on the room's video feed. "They attacked me, then a creature came off their bodies and attacked me. I trapped it in this thermos. I think they're both dead."

"What creature?" They were circling the room, looking for threats.

"It's trapped in this thermos," said Belle. "You need to declare a biohazard emergency, and these two need medical help."

The guard pulled Belle to a sitting position. "Are you hurt?"

Belle was annoyed that they'd cuffed her and treated her roughly. But what had they thought when they saw two bodies and Belle standing over them?

"I don't think so. A bump on the head and a racing heart, but that's it."

The guard looked over Belle's body.

"I didn't attack them," Belle said. "Why are you cuffing me?"

"Just stay there until we figure out what's going on."

"You need to bring Dr. Benton Valero here. He'll know how to handle this creature."

A minute later, medics arrived and began working on Kauffmann and the first guard. But Belle was sure they were both dead. The Zyd agent killed them the moment it left their bodies.

Belle had survived. The adrenaline was wearing off. Her hands shook, and she badly needed to pee. And a drink of water.

She'd captured the nimat. Not just eliminated it as a threat, but trapped it in Kaffmann's thermos. Now she just needed to convert this success into a story that would lift suspicion off her. Restore her pilot's license and her job duties.

35

About twenty minutes after the incident with Kauffmann and the guard—and the Zyd agent—Benton Valero appeared at the holding cell and took charge of the nimat and of Belle.

She found out that Grant was also being held. He had been detained at the same time as Belle, though Kauffmann hadn't visited him yet.

Benton used his authority and influence to get Belle uncuffed and both of them released from detention. Especially now that Kauffmann was out of the picture.

He brought them and Madhur to his spacious office and said they would remain there for the next few hours while he got things sorted out with Kepler management.

Grant breathed heavily and stood with arms crossed. "Are you okay?" he said to Belle.

She nodded.

He held his hands to his head. "I can't believe you confronted Kauffmann by yourself!"

Belle was silent, not knowing what to say. She bit her lower lip, studying Grant's intense face, trying to understand his feelings.

He lowered his arms and said, "You scared me, Belle."

Suddenly it all flooded in, the realization that she had almost died. And in that moment, she realized she wasn't alone. Someone—Grant—had been with her all along. She mattered to him when she hadn't quite truly mattered to anyone other than Phil since her father's death. The realization overwhelmed her, and she burst out weeping. She tried to hold Grant's gaze, but tears streamed down her cheeks.

Grant was there in a breath, wrapping her in his strong arms. "You're safe now. I'm so happy you're safe."

Benton said, "I'll be back in five minutes." He left the room.

Belle held onto Grant, pressed her face into his chest, and cried. Not just for the scare she'd experienced with Kauffmann and Madhur. No, she also wept for the years of loneliness she'd brought on herself by pushing away others. Trusting in somebody as much as she did in Grant was such a relief.

Grant kissed her forehead. "You certainly know how to take care of yourself. Not that I had any doubts after watching you out in the jungle."

Belle pulled back slightly and looked up into his face. His eyes were warm and peaceful. After being detained for twenty-four hours, he smelled of sweat and dirt, just like her. But it was not unpleasant. The firm muscles in his back rippled under her hands. Her belly tingled pleasantly.

Benton reentered the office. Grant let go of Belle and sat in a chair. Belle wiped at her eyes with the sleeves of her shirt and sat in another chair next to Madhur's prison.

Benton said, "Belle, you gave us all quite the scare. But it turned out well in the end, thank god! How do you want to secure the nimat? That thermos won't do, I'm afraid."

Belle asked for and was given a two-liter, transparent yet shatter-proof, polycarbonate jar. Then she transferred Madhur from the thermos to the jar. It tried to escape when she made the transfer, but Belle squeezed it into the jar. The nimat lost a little more of its body.

Kepler management went bonkers when they discovered a real live *intelligent* alien at the base. Paralyzed in indecision between a desire to lockdown all employees to minimize liability and looking for ways they could leverage the potential intellectual property.

At one point, a corporate lawyer with a couple security guards in tow came to Benton's office, seeking to take Grant and her back into custody again for having mishandled company proprietary information. Benton smoothed over the situation by pointing out the benefits of the publicity that would come from a more friendly attitude toward them. Soon, Belle and Grant would be immortalized as the humans who achieved First Contact.

While sitting in Benton's office, Belle was contacted by Iron Seer in a simple text message to her neural implant.

Belle Machado, this is Iron Seer. Please confirm the elimination of the Zyd threat.

She responded back, *I confirm that a Zyd nimat agent named Madhur has been captured and its influence on humans eliminated. I await your instructions regarding the final disposition of the prisoner.*

Iron Seer: *Excellent results! You will receive further instructions via diplomatic channels.*

Belle wondered what Iron Seer could possibly mean by "diplomatic channels."

Fifty thousand kilometers above Clinton Base, a point in space began to expand. Where there was nothing a moment ago, in less than a picosecond, a dot expanded to a kilometer-long cylinder, eighty meters in diameter, with domed ends. Its black surface reflected no visible light, a shape betrayed only by occulted stars.

Moments later, a multitude of hatches opened. Through them, extended sensor apertures, communication arrays, ports of unknown purpose, and a reaction mass propulsive cone at the stern. Its engine lit, and the vehicle placed itself in a supersynchronous orbit directly above Clinton Base. It thrusted downward toward Clinton to maintain its orbital position relative to the base while keeping sensors and ports ominously facing the planet.

A few minutes later, an identical cylinder appeared ten thousand kilometers above the monolithic ruin, Iron Seer's listening post. The second ship also deployed in like manner to the first, though facing away from the planet and accelerating upward to maintain its protective position covering the post.

Shortly thereafter, a third identical cylinder materialized one thousand kilometers above the northern hemisphere of Clinton and accelerated into a sun-synchronous polar orbit. Then a fourth appeared, accelerating to another sun-synchronous orbit whose ascending node was rotated one hundred eighty degrees from the previous.

"To the humans on Clinton," sounded the speakers over the traffic controller's console, "this is Squadron Commander Burned Silica of the Quynh Federation. Listener Iron Seer has informed my superiors of an agent of the Zyd Hegemony whom you have captured. Subject to Quynh Federation orders, I have quarantined this planet with my squadron's warships. You are required to surrender this agent to my forces without delay. Please respond on this frequency."

The on-duty traffic controller listened to the incoming radio message in confused astonishment. She didn't know Burned Silica, Iron Seer, the Quynh, or the Zyd, and knew nothing about a captured agent. What's more, the four massive warships that had just appeared on her radar screens were setting off all sorts of traffic conflict alarms. Especially the two in the low polar orbits.

"Squadron Commander Burned Silica, this is Clinton Base Control. Message heard, but I must forward it up my management chain for instructions. Please stand by for a response, and be advised of potential polar orbit traffic conflict."

The controller called her boss about the received message, who in turn requested instructions from the corporate offices and was told that a Kepler representative would come to the controller's station.

Ten minutes later, the base leader and chairman of the Clinton Base Executive Committee, Gerald Hillam, arrived at the controller's desk with an assistant, two armed security staff, and the chief DPE representative for Clinton, Lisa Poulsen. The controller jumped to her feet.

"Hello, sir. The senders are standing by for your response."

"How long have they been waiting?" Hillam asked.

"A little over ten minutes," said the controller.

"Have they sent any further messages since the one you forwarded to us?"

"No, sir."

Poulsen asked Hillam, "Could this be related to that biohazard incident this morning?"

"I don't know," he responded. "We're still investigating. My director of operations, Kennedy Kauffmann, suffered a fatal accident, and there are claims of an alien organism being released at the same time at the security center. However, I've been assured the situation is currently under control. Well, at least it was." He looked at the controller and said, "Okay, how do I talk into this thing?"

The controller gave Hillam instructions on using the radio. Then Hillam pressed the transmit button and spoke into the microphone.

"Squadron Commander Burned Silica, this is Director Gerald Hillam of Kepler Research Corporation, chairman of the Clinton Base Executive Committee. I understand you believe we have something of yours in our custody and would like it returned. Unfortunately, we've never heard of the Quynh Federation or the Zyd Hegemony, nor am I aware of any agent of the latter being captured. We of course want to help you in any way within our means. Please send us additional information."

"Director Gerald Hillam, this is Squadron Commander Burned Silica. Our agent on Clinton, Listener Iron Seer, collaborated with two humans to successfully locate, neutralize, and capture a Zyd agent who infiltrated your leadership. The names of the humans are Belle Machado and Grant Stewart. Machado made the capture.

"Per a prior agreement made between Iron Seer and your agents, you are required to surrender the Zyd agent immediately."

Hillam looked at his assistant and asked, "Who are these people he's talking about?"

The assistant studied his tablet briefly and responded, "Belle Machado is a junior pilot from the sensor tender group, and Grant Stewart is a pararescue team leader for Special Missions."

He looked up at Hillam. "I remember them both, sir. They were involved in a couple fatal vehicle mishaps last week, and these two were rescued from the jungle three days ago. Belle Machado seems to have been involved with the Kauffmann biohazard incident that just occurred."

Hillam then looked at the security persons and said, "Find out where Machado is currently located."

They nodded, and one of them stepped away and began making calls on a hand-held radio.

Hillam was embarrassed for seeming to know so little about the situation while standing in front of Poulsen. He looked at her meekly and said, "Looks like it's going to be one of *those* days."

Poulsen said, "Director Hillam, we need to find out who these Quynh Federation and Zyd Hegemony are. It also sounds like we may have a First Contact situation on our hands. These don't sound like humans. Have the First Contact protocols been put into action?"

"No, they have not. This is the first I am hearing of these events."

"It looks to me like we have a potentially hostile alien fleet orbiting our planet, expressing demands. We don't know them, and saying the wrong thing could spring us into a conflict. I recommend you bring this Machado here immediately to assist with communications. It seems she has prior experience dealing with this Quynh Federation."

"Normally I would agree, but Machado has clearly violated multiple corporate rules and possibly even some federal criminal statutes. Furthermore, she's a very junior member of my staff. I don't believe it appropriate to involve her to any further degree than she already is."

"I see. So you would prefer to wing it instead and communicate yourself with this squadron of alien warships from a culture we do not understand? Or did you have a specialist in alien diplomacy hidden somewhere on the base?"

Hillam mentally cringed at hearing his reasoning echo back at him. And no, he did not have a hidden diplomat, if somebody was even trained to deal with an alien civilization. He waved at his security team again. "Bring Belle Machado here as soon as possible. And anybody else involved with this Iron Seer."

He sighed. This was one of those moments when being the guy in charge was bad. He held his hand up to quiet everybody, pressed the radio transmit button, and spoke again into the microphone.

"Squadron Commander Burned Silica, we are consulting with Belle Machado and Grant Stewart to verify your stated facts. Please forgive the delay, but I hope you understand that I must perform my due diligence as leader of this installation."

"Director Gerald Hillam, this is acceptable. However, until the Zyd agent is in our custody, we will interdict any interplanetary traffic to or from Clinton. Intraplanetary traffic below two thousand kilometers is permitted. We await your decision."

36

Belle, Grant, and Benton sat in Benton's office with Madhur. The gelatinous mass in the jar lay still.

Belle had seen no movement from Madhur since she'd replaced the thermos with the jar. They seemed to feel no pain or be overly concerned with losing parts of their body. However, the nimat was not a distributed organism. Any parts separated from the main mass appeared to die, becoming still, turning gray, and drying out.

Belle wondered if Madhur would suffocate with the lid on the jar. What were their atmospheric needs? After they had been still for about twenty minutes, she decided to open the jar slightly to test if they were still alive. She opened a tiny gap, about a millimeter, but nothing happened. She began widening the gap but still saw no motion.

When the lid was almost completely removed, Madhur ran for it, shooting multiple pseudopods out through the neck of the jar, gripping its outside surface, trying to pull itself out. Belle did her best to scoop it back in, then slammed the lid back in place and screwed it down tight.

"So, they seem not to need much atmosphere," said Benton, "and possess some characteristics of slime molds.

Their biology appears much like some of Earth's fungal lifeforms."

"Fungal, like mushrooms?" Grant asked.

"No, not quite. This nimat could be an analog to some of Earth's parasitic molds. They invade a host's nervous system and take control of it. This organism infected Kauffmann, but we don't know for how long. It could have been years! Does it replace the host's nervous system? Probably not, but if so, then how much does it replace? Is the host still conscious of what is happening, or does the nimat become the new consciousness?"

Belle shook her head. "I don't know, and sadly, neither does Iron Seer or her people. I think that's why they're so interested in getting their hands on Madhur."

She looked at Benton. "Do you think it can hear us? Understand what we're saying right now?"

"It's likely," Benton said. "It can certainly feel vibrations through its body being pressed up against the walls of the jar. What are you sensing through the auger?"

"Just a second." She still had it in defense mode, which wouldn't allow her to sense at the same time. She switched to sensing mode. "Sweetness, and the scent of chlorine. That's what I've smelled in people who are listening and absorbing information. Without knowing more, I would say it's listening carefully to everything we're saying."

"Then we should take great care in our conversation," Grant said. "It could have infiltrated us for years and years! Think of all the secrets it's probably learned."

"Iron Seer said it's possible nimat infiltration of humanity is widespread," Belle said, "going back centuries. The Zyd Hegemony may know the deepest secrets of our civilization."

"The possible implications leave me almost speechless,"

Benton said. "The Zyd could be the greatest threat faced by humanity in centuries. We need to make the Quynh our allies. We need friends!" Benton was pounding his knee, emphasizing each point.

Benton's mobile sounded. "Yes, she and Grant Stewart are here with me in my office... Yes, the nimat is in her possession... No, I believe she is the only person who can safely handle the alien... Iron Seer granted Belle special defensive skills... Yes. We can carry it, though I suggest taking special biohazard precautions... Okay, we'll wait here for them."

He ended the call and looked at them. "That was security command. Director Hillam is requesting our presence at the base traffic control room. Apparently, they are in contact with a fleet of warships whose commander demands we surrender a captured foreign agent. Our help is needed."

"That must be the diplomatic channel that Iron Seer mentioned. Not subtle at all," Belle said.

"Indeed. Security is sending a team to escort us—and the nimat—to the control room. You sure you're okay transporting that thing?"

She nodded but looked for a bag or something to cover the jar with. No need to let it see more than was necessary. Benton sacrificed a nice-looking lunch bag to the cause, and she soon had the jar hidden inside. She re-enabled her auger defenses, chilled by the thought of the nimat escaping while her defenses were down.

A few minutes later, there was a knock at the office door, and a heavily armed and armored security officer entered. After he and another did a quick sweep of the office with their weapons—they were taking no chances—and verified that Madhur was properly secured, the eight-man team surrounded Belle, Grant, and Benton and escorted them to the traffic control building.

There was additional armed security deployed along their path, securing their route.

At this hour, dozens of Kepler employees normally walked between buildings, but the facility must have been in lockdown. Only security staff and a few biohazard specialists standing by in the shadows were present.

Belle feared for her job after today. She'd broken too many company rules over the last week. Who would care that she hadn't had a choice? The corporation would have preferred she'd died in C195 with the rest of her crew rather than get them mixed up. If she was lucky, the mitigating circumstances involving the aliens would help her escape criminal prosecution, but the coming weeks were going to be messy. Perhaps she still needed a lawyer.

They arrived at the control room, which was crowded with too many people. Benton greeted Director Hillam and introduced Belle and Grant to him. No handshake was offered, not even a nod of acknowledgment. She didn't know the director but could tell he was embarrassed and angry.

Hillam spoke to Benton. "Where is this Zyd agent?"

"In Pilot Belle Machado's custody." Benton was gesturing toward her. "We believe she is the only person able to safely handle it. Indeed, we are all probably in danger even being here in the same room with it, an unknown threat, though proven deadly."

"Did it kill Kennedy Kauffmann?" asked Lisa Poulsen, the DPE representative.

"A thorough investigation will determine that in time," Hillam said.

But Belle contradicted him. "Yes, ma'am, I saw it with my own eyes. It also killed a security guard. It tried to overcome me, but I fought it off and trapped it in this jar." She nodded to the lunch bag hanging on her shoulder.

"That must have been frightening," Poulsen said.

Belle nodded.

"Let's have a look at it." Poulsen pointed to the bag. "Assuming you think it's safe enough."

"Yes, it should be fine. Nobody remove the lid." Belle briefly lifted the jar from the bag, let the people gaze at it, and then placed it back. "The nimat's name is Madhur. I got that out of them."

"It—They talked to you?"

"When they were in Kauffmann's body. Then later, when they took the guard as host. I don't believe they can communicate when outside a host."

"They're not much to look at," Benton said, "but I assure you it is dangerous. I observed Pilot Machado on two occasions re-securing it, and each time, she had to defend herself and force it back into the container."

"And how does it attack? How do you defend?" Poulsen asked.

Benton interjected, "That is a complicated conversation that perhaps we should save for a less tense occasion. Do you agree?"

Poulsen nodded and gestured to Hillam. "Please, Director Hillam, what do you plan to do next?"

Still ignoring Belle, he asked Benton, "Dr. Valero, what are these Quynh and Zyd, and who is this Iron Seer?"

"I think it would be best if Pilot Machado and Team Leader Stewart answered. They are by far the most knowledgeable of any of us."

Hillam sighed, finally looked at Grant, and nodded, waving a hand at him and rubbing his forehead.

Grant gestured to Belle.

"Iron Seer is a sentient alien being who's been living on Clinton for decades," Belle said. "She operates a listening post for the Quynh Federation. Kepler originally concluded the post was just an anomalous stone monolith in the jungle."

It was almost completely silent in the control room, except for soft words from a controller across the room who was trying to do his job controlling atmospheric traffic, despite the commotion in his workspace. Everybody else was hanging on Belle's words.

"Iron Seer rescued pararescueman Grant Stewart"—she pointed to him—"and I after mishaps with our Kepler vehicles last week." She was glossing over the truth, particularly the part about Iron Seer having a part in their destruction, but there would be time for the full truth later.

"After meeting Iron Seer, but before we could inform Clinton Base, she warned us of the severe threat presented by a Zyd agent that had infiltrated our organization. We came to understand that if we told anybody about the monolith's true nature or the existence of Iron Seer, it would likely get back to the Zyd Hegemony and cause significant harm to the Quynh Federation, probably including the death of Iron Seer and the loss of their listening post on Clinton.

"In return for our promise of secrecy, Iron Seer promised us safety and the skills and knowledge to locate and eliminate the enemy agent."

"And the Quynh Federation?" Poulsen asked.

"The Quynh Federation is an organization of allied polities who are all composed of a sentient alien race called ighakans. These are Iron Seer's people, and I believe that is who crews the warships currently positioned over Clinton. This Burned Silica is the diplomatic channel through whom Iron Seer instructed me to surrender the captured agent."

"And the Zyd Hegemony?"

"It is a multi-species alien civilization headed by a race known as the nimat. The nimat are masters; all other member species are subject to them, many of them utterly enslaved. Iron Seer says that the Zyd exploit human knowledge and manipulate our civilization to play a game. A game that's at the center of their culture."

"Are they in conflict with one another?" Poulsen asked.

"The Quynh Federation and the Zyd Hegemony are enemies and at war with each other. The nature of ighakan biology apparently makes it difficult for them to be manipulated by the nimat. They are conducting a war of extermination on the Quynh, though so far without much success."

Grant stepped forward. "We know we made unilateral decisions regarding immensely weighty questions."

Hillam and Poulsen were both nodding in agreement.

"But look at it from our perspective. Our choice was an ugly death in the jungles of Clinton or to help keep both the Quynh and humanity safe."

Belle said, "I didn't know events would go as far as they did—certainly I didn't expect to capture a hostile alien—but I'm glad I made the choices I did and am prepared to face whatever consequences come as a result, be they good or bad."

"You and Stewart lied to your respective mishap investigation committees," Hillam said.

"Yes, but we planned to correct the record as soon as the Zyd threat was removed, full-well recognizing that knowingly lying to the investigators could cost us our jobs or even our freedom. However, I hope you will accept that there are mitigating circumstances that explain why we were dishonest."

"Director Hillam," Benton said, "in their defense, they

approached me with the full truth the day they returned. They arrived at the conclusion they could not do what was needed without help and trusted that I, at least, was free of influence from these Zyd. If they are guilty, then so am I for not bringing this information to your attention immediately. But we had our reasons. Belle and Grant are intelligent, persuasive, and remarkable young persons who deserve our respect and admiration for all they have done."

"I propose we shelve these accusations and charges until after we deal with the current crisis," Poulsen said, looking at Hillam. "There will be time enough to get to the bottom of all of this. For now, Machado and Stewart have convinced me that the claims being made by this so-called Quynh fleet have a valid basis. We must decide what we will do. I can tell you there are many people at DPE who will be quite angry at losing this nimat specimen if we were to surrender it."

"Ma'am," Belle said, "I believe the Quynh are acting in good faith. The Zyd are their mortal enemies, and yet, they have never successfully captured a nimat, alive or dead. Surrendering the nimat will greatly aid their efforts.

"I also believe that if humanity establishes friendly relations with them, the Quynh will gladly share with us whatever they learn about this specimen. During the few days we resided with Iron Seer, she generously shared her knowledge, skills, and technology with us, based only on the promise that we would keep her secret safe."

Belle pulled back the sleeve of her left arm and showed them the auger. "This is a gift I received from Iron Seer called an auger. With it, I managed to locate and defend against the nimat. She taught me how to use it.

"If the rest of her people are similar in nature to Iron Seer, then we want them to be our friends. Surrendering the Zyd agent will prove to them that we are worthy of that friendship and, I believe, will lead to a hundredfold increase in knowledge and security over what we could possibly learn by ourselves if we were instead to hold onto the nimat and begin our relationship with the Quynh on an adversarial footing."

Poulsen gazed at the auger, then said, "That is an alien artifact, and by law must be turned over to DPE."

"If you force me, then I will give it to you, but know that I promised Iron Seer, as a condition of receiving it, that I would not allow it to be taken. However, if you allow me to keep and control it, I will cooperate with you and teach you its capabilities. Again, given Iron Seer's easy generosity in supplying us with it, and the knowledge to use it, I suspect her people would do likewise for other humans."

"That seems like a wise course of action, but it's not up to me," Poulsen said. "The law is the law. You must get a court order protecting you or an official DPE exemption for possessing embargoed alien artifacts. However, like all the rest of this discussion, we can decide later. Right now, we must decide what to do about the nimat."

"We need to surrender it," Hillam said. "My priority is the welfare of the humans on Clinton, and that fleet up there doesn't make me feel safe."

Poulsen nodded. "I agree. Furthermore, Pilot Machado is correct. It would be wise for us to start out our relationship with the Quynh on a friendly footing, in the spirit of cooperation. Perhaps you could express to Burned Silica our desires to deepen our relationship with his people?"

"Agreed." The base director signaled he was ready to speak again on the radio.

"Squadron Commander Burned Silica, this is Director Gerald Hillam. I have consulted with my people and verified your claims to the Zyd agent. The Zyd agent is currently in our custody, and we would happily give it to you. Please send us instructions on how the prisoner transfer should occur.

"Let me also say that I hope you will accept this act as a gesture of goodwill from humanity and an expressed desire to establish a friendly relationship between our civilizations."

"Director Hillam," came Burned Silica's voice out of the overhead speakers, "it greatly pleases me to accept your generosity and the assistance of humanity. The capture of a live Zyd agent will greatly assist us in our conflict with that evil government.

"An orbit-to-ground shuttle will contact your traffic control shortly to request landing vectors.

"My superiors also authorized me to extend a hand of friendship from my people to yours. Diplomats shall be exchanged, and trade established."

Benton Valero walked over to Belle and Grant and shook their hands. "Nicely done, nicely done!"

He and everybody in the room knew they had just watched history being made. Even Hillam had a smile on his face now and was talking animatedly to Poulsen and Benton.

Belle only enjoyed the scene for a moment. The security escort team soon whisked her off to a distant landing pad where the prisoner transfer would take place. Grant tried to accompany her, but the security team wouldn't allow it.

37

The dark gray Quynh shuttle was shaped like a flattened ellipsoid, making it look like a giant river stone. Not much larger than *C195* had been, it easily fit onto the large landing pad assigned for the task. Out of the shuttle, to Belle's surprise, exited Iron Seer.

"Hello, Belle Machado, it pleases me to see you again," the small alien said to her, standing about two meters away, with her wispy arms waving around.

"My pleasure also, and I am surprised. I thought you would still be at your installation."

"No, I have been relieved of my post and a replacement installed. I must return to Ghatti to face charges for the humans killed during my stewardship over the post. This shuttle just collected me, and we are now assigned to accept the transfer of the prisoner. I was instructed to execute the transfer because of my previous contact with Grant Stewart and you."

"Oh no! Will you be in a lot of trouble? I thought the deaths were accidents?"

"Yes, they were unfortunate accidents, but preventable. Sentient lifeforms were killed. I am charged with homicide and must stand trial. I will answer truthfully and accept whatever punishment is decided."

"If guilty, what will happen to you?"

"Probably I will be dishonored, dismissed, and ordered to pay reparations. If not guilty, my status will be restored, and my government will pay reparations."

Belle nodded in understanding. The Quynh sounded like just people.

"I have the nimat Zyd agent, Madhur, trapped in a jar in this bag." She showed the jar to Iron Seer.

"I am amazed. It is so small and fragile. Is this what my people have feared for so many years?"

"Are you sure it's safe for you to handle? It tried to take me as a host, and I only could stop it when I remembered to use the auger defenses you had taught me."

"Yes, it's safe. Nimats are unable to coerce ighakan, though our scientists do not know why. This is why we are so pleased to obtain this specimen. Is it still alive?"

"Should be. It lays perfectly still until it senses an opportunity for freedom. Then it tries to flee. Be careful." She showed Iron Seer how the jar worked and explained that its surface was transparent to human vision. Then she handed the bag to Iron Seer.

"With my own auger, I can sense its intentions. Yes, this feels like the other nimat we had encountered previously, though the first time we have been in close proximity." She turned around but said, "Please wait here one moment while I secure the prisoner in the shuttle."

A minute later, Iron Seer exited the shuttle and came back to Belle. "Belle Machado, I am astounded at how quickly you learned to use the auger and that you managed to capture a live nimat. Humans seem to have an affinity for the auger and for understanding the R-field because of your flexible nervous system and rapid metabolism."

"Thank you, Iron Seer, but we could not have done it without your help. We make good partners, ighakans and humans."

"Indeed, and my superiors also believe so. I am instructed to extend an invitation to you to accompany me back to Ghatti to receive additional training in the use of the auger and to allow our scientists to study your species. We would like to recruit you as a Quynh field agent."

The offer took Belle aback. The Quynh would sacrifice their time for her? To train her? She was silent.

"I did not believe I would ever see a speechless human," Iron said.

Was that ighakan sarcasm she just heard?

"We believe the best way to help humans with the Zyd threat is to begin training human field agents. You would be trained as a Quynh field agent, but with the intention that you would eventually operate in human space for the benefit of your species."

That would be a crazy experience. It would turn her into a foreign agent, working for the Quynh government. "That is a generous offer. I need to speak with my superiors to understand their thoughts."

"In helping you, we help ourselves. Please speak with your superiors if you feel it is necessary, but this invitation is extended to Belle Machado from the grateful people of the Quynh Federation. Though I suspect there will eventually be a formal invitation of collaboration extended to all qualifying humans."

The Quynh had singled her out. She was exceptional in their eyes. Otherwise, why would they make such an offer? She was deeply honored by the recognition. But living on an alien planet for months or longer? She had her own goals.

"Can I survive on Ghatti?"

"We can easily supply you with a safe and comfortable living environment. Despite the differences in our biologies, our environment on Ghatti is not so different from the human optimal. You will have comfortable habitation and environmental suits for when outside your habitat."

Didn't sound comfortable, despite Iron's assurances. "What happens to me after I complete the training?"

"We extend an offer of permanent employment as a Quynh field agent once you complete training. Compensation will be competitive with Quynh standards, which will likely make you exceedingly wealthy by human standards."

What would exchange rates be like between human space and the Quynh? They were probably favorable to Quynh money because of their higher technological level than humans. This could get her out of poverty.

"I have a career as a pilot I'm trying to follow."

"Your skills as a pilot, though not of primary interest, will also prove valuable in the long run."

Some of her duties as a Quynh agent would require piloting. Maybe for independent deployments? That sounded interesting. Maybe she would be assigned her own ship and crew.

"At the same time," Iron said, "there will be no service obligation should you undertake the training. You may exit the service at any time, including during training, though understand that if you choose to do this before completing that, you will not be permitted to re-enter."

"How long will training take?"

"We do not yet know. For an ighakan, it takes many years, but it is an unfair comparison because of our slower metabolisms and longer lifespans. We believe your training will take somewhere between six months and three years. After you complete it, we will have a better idea, but you will serve just as much as a test subject as a student."

She imagined being away from her family for three more years. It had already been one year since she'd last seen them, and her heart ached. "I'm missing my family. In human terms, it has been a long time since I last saw them."

"You will be granted occasional leave to return to human space under reasonable terms that still need to be determined. The only requirement is you return to training after the leave is complete. However, if you accept this offer, we need you to come with us immediately. You will have to wait until your next leave to see your family."

"Now?" she asked, bewildered.

"In two days. We depart for Ghatti in thirty-six hours."

She had learned so much over the last ten days since encountering Iron Seer. Everything she had seen of the ighakans had impressed her. Their intelligence, sense of justice, respect for life, liberty, and happiness.

She could also not deny the appeal of the auger every time she used it. It made her feel more certain about the world and the people around her, and she knew that through it, she could perhaps bring the same increased certainty to others.

Plus, Iron Seer was offering her a fortune, and likely also fame, or at least an anonymous yet permanent mark on human history.

"Yes, I accept, Iron Seer."

"Excellent, I am most pleased, Belle Machado!"

"How should I pack? And where and when do I report?"

"Pack as you would for a long journey on human transport. Do not concern yourself with the habitability of your living spaces. We will accommodate. In two days, report back to this same landing pad at oh-five-hundred hours, local time."

"I will be ready. Thank you."

As Iron Seer climbed the ramp into her waiting shuttle, Belle was pretty sure Iron made an attempt to imitate a human hand wave.

"Belle, I cannot say how sorry I am for everything that happened. For how the company treated you," Danny Jephson, her group manager, said. They were alone in his office. "How are you feeling?"

"Tired, but I'll be okay. Danny, I have something to tell you."

"Before you do, I have something to tell you."

"Of course, go ahead," she said.

"Well, actually, more than one thing. First, Kepler has dropped all accusations against you regarding the deaths of Borya and Phil. Your license is reinstated. Kauffmann and Vroomen were in the wrong in how they handled the investigation."

Belle sighed in relief.

"Second," Danny said, "we have accepted Phil's evaluation of your check-flight. You are officially promoted to pilot-commander, effective immediately."

Belle clapped and smiled.

"Third, in recognition of your recent efforts in the First Contact with the Quynh Federation, you are being transferred to Kepler's Special Missions division. I'll be sad to lose you from my group, but pleased knowing it opens for you new and interesting career opportunities.

"Lastly, because of the promotion and transfer, your current salary will increase by one hundred twenty percent." Danny had a big smile on his face. "I hope this good news will compensate for whatever suffering the corporation has put you through in recent weeks. My congratulations to you!"

Belle was blown away. Kepler had really done their best to make up for everything bad that happened to Belle. It made what she planned to do even more difficult.

"That is generous. Thank you, Danny," Belle said.

She paused for a few seconds to gather her thoughts. "I've been offered an employment opportunity with the Quynh Federation. And I've accepted."

"Will you not reconsider, given your recent promotion?" said Danny.

"The promotion and salary increase is generous, and I would welcome the opportunity to work on Special Missions. But working with the Quynh allows me to continue developing relationships with Iron Seer and others like her. A relationship I enjoy and have great hopes for. Therefore, my answer is no. I am submitting my resignation, effective in two days."

"Oh, that is unfortunate for Kepler. But I completely understand. Let me offer you my congratulations on your new job."

"You are too kind."

Danny helped her start the paperwork for leaving Kepler.

Belle's bags were stuffed full of all her belongings. In the first, she had packed clothing, shoes, and toiletries. In the second were books, office supplies, electronics, and a few of her most precious keepsakes. The rest she was shipping back to her family.

The evening after her chat with Danny, she had dinner

again with Grant and Benton and told them of the news. They were excited for her.

Benton said that Kepler was losing one of their best employees and DPE had missed out on an opportunity to recruit her as soon as they knew about the auger. He was happy for her though, and said he wished he could trade places with her. He also said not to worry about criminal charges for violating First Contact protocols. He had already heard firsthand from the DPE rep that they would not press charges for any mishandling of aliens or their artifacts.

Grant was quieter, though he seemed content with the outcome of everything. She felt torn about her feelings for Grant. A new desire to be with him. A newly discovered relationship she wanted to explore. Her heart ached, knowing she had to choose between him and the Quynh.

Belle also felt ashamed that so much of the glory was falling at her feet when Grant had played such a huge role in their success. She told him that it was unfair and only because she had been compatible with the auger.

"Don't worry," he said. "Unlike Benton here, I *don't* want to trade places with you. I'm pretty happy with the work I'm doing right now. This was a great trade, and I can't think of a better person I would rather enjoy it than you.

"Besides, Lisa Poulsen asked me to take a leave of absence from Kepler to help DPE develop a contact plan for the Quynh. I guess I'm the next best thing since you and the aliens are leaving town. It may be temporary, but it looks like I'll be a diplomat to the Quynh for the foreseeable future." He laughed. "Imagine me doing this. My father will die of envy."

Belle congratulated him on the opportunity. Perhaps they would encounter each other again sooner than she had believed.

After dinner, she bid them all farewell, embraced them, and shed tears. But she held hopes of meeting again someday.

The next day, her last with Kepler, was spent in several long meetings with the mishap committees and another committee investigating Kauffmann and the guard's deaths. Seeing that she was about to depart human space for an indefinite period, they knew it was their last chance to grill her. She gave them the whole truth.

She spoke with her family the night before. She wasn't allowed to tell them much. Despite the Xenology Accords, DPE had sworn everybody involved with the aliens to secrecy. But she told her family in broad strokes everything that happened and that she was headed to a foreign country for training. They didn't fully comprehend it, but who could blame them? Belle still wasn't certain about what she was getting herself into. But she did promise them she would be given leave to visit them sometime within the next six months. They were happy to hear that and wished her good travels.

Now her bags were all packed, and a ground car was picking her up in ten minutes to take her to the landing pad where a Quynh ground-to-orbit shuttle would take her to orbit.

There was a knock at her door. It was Grant, wearing workout clothes.

"Grant Stewart, what are you doing at oh-four-thirty in the morning?!"

"This is my normal morning time. It's when I work out. Was on the way to the gym, but thought I'd stop by and wish you one last goodbye."

Tears again welled up in Belle's eyes, and all she could do was go to him, wrap her arms around him, and hold him.

They had been through so much together, and he had proved himself to be loyal, good-hearted, diligent, and gentle.

"What are these tears for, Agent Machado?" he joked with her.

She playfully punched him in the chest. "We never did get the chance to go to dinner together. Remember, you invited me."

"I didn't think my date was, after spending a week in the jungle, going to leave human space altogether four days later. Never had the chance!" He leaned his head against hers and said softly, "The invitation is still open next time you're around these parts."

The ground car arrived outside. Leaning into Grant, she squeezed him tight, then tilted her head and gave him a long kiss on the lips. He held her close, and the moment stretched on.

"Thank you, Grant Stewart, for changing my life. For being a good man. I want to see you again. I insist."

Grant was blushing, and his eyes were shiny. "Then find a way to stay in contact when you get to Quynh space."

He gave her another long kiss, and she pressed her body against his.

"I wish we had more time, but I must go."

"Goodbye, and be safe. Say hi to Iron Seer for me. And kill a few nimat if you get the chance!"

She laughed at his exaggerations.

The Quynh shuttle was already waiting for her when the ground car arrived. It looked like the same model as the one that picked up the Zyd prisoner, though it had no markings.

Iron Seer was there and escorted her into the vehicle. Just

like the transport from the monolith to the outpost, it was a tight fit. Human bodies were larger than ighakans, and she realized this would be a continuing problem if she lived in their society for the next few years.

She was given an environmental suit and told to put it on and not remove it until told to. The shuttle was going to be pressurized with an ighakan atmosphere. She was told it consisted of a nitrogen, carbon dioxide, carbon monoxide, and argon mix. Ighakans didn't require an oxidizing atmosphere.

Interesting. She looked forward to learning more about their biology.

The shuttle lifted off. Out a small window, she watched Clinton Base quickly disappear into the distance. She felt almost no movement or pressure, even though they must be accelerating at well over three Gs. The Quynh had better gravity control technology than humans.

After the lift-off, Iron Seer excused herself for a few minutes. When she returned, she looked different. Her shiny dark gray exoskeleton was gone. Underneath was beautiful silver skin. Thick and tough, but skin it was.

Iron Seer explained that the exoskeleton was made of silicon carbide, protecting her from oxidizing atmospheres. But it was heavy and uncomfortable to wear for long periods of time.

It was also scorching in the cabin. Though Belle's environmental suit kept her cool, it had to be well over fifty degrees centigrade here.

After a two-hour flight, they arrived at the flotilla's flagship, *Summertide*. In a voluminous hangar, Burned Silica himself welcomed her onto the ship. If she was not mistaken, there was even an honor guard.

All the ighakans looked the same to her. There was a

slight variation in size and body shape, but it would take Belle time to recognize these.

She was taken to a large box in one corner of the hangar and told this was her personal living quarters while they transited to the ighakan home planet, Ghatti. It had been constructed over the last twenty-four hours. The hangar was the only space on the ship where it would fit.

There was a one-person airlock. The interior had a nitrogen-oxygen atmosphere and was air-conditioned to a comfortable temperature. It was cramped but comfortable. They had added a bed, a human-style chair, a small desk, and an ighakan-style chair. There was also a small kitchenette and a separate bathroom with a shower.

There was a small fridge, and in it were packages that must be food of some type. She had running water, and the air was fresh.

Belle was amazed at how quickly her hosts had prepared all this for her. Human biology was distinct from ighakan, and yet the small room had all the comforts of a modest hotel room. *The ighakans must know more about humanity than we suspected.*

Iron Seer told Belle that the trip to Ghatti would take about twenty-four hours. That she should remain in this room the entire time because the rest of the ship had not been prepared to accommodate her. But that she would come to visit Belle in a few hours.

Belle considered what awaited her on Ghatti. What would the training be like? Who would be her classmates? Would she even have any? Who would be her teachers? What would happen at Iron Seer's trial? When would she next see Grant?

Would she come out of this experience a better person than she was now?

She hoped that was the case. The future held the answer.

THE END

Belle Machado returns for more adventures in *Quynh Recruit*.

As an indie author, I depend on your reviews to legitimize my books in the eyes of those who have not read them. Please rate and review this book online. Thank you!

Sign up for my newsletter at www.josephmcraepalmer.com to receive monthly updates on my current works in progress, and invites to be a beta-reader or advanced reviewer for my upcoming titles.

About Joseph McRae Palmer

Joseph McRae Palmer's debut novel is *Belle's Ruin*. Joseph writes speculative science fiction and fantasy novels.

He earned a Ph.D. in Electrical Engineering from Brigham Young University. Joseph was employed at Los Alamos National Laboratory for thirteen years as an engineer who designed nanosatellite modems. He was privileged to see several of his designs fly and operate in space.

In 2023, Joseph wrote his first novel, *Belle's Ruin*, after being diagnosed with Autism Spectrum Disorder (ASD). As a neurodiverse person with ASD and ADHD, he finds being an eccentric author to best fit his mental and physical needs. However, he's still happy to chat anytime about modulation theory, error correction codes, or orbital mechanics.

Joseph and his wife of more than two decades, Beatriz Palmer, are parents to one son and three daughters. As of 2023, they reside in northern Utah, USA.

Joseph's fiction site: www.josephmcraepalmer.com

Made in the USA
Middletown, DE
20 September 2023

38867132R00166